Hai

A Journey from Laos to America

A Novel

Ninsavang
Pravisay

This book is a novel inspired by many true stories and factual events. The names and identifying details of the characters, places, and incidents are products of the author's imagination and some of her life experiences.

Cover: Artwork by Laura Bird Miller

Photography by Nadine Nasby Photography

Email: **haventoheavenbook@gmail.com**

Library of Congress Cataloging-in-Publication Data

ISBN-13: 978-1985108721

ISBN-10: 1985108720

ACKNOWLEDGMENTS & DEDICATION

This book is dedicated to my Mom, without whom I would not have a story to tell. Sadly, I was not able to finish the book while she was living. I hope she enjoys reading it from heaven. My hope is to pass on the story to my children and theirs so that they can get a glimpse of "my world" and their roots, a world of a multiplicity of issues in all aspects of life: cultural, religious, political, racial, gender, educational, and generational. They were relevant then, and they are still relevant today.

I am truly thankful to my husband Raymond for his love and constant support for writing this book. Year after year, he encouraged me to make it happen. My inspiration goes to my children -- Karina, Cameron, and Kaitlin - my pride and joy, whom I continue to be inspired by and learn from every day, in more ways than they'll ever know -- they are my "Mekong lifeline" and my beating heart.

Reflecting on the journey of writing this book, I would be remiss not to mention my parents-in-law, specifically the late Rev. Yap Kim Hao, from whom I have gained a great deal of knowledge and wisdom, especially about the world we live in where equality and justice remain in peril. His life was his message to us all, and we must strive to carry on his legacy. Sadly, he did not live to read my finished book; but I hope he, like my mom, will have the pleasure of reading it from heaven.

I am fortunate to have a team of creative and talented friends – without them, this book would not have been published this year. Special thanks to my friends, Laura and Nadine, for their incredibly amazing talents for blessing the book cover with Laura's painting and Nadine's photography skills. My unfailing appreciation goes to my consultant friend, Alan, for his enthusiasm and creativity, who always had faith in me and helped make my work alive. Huge

i

gratitude goes to my editor/faithful friends and first readers – Ken, Cindy, Myra, and Corrine – their suggestions and opinions are much valued and appreciated. I'm blessed with my close circles of friends – from childhood to adulthood friends – from JLS to book club friends – and all in between in every walk of life.

Last but certainly not least, I dedicate this story to those who lost their lives during the escape, and to those who survived, so that the story is never forgotten. I am most thankful to my refugee family – for my parents' sacrifices – for the extraordinary life experiences, both fortunate and sad. They make up a part of me that only deepens my story and my desire to share it. My parents, my brother, and I are forever indebted to my altruistic Uncle Kheu, who saved us and brought us over on his boat to become refugees in Thailand. He gave us the taste of our "first freedom." I am forevermore grateful to our home country – the USA – along with the U.S. Catholic Charity, co-sponsored with my Aunt Nom. They all led us to our "second freedom" home in the USA. With all of its greatness and in spite of its shortcomings, I do so love this country with all of my heart. It is a place of haven and a gateway to heaven.

~Ninsavang Pravisay

Table of Contents

Foreword

"Life is as good as the freedom that you can trust."

~Kim Champa

Friday, 25-November-1977

Today is the day after Thanksgiving. It has been a clear, chilly, but rainless day here in the Bay Area, and now at about nine o'clock at night, even the wind has died down.

Even though this is the first time we are celebrating Thanksgiving, I believe the Champa family has adopted this American holiday as if it were its own. We are thankful every day for the safe haven that we have found in the United States, from the tyranny that we barely escaped in Laos, and the poverty that we endured as stateless refugees in Thailand. Yesterday, we gathered at our new home in California, where we hope, soon, to become U.S. citizens.

I was born on the 27th of December in 1940. Now, at almost 37 years old, I have finally decided to start writing the book that I have been preparing all these years.

As far back as 1966, I was able to buy a Kodak Brownie 127 Model 3 camera, just before it was discontinued. I bought it to take pictures of my daughter Kasi, who was on her way into this world. I loved that camera, because it allowed me to remember things that I might otherwise have forgotten. Until a month before we left Laos – and to avoid the appearance that they were coming from me – I had been asking friends to send boxes of 127 film rolls to my sister in the refugee camp. I had been buying and stockpiling them for over a year. I put the camera in a plastic bag to keep it safe when we jumped into the Mekong River.

1

Haven to Heaven

Tonight, I have taken out all of the photo albums from our years in Laos and Thailand. All of the copies of letters that I sent to so many people are neatly stored in folders by year. In a separate folder, I have kept my notes collected over the years containing snippets of ideas I had or complaints that I thought no one would hear or care about.

When we were refugees, we had no space that we could consider our home. In the refugee camp in Thailand, we knew that we were transients. Of course, then, except for the activities that were required for us to live, our time was our own. That is what permitted me to create a small business selling food and wares in the camp. Now that we are settled in the U.S. we have a place that we can feel is our home. However, our time is not our own. Both Khamphet (my husband) and I spend all of our time working multiple jobs, and I have the house work and the children to take care of, too. Transportation is a big problem. We can't afford a car yet. So, I must ride a bicycle to work every day.

Despite all of these challenges, I am determined to write this book documenting our journey. While I may not have much time to work on it, I will make as much progress as I can every day. I know that it will take me a long time to complete. That is how it is with all goals or desires that matter to the heart. The important thing is that I had the presence of mind, ever since contemplating our escape from Laos, to dedicate myself to the recording of facts. It is my dedication to truth-telling that lies at the root of that recording effort.

Every truth-teller has a trusted source. Kasi was mine, even though she was very young when we were in Laos. She took to writing her daily thoughts as soon as I got her that first diary. Unlike me, she is a creature of habit and a very dedicated worker. She approached her writing as if it were her job. I am not like that. I write only when I am inspired and only if I have time. I did not keep a journal, as Kasi did, but I did take photographs and make notes, such as the one I wrote in Laos when I was considering our escape:

"I gave Kasi a little notebook for her ninth birthday so that she can keep a journal. I talked to her a little bit about the past, the present, and the future. I told her that she could send messages to herself when she is older by writing in her journal now. She seemed to understand that immediately. I am writing this down, because think I may be able to write a book when (not if) we get to the U.S. If little Kasi is as meticulous and dependable as I think she will be, I will be able to use her journal to help me with that book."

Information is not free. Truthful information is as costly as it is precious. Memory is fickle. I vowed not to let reliable information escape me. Kasi and my camera were my sources of reliable information. She did not, and has not, disappointed me. However, I owe you, my readers, a little bit of the truth about how I preserved that information.

First, I came up with a plan. I could have decided that letting Kasi preserve the information in her journal was enough. I didn't do that because I had to think ahead. I imagine terrible things, sometimes. However, that imagination sometimes protects me from the worst effects of chance. I imagined that Kasi might lose her journal or that it might be destroyed by the unpredictable nature of our journey. I also knew that I would have very little time to read and copy her journal. Yes, I know that her journal should have been private. I even told her that. But my desire to preserve the truth superseded my respect for her privacy. That was my decision, and this book would have been full of fictions of my imagination if I had permitted that respect to deprive me of truthful information.

To solve the problem that I imagined of not having time to copy her journal by hand, I decided to photograph the pages. That was a natural solution because photography is my hobby and my second love after my family. You may think that it would be difficult for me to do this without being discovered. But you don't know Kasi yet. Once I understood her daily routines, I had unfettered access to her journal. Besides, I was able to control her behavior while she was still young. I taught Kasi the daily routine of setting up the shop in the refugee camp. That typically took at least half an hour. Every other day, while she opened the shop, I would go to her hiding place in the hut and take pictures of the new pages in her diary. I considered this collection to be part of my job as a writer. If not for the pictures of Kasi's diary pages—which I developed only after we got to the United States—I would not have been able to write this book.

Most of the other details came from the letters that I sent to relatives and friends who emigrated to France, Australia, and the United States. Naturally, I kept copies of those letters. My notes to myself will also make their way into my story at some point.

I don't know yet if this book will be worth all of the effort that I have put into documenting the details of our journey. I am not sure how much more effort will be required to complete my story, either. That was exactly how I felt in Laos about the project of bringing my family to the USA. That project is complete, and I think it was worth it. This project has just begun and you, my readers, will be the judge of its worth.

No matter what, this book is the legacy that I leave to my children.

~Kim Champa

Part I: KIM

Haven to Heaven

Birth ~ Laos

"Good evening, folks! This is your Friendly Fred Fry disc jockey and newsman extraordinaire, and I will have news and rock tunes for you from now till midnight, right here at WTWR 99.3 FM Seattle, Washington. Now, for those of you who have dropped out this weekend, here are some of the things that you have missed.

On Friday, The Monterey Pop Festival began. We heard Jimi Hendrix, Laura Nyro, The Byrds, Jefferson Airplane, the Grateful Dead, and Simon and Garfunkel among others.

On Saturday, Red China announced a successful test-detonation of their first hydrogen bomb.

And today, Tuesday, June 20, 1967, heavyweight boxing champion Muhammed Ali was sentenced to five years in prison and fined $10,000 for draft evasion.... Welcome to the summer of love!"

"Only mothers can think of the future - because they give birth to it in their children." ~Maxim Gorky

My name is Kim Champa and I am responsible for turning our family into refugees. I chose this path. No one else did. For you to understand why I did so, I will have to tell you the story of my daughter, Kasi Champa, because I did it for her. Of course, you won't be able to understand Kasi unless you understand the family that she grew up in and the culture that nourished our family.

I was born in Laos to Chinese immigrant parents. Laos is a beautiful country but with a difficult history. Colonized by the French in the late 19th century, various factions jostled for governmental power for decades until 1954. In the IndoChina War between the North Vietnamese and the U.S.-backed South Vietnamese, the U.S. recruited Lao rebel fighters in their war, thereby drawing Laos into the conflict. With the 1975 Fall of Saigon and the withdrawal of U.S. forces, the North Vietnamese-backed Pathet Lao Communist took control and began enforcing their communist policies in Laos. Many former government and military officials were arrested and sent to re-education camps. As a result of these harsh policies, 10% of the population fled Laos as refugees. Our family was one of the many that fled.

Once I had decided that we must leave Laos, I told my husband, Khamphet, that he could stay if he chose to but that I was taking the children with me to give them a better life. He saw reason and decided to come with us. There was little choice, really. If we had stayed in Laos much longer, we would have been sent to the Communist Reeducation Camps like his brother. I will tell you how we came to know about that a little later in this story.

Let me begin with our names. Kim is not a name of Lao origin. It is Chinese, actually, and so am I. It's not that I was born in China. I was born in the royal city of Luang Prabang of Laos. However, my parents emigrated to Laos from China ten years before I was born. So, my parents were refugees, too. I have relatives that still live in China. The Laotians can tell that I am Chinese. I am proud of being Chinese. That's why I have kept my Chinese first name. Coincidentally, it is like the Lao name "Kham" which means "gold" or "golden".

Khamphet (pronounced 'kam-pait'), my husband, has a true Lao name. It means "golden diamond".

My daughter, Kasi (pronounced 'kha-see'), which means brilliant and brightly colored, is named after the city (ເມືອງກາສີ) of her birth. As you will see, her personality is brilliant and brightly colored. So, her name suits her character well.

My son, Huck, also has a Lao name. Huck reminds me of my

favorite American novel, *Adventures of Huckleberry Finn* by Mark Twain, but really, the name in Lao means "love". My hope is for him to be filled with love and to give abundantly.

All of these name origins and meanings remind me that the Lao society is quite insular. It is not insular in the way that the United States is, though. For example, almost every Lao citizen knows at least two languages, and some know many more. That cannot be said of the citizens of the United States. However, in Laos, if your last name is not a Lao name, you might not get too far in life. This discrimination based on last name can be quite subtle or blatantly brazen.

Our last name, Champa, is a Lao name. *Dok* means "flower" in Lao. *Dok Champa* is the name of the Laos national flower (Plumeria frangipani). The *dok champa* and our family, I think, represent Laos in symbolic ways. The bright colors of the flower — yellow (gold), white, red, and pink — are like the distinct personalities in our family.

The yellow Champa variety represents the Sun which is the source of all the resources on Earth. In our family, I am like the Sun because I am the true provider of all resources.

The white Champa variety represents the Moon, and it shines by reflecting the light of the Sun. My husband, Khamphet, provides for the family, too. However, he would not be able to do it without my strength and discipline. In the patriarchal society in Laos, Khamphet must be the face of the family.

The red Champa variety represents blood and the passion of struggle. Even now, I know that Kasi is the passionate one in our family.

The pink Champa variety represents modesty and humility. That, I suspect, will be the way of Kasi's brother, Huck. They are only children as I write this. When I know them better, we will come back to how they represent Laos.

Our culture is uniquely the culture of Laos. Laos, a land-locked country in Southeast Asia, is about the size of the state of Kansas. It is known as the "Land of a Million Elephants". The elephant symbolizes the ancient Kingdom of Lan Xang (ລ້ານຊ້າງ) and is supposed to bring prosperity to the country. I must confess, however, that I have not seen more than a few dozen elephants since I was born. Neither is Laos a prosperous country.

We can learn much from these few facts. Laos has a long cultural tradition. For three and a half centuries (1354-1707), Lan Xang was one of the largest kingdoms in Southeast Asia. Unfortunately, the reason that I have seen so few elephants is because there are fewer than 400 left in Laos (2018). At their current rate of decline, they will soon be extinct. Just as the real elephant population has diminished over time, so too has the prosperity of the Lao culture that identified with a large population of elephants.

Since our marriage, Khamphet and I had always planned to start a family. We did not wait long and soon I was with child. My first two children died in infancy – one from stillbirth and another from malaria at just eleven months old. In Laos at that time, the infant mortality rate was 50%, so our children fell into that statistic. I was every hopeful when I got pregnant for the third time. This time, I swore that I would take every precaution to ensure a successful delivery and childhood.

On one particular day, June 20th, 1966, Khamphet was away on one of those district meeting trips. So, I came home to our empty house in Kasi. Soon, I knew it was time. I calmly began to prepare the water on the stove. In between the contraction intervals, I boiled the cloths and a pair of scissors that I knew I would need. Many Lao women still give birth alone. It wasn't a big deal, really.

When Kasi arrived, as I cut the cord and cleaned her up, I knew she was something special. I wanted to name her Kasi, not because of the unremarkable town, but because her spirit seemed to shine brightly, even brilliantly. When I looked in her eyes, I could feel her intelligence and willfulness looking back at me. Truthfully, it frightened me. I was sure that she would be better than me when she grew up. I lectured her on that day of her birth. I told her she should not be so proud and independent. It was dangerous to be so, I told her. She just smiled at me, and I let her nurse. There would be time for explanations later, I thought.

You may judge me harshly for what I am going to tell you now. However, every culture has its norms and the Lao culture is no different. We are called to be humble. Humility does not come naturally to everyone. When the parents of a Lao child see that the child is too proud or is a show off, they need to correct the situation or lose face in the community. That's all I did, really. I saved face for the Champa family. I told Kasi, when she had attained the age of reason and asked where she came from, that we found her in a garbage dump. I told her that we cleaned her up and brought her home to give her a better life. I didn't think much about it at the time, and I had no idea that Kasi would take it so seriously until I looked at her diary entry for the 9th of December of 1975. (You may judge me more harshly for this, too.) She seems to think she needs to work extra hard so that we won't regret picking her up and bringing her home. At least she is not too proud. I only wanted to protect her.

By 1954, twelve years before Kasi was born, my lovely Laos got a new constitution. Consequently, Civil War broke out between Royalists and the Communist group, the Pathet Lao. That provided the framework for all of the events that would cast our family into the winds of change and on the mercies of strangers. Of course, there were groups that used that institutional framework to gain advantages of various kinds. Some of those groups were political parties; others were networks of kinship. Everybody was just looking for safety or power. We sought safety. Let me tell you how our journey out of Laos began.

Thirteen years after the adoption of the new constitution, in 1967, when Kasi was only a year old, we were happily oblivious to the threat that looms so large now. Then, our future looked bright. My husband was the principal of a regional school system, and I was a Lao and French language teacher in one of the schools. We were living temporarily in the small town of Kasi while waiting for positions to open up in the new school that they were building in Vientiane (ວຽງຈັນ), the capital city just a few hours away by car. Kasi, as I said, means "bright, brilliant, and colorful." Unfortunately, although the view of the mountains was breathtaking, the town itself was quite ordinary.

Being a principal in Laos was a high-profile, prestigious position. Khamphet often travelled in a helicopter to visit all of the far-flung schools in the region. Although he certainly worked hard to get that position—and he deserved it—he did not do it all on his own. Without my help, he would never have succeeded. Of course, women in Laos at that time could not have such high positions. I lived vicariously through his success.

I had to take some time off after Kasi's birth. I didn't take much, though. Just as I had the year before, I was teaching French 1 and French 2. That year, I was asked to propose a new course in French literature for the upper-class students. I was ambitious; and I was interested in French Literature, so I jumped at the opportunity. However, it was a struggle to fit in the research to prepare the classes when I already had so much else to do. I would borrow French fiction from the school library and—while nursing Kasi— I would read. Khamphet and I were thinking about having another child. I was not taking any form of birth control; and I knew that, as long as I was nursing Kasi, our relations would be unproductive. He didn't exactly lose interest. Still, taking care of the baby and doing all of the housework distracted me. He got into the habit of reading before bedtime and, naturally, he would end up falling asleep before I finished all of the house work and child care. That gave me time to read the French fiction that I had brought home. I read Baudelaire and Flaubert. Then, I started with Camus. I was captivated and moved on to Simone de Beauvoir and Sartre. It was their conception of freedom that deeply fascinated me. Was I free? Was Kasi or Khamphet free?

One day, I looked down at the nursing Kasi. She was hungry. She fed greedily, and her eyes watched me. I smiled, and she smiled back. I tickled her, and she lost her grip on my breast as she giggled. She found it quickly enough though. Now, she watched me more intently with a little impishness in her stare. If I tried to tickle her she would grip my breast ever so slightly harder and push my hand away with hers. She was learning to defend herself. That was good. I understood how I could teach her.

As Kasi grew older, past her first birthday and beyond, month after month, I became more and more fascinated with an American author who also spoke about freedom: Ayn Rand. Of course, I couldn't use a French translation of an American author in the classroom, but her outlook influenced the way I guided discussions about the French authors. Why were the French so focused on class solidarity? I felt that this was all an aspect of the rich French culture that was a part—however small—of the Lao cultural heritage, which the Laotians still embraced.

The students in the French Literature course blossomed. Our discussions were heated and made the class time pass quickly for all of us. I grew to have a certain affection for some of the girls in the class. The boys seemed much more interested in the girls than in the literature. Except for one. He was quiet and I thought, at first, that he was rather dull. Gradually, as the course progressed, he began to become less timid. He asked good questions; and the others seemed to sense that he was different. Then, when I was writing on the blackboard with my back to them and they thought that I couldn't hear, they began to make hurtful comments about him. I let it go on. Boys needed to learn to defend themselves, just the way Kasi did. One day, however, there was a slightly older girl that stood up for him against the other girls. I turned around just in time to see the glance that passed between them. That was it! That was the solidarity that the French raconteurs so admired. That was a lesson that I wanted to bring home to Kasi.

During the second summer after Kasi's birth, when school was out, Khamphet and I naturally had more time to be together. Consequently, Kasi's brother, Huck, was born in March of 1968. Kasi's little brother is two years younger than she is. By the time he came along, we had moved to the capital city of Vientiane, where my three younger sisters were living at the time.

Vientiane was still mostly crisscrossed with dirt roads; and it suffered from polluted air largely due to the factories that manufactured wood products, garments, coffee, copper, sugarcane, and tobacco. The roads were filled with many motorcycles and *tuk-tuks* (auto rickshaws) but few cars. Here and there, *dok champa* flowers filled the landscape with colorful blossoms and sweet fragrances. Any passerby that took in a whiff of that sweetness would never forget it. I couldn't.

I had encouraged Khamphet to buy a house in Vientiane, because I was sure it would be better to pay a mortgage and to eventually own property than to throw away our money on rent. Of course, the prices for a nice place in the capital city were prohibitive. So, we had to settle for something less than we would have liked. Still, it was comfortable and even had a nice storage room in the back, which would later come in handy. The entrance was too steep to park a car, but of course, we didn't even have a car in the beginning. The house was a sturdy and handsome house - more or less like all of the others - on that quasi-suburban street. It was painted sky blue and had a big picture window that looked out over the street to give us a magnificent view of the city.

From the east side, we could see the capital's iconic *That Luang* temple (ທາດຫຼວງ) or the Great Stupa – a national symbol (its image is on Laos official seal), also the most sacred monument in the country. From the west side of our house, we could spot the Patuxai Victory Monument; and we were also within a walking distance of the Night Market. We had a splendid view of the neighbors' houses, and the flowers and trees, all in a straight line along both sides of the street.

At that time, it was a solid middle-class neighborhood. It was nothing fancy, but it was safe.

Haven to Heaven

Gold Necklace

Necklaces may have been one of the earliest types of adornment worn by humans. As was true of jewelry in general, necklaces were often used as symbols of wealth and status. That was especially true when the jewelry was made of precious metals and stones. Gold jewelry became even more precious because of the value added by the skilled crafts people that design and create it. In the Lao tradition, gold is also used as a gift on special occasions such as weddings and births.

The particular gold necklace that I had was especially precious. I had purchased it clandestinely on the black market in Laos with all of the money we had earned from the sale of our possessions, such as furniture, bikes, and clothes and most of the money we had saved until then. It was made entirely of pure 24 karat gold as is common in the East. It was also symbolic of Laos. The centerpiece of the necklace was the pendant. It was a solid gold coin embossed with the image of the *That Luang* temple. The necklace, with its coin pendant, weighed about 1.7 ounces. It was worth enough at that time to feed a whole family in Laos for at least a decade! Ten years' worth of food, and it weighed less than six quarters. It is obvious why I chose it.

Of course, for that very reason, many people—if they could afford it—would choose to convert and carry value in that way. I had to be smart about how I carried it if we were going to get away with it. Most people would try to make it invisible. I wanted to make it invisible in plain sight. Because gold is valued by people who use conspicuous consumption to gain social status, I had to do the opposite. I wanted our whole family to appear to others to be the most ordinary, humble people imaginable. I chose everyone's clothes with that in mind. Every one of my blouses was drab and ordinary. Some were even frayed or torn and appeared to have been worn and washed many times. I chose loose-fitting pants for myself and for Khamphet. The colors would not attract any attention. For Kasi, I was a little more relaxed. Even poor people like to dress their children nicely. Still, I didn't choose any bright colors or designs that might call attention to her. She didn't mind any of the clothes I chose for her and that made me happy. Huck was easy to buy clothes for. He was so young that he didn't care, and I just chose his clothes with the same guidelines that I had developed for all of the rest of us. When we were all assembled in our outfits we looked more like peasants than intellectuals. That was what I wanted.

For obvious reasons, I removed the coin from the chain and stored the separate parts in different places. That way, if seized by people of authority, even if they got one part they might not get the other. I carefully sewed the necklace itself into the seam of my bra. Then, I carefully sewed the coin into the seam of my underwear. I was careful never to wear them together. However, I always wore one just in case someone got to the one that was packed.

Before I had hidden the gold necklace, I realized that it would be useless for me to be the only one that knew about it. If I were killed or abducted, my family would not be able to benefit from all of my preparations. I had to tell someone. It would be natural for me to tell my husband. As with everything else, I did not want to do the obvious. Instead of telling my husband, I chose to tell Kasi. This choice was motivated not only by it being unusual, but because I knew that she needed some reassurance that we would be okay even if things got very difficult. I didn't want her to think that she would have to worry about all these grown-up things. I wanted her to have the assurance that the adults, her parents, had thought about the future and prepared for it in the most thorough way possible. So, I decided to tell her, but I didn't know exactly how or when I would do that.

It's not that I didn't trust Kasi. I did, but still, she was only a school girl. I didn't think that I should tell her while she was still attending school every day. One little slip, one little temptation accepted, and we would all be at risk. There were plenty of people in Laos who always had a need of some money or gold and might be willing to risk a lot to get ahead. I would have to wait until I would have her under my control at all times before I could tell her.

I also had to consider the place that I could tell her. Naturally, the conversation had to be private, so it couldn't be outside. Inside, I would have to be careful that Khamphet didn't overhear. It seemed to me that the best time would be before Khamphet came home on the day before we were to leave. I could speak to her freely then, and I would also be able to answer any questions that she might have. Besides, that would give me the additional opportunity to reinforce the message of security when I tucked her into bed and told her a bedtime story as I often did. So, that was how I settled it.

Just before sunset on Monday, the first of December 1975, we had our talk.

"Kasi, come in here for a minute." I called to her from the kitchen. She was playing in her room.

"What is it, Mai?" she asked.

Mai is Lao for *Mom*. It is just as informal as *Mom* is in English.

"Just come in. I don't want to have to yell."

She came in reluctantly, I could tell.

"What were you doing?" I asked.

"I was writing in my diary," she answered. That explained why she was reluctant to come in. I had seen her cuddle up in bed when she was writing and get totally involved in whatever narrative she was expressing. I felt sorry that I had interrupted her in that creative process, but I knew we had to have this conversation before her father came home.

"Do you want to talk about it?" I probed curiously. She looked at me directly.

"I would rather finish it before I talk about it. Some of the stuff is sort of private," she said seriously. I knew I shouldn't have even asked. I am curious by nature and I couldn't help myself.

"Are you worried about the vacation that we are going on tomorrow?" I asked.

She looked away, at the door, and then back at me. "Yes Mai. Everything will be different. I won't have any friends anymore, and I don't know what is going to happen to us."

"I want to tell you something that should put your mind at ease a bit. Would you like that?"

She had something in her hands and was playing with it. She looked down at it and then said, "I think so. Will it really help?"

"Well, let's see," I wiped my hands dry from washing the dishes, and I went over to her and held her hands.

"What is the scariest thing about our trip?" I asked.

"I am afraid that we will get separated, and I won't be able to eat anymore. I don't like to be hungry," she said on the verge of tears. She was a little hypoglycemic and would tremble from the adrenalin in her body when she was hungry and had low blood sugar. I understood how the fear of being hungry might be of concern to her.

"I understand," I said. "Well, this may help. You know that your father and I always try to protect you and your brother and to provide what you need, don't you?"

"Yes," she said still looking at her hands.

"Well, I am going to tell you a secret about how I am doing that for our trip. Okay?"

"Yes, Mai."

"So, come with me into the bedroom for a minute." She followed me in. I went over to my jewelry box and opened it. I reached into a little compartment with a sliding door, and I took out the golden necklace with its large coin pendant. I looked at Kasi, and her eyes were wide with disbelief. I let her stay that way for a little while. Then, I continued.

"I am going to take this with us. This little necklace is worth enough for us to eat for ten years. Ten years, Kasi, all of us! I am going to hide it and no one but you and I will know where it is. Okay?" She was trembling now. I could feel it in her arms. I continued anyway, because I didn't know how much time we had left.

"I have to tell you and not Pa because if anything happens to us, they will think he knows. They will not suspect you. But you have to know because – if something happens to me, you have to take care of your brother. Can you promise me that you will do that?"

She was crying and nodding. She told me that she didn't know how to take care of her brother. I told her that she would find a way if she had to. I told her that I trusted her. We held each other for a little while, and then I told her that we didn't have much time. I needed to show her where I would hide it before Pa got home. That was what I did. That little knowledge was a large burden for that little nine-year-old girl to carry. She grew up a lot that day. Maybe, she grew up too much.

I hoped she would never have to look for the gold necklace for both our sakes.

Haven to Heaven

That night, at bedtime, I went into her bedroom to read her a story. After the story, I looked at her and said, "Everything is going to be all right. You know that now, don't you?"

"I know we will be alright, Mai. No matter what. Thank you. Good night," she said. I turned out the light and kissed her good night. I was ready to face tomorrow.

Bicycle Ride

"Good evening, folks! This is your Friendly Fred Fry disc jockey and newsman. I will have news and rock tunes for you from now till midnight, right here at WTWR 99.3 FM Seattle, Washington. For our long-time listeners, this day, June 20th, 1975 marks our eighth anniversary!

All you listeners will be happy to know that the new film *Jaws* is being released today and if you want to get scared out of your wits, it's a must-see film.

Also, we got news today that Ronald Reagan, the former governor of California, declared his intention to run for president in 1976."

"Life is like riding a bicycle: you don't fall off unless you stop pedaling." ~Claude Pepper

By 1975, especially after May of that year, events in Laos took a turn for the worse. In early June, sometime after the Pathet Lao ("Lao Nation") seized control of that part of Laos closest to Vietnam, Khamphet's brother, who lived near Phongsali and was in the Lao military, was put into a Communist Reeducation Camp without warning or fair trial. We thought it was the influence of Lao Nation allies, the Vietnamese communists.

Unless you are from Laos or other similar countries, you may not have a very clear idea of what the Communist Reeducation Camps in Laos were like. Let me tell you just the slightest bit about them. The Lao Communist Reeducation Camps were somewhat different from camps elsewhere in some very important ways. They are certainly not the "appreciate nature" type of camp that might come to mind when we hear the word "camp."

Khamphet's brother was able to get one letter to us that escaped the censors. We think it was intentionally allowed because the Pathet Lao wanted all opponents of the regime to flee or be sent to a reeducation camp. Allowing letters to escape censorship encouraged the family and friends of the captured to flee. It certainly had that effect on our family. Here is what he told us:

Dear family and friends,

I don't want to mention any names, but my hope is that whoever gets this will share it with everyone.

I am in the reeducation camp here in Xieng Khouang. The most notable thing is the length of the day. They wake us at 5 AM and we work or "study" the new Constitution until 11 PM and sometimes past midnight. For me, the first few days getting only 5 or 6 hours of sleep were Okay. But as it continued, I began to fall into an inescapable depression. The discipline is harsh so there is no way to avoid the sleep deprivation. It saps our strength and—for many of us—our will to live.

The meals are never enough to satisfy your hunger and there is very little variety. Usually we get rice, not even well cooked, and some vegetables. Rarely, they provide some meat. However, it never smells very good, and it is impossible to know what it comes from. At first, I did not eat it. However, without protein, your health suffers. Gradually, I began to eat it. I only got sick once. I had terrible stomach pains, but they will not let you take time off from your schedule. So, being sick is very tough.

The physical work is exhausting! It is often strenuous. Then, when they finally let you try to sleep, your whole body hurts, and it is even harder to go to sleep. But it is necessary that we follow orders. The strenuous work is done in the hot sun with very little water. My fellow workers often pass out next to me from

*heat exhaustion or dehydration. It has happened to me,
too. We all try to cover for each other when it happens.
We help each other up and share water. But, that is not
always possible. If they find that you have passed out or
left your post to get water without permission, they make
an example of you. They drag you to some place where
everyone can see you. They strip off your clothes, and
they take turns whipping you with bamboo switches or
beating you with bamboo sticks filled with sand or other
ballast. Sometimes, they do both. They are actually
careful not to wound you so that you can't work. They
just want to inflict pain, not damage your function. That
is the nature of their careful, sadistic, ruthlessness.*

*I thought about that a lot. Why do they do that? The
answer that comes to me is that they are trying to break
us. They want to destroy our hope. They don't stop until
they conclude that you have no hope. Then, they leave
you alone to just work and study and almost starve. They
seem to be able to accomplish that in just a few months
with some. Others it takes longer. All of us were
promised that we would only be in the camp for several
months, and yet we are here year after year. That, in
itself, crushes your hope. It seems to me that the
education they are providing is an education in
hopelessness. Hopelessness kills all ambition. Escape is
impossible, and they make sure that we all know it.
There are no walls around the camp. No one would be
able to survive the journey to the nearest source of food
and clean water. So, they know we will not even try to
escape.*

*Of course, we could escape if we could commandeer
a vehicle. However, they keep the vehicles under heavily
armed guard all the time. In addition, we learned—when
one captive was able to take a vehicle—that they keep
the tanks almost empty. That way, the captive won't get
far, anyway.*

Haven to Heaven

Then, there are the "classes" where we learn how wonderful the Vietnam communists are and how evil the United States and its allies are. For example, they showed a crude black-and-white movie that included an American airplane spraying a defoliant all over the crops and cattle of a farming community. It was not even a community in Vietnam that they were trying to pawn off as a Lao community. It was a Lao community that many of us recognized. The Americans really did do that. All the crops died, and the cattle died horrible deaths. Of course, the people that were exposed to that defoliant also died horrible deaths. I was hurt that the Americans would do something like that. It gives the Pathet Lao ammunition to use in their propaganda. They don't fool me. I can see what they are doing in this camp, and it makes me sick to my stomach.

We are captured here and will not be able to help you out there to combat these criminals. If all of the good Lao people are either in reeducation camps or on their way out of Laos to the refugee camps — perhaps in Thailand, our only free neighboring country — who will fight these ruthless monsters? What will happen to our beloved Laos?

These are not happy thoughts. However, I wanted you to know as much as I can understand of the plight of our people. Perhaps you can see some way out. I don't. I am not sure if I will die here. I really don't know how long I will be able to survive without the will to live. I hope you will flee, even if that is what they want. Go live a good and full life rather than die enslaved by masters with guns or our own fears. Flee! Raise your children where they can breathe the air of liberty! Be safe.

Yours,

Sachack

That was the best of the alternatives.

When my husband told me about his brother (long before I read his letter), I knew it was time for us to leave.

"You know what this means?" I asked him.

"It means he will face inhumane conditions for many years," he replied sadly.

"Khamphet, I am not talking about what it means for him. I am talking about what it means for you, for me, for our family."

"Oh Kim, we are fine," he replied with that dismissive tone that I have always hated. "I am not a military man. Even the communists need schools. We will be fine."

Fine, I thought, is absolutely not what we would be. It was obvious to me that if the communists were opening reeducation camps, then the educational system under capitalism must not satisfy them. We would be next. Teachers, principals, writers, journalists…we were all in danger. Khamphet was often a little slow in some ways, and he was often stubborn, too. He never admitted that he was wrong and had difficulty accepting any idea that wasn't his own. These traits were important and needed to be taken into account as I planned my strategy to convince him that we had to leave.

Of course, getting ready was taking quite a while. There was much to do. In the meantime, there were meals to make and eat, children to take to school, and classes to teach. All that, I did. However, my focus was on preparations. I wrote encoded letters to my little sisters: one in France and one in the United States. When times were better, and it was still possible, we had agreed upon some simple but ingenious cryptographic rules. Each message I sent informed them of the recent news. The first was of my brother-in-law and of the stormy times I could tell were ahead. The next was my complaint about Khamphet's resistance. We used the weather to disguise our descriptions of social and economic conditions. "If the rain is too harsh," I wrote, "they say that boats may be necessary to navigate the roads." That was an encoded way to say that we would leave by boat during the rainy season between May to late September. Naturally, everything was delayed.

The Mekong River is the largest river that flows from north to south in Laos. It flows from the southern part of China south along the border between Laos and Thailand and finally empties into the Mekong delta, one of the most prolific agricultural areas in Southeast Asia. It provides the livelihood and food security for most of the people of Laos. My brother had his own commercial boat that he used to transport dry goods and other necessities to and from the southern part of China and ports all along the border between Laos and Thailand. I began to communicate with him carefully in code. Everything took so long. The mail was slow and undependable. Still, I was determined to make my plan happen.

We had only two bicycles. Late in August, even though we used them every day to take the children to school, I went into the storage area under the cover of darkness and checked them with a flashlight. I oiled them and tested the brakes. I tightened those that needed it and filled the tires that were low. I put the wheels in troughs of water to look for leaks. I was determined to leave no stone unturned.

In early September of 1975, I caught Kasi watching from her bedroom window as some neighbors hoisted their belongings over a wall in the back of their house. I was not gentle with her. I pulled her away from the window and slapped her face. I ordered her to get back in bed and mind her own business. I pulled down the shades on her window and left the door open so that I could hear her sobbing when I left.

Bicycle Ride

I went into the bedroom where Khamphet was already in bed. "Kasi was watching as the neighbors passed their belongings over the wall in the back," I told him. "Khamphet, please. We have to make preparations. You always say that the wise man conserves water during the rainy season to use in the dry season. That is your idea, and a good one. We don't know if the dry season will come but why not conserve water now, while we have it?"

He looked at me carefully. "Yes. I do say that. How does it apply to us now?" That gives you an example of that slowness I mentioned.

"We should give some of the things that we have and don't need to those who are willing to pay us for them. Money is easier to move than furniture."

"Why do you want us to sell our furniture?" he asked.

"Khamphet, we may not need to leave now but we need to be ready to leave when the time comes. Help me to get ready, please."

"What do you want me to do, Kim?" That was the breakthrough that I was waiting for. I calmly explained that he knew many people that might want some of the things we had. If we could sell things now, we would have a better chance at escaping when the moment arrived. He finally relented but said we should not sell too much because we are just getting ready in case something happened. He didn't believe it would happen. So, he wanted to be conservative.

I didn't wait for him to contact anyone. The whole conversation was just a way for me to bend his thinking and cover the things that I knew had to be done. I contacted people in the neighborhood with the excuse that we were soon to move to another place and there wouldn't be room for all of our furniture. What we could not sell, I gave to our relatives and some friendly neighbors. I knew it was risky, but it had to be done.

Haven to Heaven

Two weeks later, we were the ones that were passing things over that back wall. I told Kasi that we were just giving our things to people who were less fortunate than we were. She seemed to believe it.

So, it was that we were ready to leave Laos by December of 1975 when the Pathet Lao took over in Vientiane. As we listened to the abdication speech of King Sisavang Vatthana on the radio, we were all packing. Well, the three of us were packing. Khamphet was still procrastinating.

"Khamphet, you must pack up your things right now. Where is your wallet?" I goaded and cajoled him.

"I don't think we should go," he said, stubbornly. That was the last straw as far as I was concerned.

"You can stay here if that is your choice. I am taking the children with me and we are leaving tomorrow morning. Do you want to stay here alone with no wife and no children? What kind of life will that be?"

He refused to concede the point, but he got up and started packing his things. That was all I wanted.

The next morning a cascade of events began that carried our whole family away as if it were a riptide in the ocean. At first, the movement was gentle, a comfortable drifting. Then, it suddenly became irresistible. That was how it was for us that morning.

I explained to Kasi and Huck that we were going to go on a vacation. However, I told them, "This is a secret vacation, and no one can know that we are leaving". Huck was seven and a half and probably too young to have any questions. Kasi was all eyes. Her whole being formed a question mark, really. She began asking me questions as I laid out the special clothes that I wanted her and her brother to wear today.

Bicycle Ride

"Where are we going, Mai?" she asked.

I told her that it was better for her not to know until we arrived there. I stressed again how important it was for her not to tell anyone about our vacation.

"Who will ask us about our vacation, Mai? I won't tell my friends at school today," she said.

I told her that we were going to start the vacation immediately. So, she would not be going to school and did not have to worry about her friends' questions. I told her that we needed to be careful of all adults, especially if they are wearing a uniform. She didn't understand the word I used for uniform. So, I had to explain that to her, too. She seemed to be getting the idea, now.

I got out the bicycles. I did my standard check again. Everything was good, and I stowed the compact bicycle toolkit in a little basket under my seat. The bicycles each had a child seat attached. They would be reasonably comfortable during the first part of the journey. Of course, Kasi was getting a little big for her seat. This would be the last time she would have to use it, though.

What troubled me most was the fact that we could not afford the time, or the risk associated with selling the house. We needed to leave now and could not wait for a buyer. In addition, seeking a buyer would call attention to us. Why were we selling our house? All house sales were suspicious to the communists. No. We had to accept the fact that we would have to abandon our beautiful little house. So much of what we had worked for was bound up in our house. Leaving it was accepting that all that work was wasted. All that life time was gone forever and would bear none of the fruits we had expected from it when we got married and had our children.

People look at refugees as poor people. They are typically only poor because they had to make themselves poor to pay for their freedom. *You are only as free as you can afford to be. You own your freedom only after you have paid for it.* We bought our freedom with the value of the house that we lost.

When we got on the bicycles that morning, neither Khamphet nor I knew if our losing the house would actually purchase our freedom. First, you have to pay. Then, there is a delay before you get your freedom. I believed that we would get our freedom and that is what kept my spirits high that morning as I sat Kasi in her bike seat. I asked her if she had her diary in her bag, which she wore crossed over her shoulder. She did. I bought her that diary in June when I was sure we would be leaving. It would be the only record she would have of her time in Laos before we were refugees. I wasn't sure how that would be important, but I was sure that it would be. I told her that she should record everything that she had questions about. Then, we could answer them when she was old enough to understand.

Our plan was for Khamphet to wait five minutes and then follow with Huck. I knew that Khamphet was not so convinced that our purchase of our freedom would be successful. He felt the loss of the house terribly. Just before I got on the bicycle in front of Kasi, I could see that Khamphet was hiding his tears from us all. He was choosing to become a man with a family but no home. It hurt his pride and his honor. I knew I was indebted to him for his consent and participation. There was no time to dwell on that now. I pushed the bike onto the path toward the boat and began to pedal just quickly enough not to raise any suspicions.

"Kasi, remember what I said!" I whispered. I felt her nod her head because she was hugging me around the waist and her cheek was against my back. Her bravery was clear from her silence despite her terror.

I only asked her once to turn around. I wanted to know if she could see Khamphet and Huck. "Yes," she whispered.

We were on our way.

Boat Ride

"The only real prison is fear, and the only real freedom is freedom from fear." ~Aung San Suu Kyi

My little obedient jewel, Kasi, was quiet and watchful when we arrived at the boat dock on the 2nd of December 1975. We were the first ones there. We chose a Tuesday for our departure because it is the most unpretentious of all the days of the week. It is neither first nor last, and one hasn't even had a Wednesday yet to begin to mark the time until the weekend. Nobody notices Tuesday. We hoped that nobody would notice us, either.

Khamphet and Huck would be along in just a few minutes, I knew, but I hurried, nevertheless. I had scouted the dock some time ago because I knew that Kasi might have to go to the bathroom about now. I had found a group of low bushes that she would be able to hide within, so that no one could see her from any side. I parked the bicycle and took Kasi down from the seat on the back. Then, I rushed her to the bushes and told her what to do, reassuring her that no one would see and that I would keep a lookout. She relieved herself, and I could see that she was grateful for that. I straightened her dress and whispered praise in her little ear. I wanted her to know how proud I was of her. Still, we couldn't let our guard down.

Naturally, everyone everywhere has secrets and keeps secrets. Still, when you are seeking refuge from a hostile, punitive state like the one in Laos under the Pathet Lao, secrets take on a whole new dimension. Usually, when someone discovers something that you are trying to keep secret, you will be embarrassed. In Laos, on the day we were escaping, the discovery of our secret could mean the difference between life and death. Perhaps, it could mean something worse than death for a little girl like Kasi. I missed nothing as I scanned the horizon. Adrenalin was my life blood, and my mind was racing as fast as any mind could. I had to keep her safe.

I looked back toward the road, and I could see that Khamphet and Huck were coming. We would not wait for them, though, because we did not want anyone to know that we were together. I took Kasi, and we scurried to stand far behind the others, and waited until they had gone in the boat before we approached the dock. I reminded her that she must not talk to anyone or trust anyone. I especially reminded her to hold on to me and never let go unless I told her to. "No candy from anyone!" I whispered energetically.

Promptly, my brother, Seng, appeared at the boarding place and he looked around nervously before motioning to the passengers to board quickly. He was always willing to help as many families as his little commercial boat could carry. Every time he did that, he was risking his own life, but he never saw it that way, as all people's lives mattered to him. As I passed him, we exchanged silent glances, but no more. No one was to know that we were related. That was safer for everyone.

Let me tell you a little bit about my brother, Seng. He is of average height and sturdily built. He usually wears a cap or a hat. He has a whole collection. He has a broad and handsome face and he keeps his hair just a little bit longer than he ought too, I think. His hands are the hands of a seaman, dark from the sun, wrinkled from age, and tough from the calluses he gets from his work on the boat. He has an incredibly brave and generous heart. He is kind, and he is smart.

Brother Seng is 18 years older than I am, so he has always been like a father figure, not only to me but also to all my little sisters. It has been that way ever since our parents died. We were orphans when my youngest sister was only about five years old.

Seng had a certain presence of mind that made him impossible to ignore when he was in a room with you. Once, when I was only 13, an older boy came into our house and looked at me the wrong way. He ordered me to come with him and gave an excuse that I don't remember. Seng took my hand and drew me slowly behind him. "No," he said, looking straight into the older boy's eyes. "She's staying with me. Get out before I tell your parents what you came here to do." The older boy hesitated for just a fraction of a second, and Seng shouted at him, "Now!" The boy turned and fled.

He had always been protective of me in that fatherly way. I had always looked up to my brother Seng.

Seng had worked on a boat for as long as I have known him. He inherited the boat from our father and has managed the customers, cargo, and income well. He did not live ostentatiously, although he could. He lived in accordance with the Aristotelian idea of the golden mean: moderation in all things, not too much of anything or too little. This served him well in business. He developed a reputation for being fair and honest. His customers always returned to do more business with him, and his clientele grew by word of mouth. Seng represented a whole class of Lao people that works hard, lives simply, and helps others whenever possible. I think of my brother as the epitome of an altruist in the best sense of that word.

As I looked to my left, I could see the Mekong River streaming past and rocking the boat that we would soon be on. I hadn't been to the river in a long time, and I had forgotten what a presence it had. The Mekong River is not just a body of water. Of course, from outer space or on a map, that is what it looks like. But, for those whose livelihoods depend on it, the Mekong River is a living thing. It can be healthy, or it can be sick. Ask the old fishermen that have been pulling fish from the river their whole lives whether the

Mekong River is healthy now, or sick. Ask them if it was ever more healthy or more sick than it is now. They will remember, and they will tell you. The Mekong River is much more than just a river. It is the border between countries and cultures. When you cross from one side to the other, you cross from one language community to another. You cross from one culture to another.

As I looked to my right, I saw Khamphet setting our son on the ground and marching him, like a little soldier, to the boat. I permitted myself a sigh of relief and hurried Kasi along.

Khamphet and I had long agreed for each to focus on one child. I handled Kasi, and he handled Huck. We thought that would be a more efficient and effective escape plan. It turned out to be a perfect plan.

Seventeen people, including us, got on the boat at the first stop. Seng and I had made a deal a long time ago as we were planning this voyage. We promised not to be like the communists who were indifferent to the loss of individual lives. What my brother and I decided was that he would carefully count the number of passengers as they boarded. I would be the last one off the boat. Just before I threw Kasi into the river, he would tell me how many we were so that I could do a count on the shoreline to see if anyone was lost. Everyone mattered.

Once we were inside the boat, we formed a single-file queue to enter its bowels. The inside of the ship was an incredible sight. As I passed along the narrow passageway to our place, I noticed the variety of cargo that we were carrying. There were all sorts of merchandise. I noticed bags of rice, boxes of flour, water and soda cases to be shipped to food vendors. There were rubber materials and rows of tires—there must have been at least two dozen of them—stacked up from the floor to the ceiling of the boat, to be shipped to automotive customers.

We had to squat down to get through the tiny opening that must have been intended only for cargo. As we each got to the hatch, Seng or one of his three trusted hired crew gave us an inflated inner tube. That inner tube, among the items carried in the boat, was our only life preserver.

I passed Kasi to the person ahead of me, and without letting go of her hand, I jumped down as if I were ten years younger. This part of the ship was called the hold, and it was dark, uneven, and smelled of the grains that were held on the deck above. I could also smell urine and feces. So, I walked carefully and carried Kasi in my arms. I chose a place as high up as I could and squatted there, so that Kasi would have a place to sit on my lap.

We each had only a shoulder bag that we carried with us from home. Each one had small variations of color and fabric, but they were all essentially the same. They had broad cloth straps that went over our shoulders and a fold-over flap that kept things from falling out or the rain getting in. Some had fringes, and some were larger than others, but they all served the same purpose for us. They held the few—hopefully waterproof—things that we would take with us to our refugee camp in Thailand.

Kasi asked if she could have a drink. "You can have a drink just as soon as the boat starts moving," I said. I didn't know how long we would be here at the dock, but the trip to Thailand was about eight hours. By that time, a drink would force her to contribute to the squalor of the boat and be seen by strangers. Sometimes, as a refugee, you have no choice but to contribute to the squalor or have your privacy invaded by strangers who cannot help seeing you.

It was just a few minutes later that they closed that tiny hatch, and the little bit of light it had provided was snuffed out like a candle. I could hear the crew and my brother moving those bags and boxes around above us, so the hatch openings would not be visible. I was not sure where Khamphet had found a place in the dark, crowded confines of the hold. I was confident that he and

Huck were on board.

"Can we play a game, Mai?" Kasi asked in a whisper. I hushed her and said as kindly as I could, that we had to be absolutely quiet now because any noise that anyone made could put us all in danger. In fact, all of the families with younger children had brought medicine to put them to sleep. I prayed that they all knew how much to give them, so that the sleep would not be permanent.

In the dark, in the silent presence of strangers, time passed slowly. I had no way to know how long we were there, but it was uncomfortably long. I hugged Kasi and rocked her silently to pass the time.

Finally, the engines coughed to life. Then, the propellers under the boat burbled, and the boat rocked from side to side as the captain navigated away from the dock with the heavy load of passengers and cargo. I prayed that none of the officials that we passed as we travelled along the Mekong River would notice how deeply the boat sat in the river water. I gave Kasi the drink I had promised her.

The boat was scheduled to make two more stops to take on cargo and, secretly, passengers. As the engine and the rotors came to life, a cold shudder passed over me. It was the realization that the dangerous part of the trip was just ahead of us, and there was no turning back now.

That often happens in life. You come to a fork in the road, and you must choose. Some choices can be rescinded, and others cannot. This one was forever. The shudder settled in the pit of my stomach as I braced to be proven wrong by circumstances. As we steamed toward the next stop, I knew that it was relatively safe. We would take on cargo and passengers, but there would be no inspections. I tried to relax and smile a little. We were alive, and we were together. If only that dull anxiety in the pit of my stomach would let up for a bit.

Boat Ride

The boat began to slow and to rock back and forth as we swung around to dock at the second stop. The idling engines were just grumbling instead of screaming, and that was comforting. We could hear the new passengers getting on and after a moment, the hatch opened, and they poured in. I couldn't tell for sure, but it seemed like it was just one family.

With the light that was coming through the open hatch, we could see the new passengers jumping down into the hold just as I had. At this stop, Chansy, the fifteen-year-old daughter of my sister, was supposed to get on. I opened the zipper on Kasi's shoulder bag and took out a little flashlight. We had agreed that I would signal to her that way. As they closed up the hatch, Chansy found us and we all embraced. Chansy's father, a military official, was sent to a Communist Reeducation Camp a year ago, and no one had heard from him since. Fearing for their lives, my sister decided to flee Laos with her seven children. Leaving with the entire family would arouse suspicion – so she paid people to leave, a week apart, with two children at a time. Then she left with two more before Chansy, the oldest of the seven and the last to escape, met us on the boat. An older man had been hired by my sister to escort Chansy to us. After she found us, I put the flashlight away in my bag, and we settled in for the rest of the trip.

Soon, the boat started to leave the dock for the final stop in Laos. We idled and rocked for a bit longer, before the engines got serious and began to scream again. This was the time for Chansy and Kasi to meet and find a way to bond, in spite of the circumstances.

I wasn't able to stop myself from thinking of all that could happen when we stopped for the last time in Laos, and they boarded us to inspect the cargo. I didn't know if my brother had paid off the inspectors or if he would. He never discussed his business with me in that way. In some ways, I hoped that he had paid off the inspectors. In other ways, I hoped that he hadn't. Payoffs are good because the payoffs appeal to something universal: greed. However, the greedy tend to be unscrupulous and once they have the money, they are quite open to betrayal if it can get them power. The greedy prefer power to any other reward. Power allows them to take what they want.

The danger was clearly becoming more and more imminent. We had to remain quiet and calm. I reached over and brought Kasi close to me. I stopped her from playing with her cousin, but Chansy was still closely at arms-length from me. I took out a towel from my bag and handed it to Chansy in case she needed it to keep quiet, sneeze or cough, or use it just as an object of comfort.

Finally, we were coming into that last stop in Laos. This was the most dangerous one. The boat was drifting into the dock and rocking innocently while the idling engine, again, gargled as if it had a cold. Now, I could hear the footsteps of the inspectors. They were just slightly louder than my heartbeats.

I felt Kasi's heartbeat under the palm of my right hand. Mine began beating faster and almost drowned out the conversation from above.

"What is in that sack?" one of them asked. My brother answered. From what I could hear, he told them that it was part of a larger order and showed them the inventory list.

"Do you have any passengers on the boat?" I distinctly heard one of them ask.

"No, Sir," came my brother's charismatic reply. I could imagine his serious face and unwavering eyes looking into the eyes of the inspector. There was silence, then, footsteps.

"Navigate carefully," one of them said as he left.

I couldn't tell whether I just overheard a payoff or not. No matter. I breathed a sigh of relief and released the right shoulder of

Kasi that I had been squeezing with my right hand. The boat began to rock again, and the engine's gargle turned to a whine, and then a scream again. We would make it to the coast of Thailand.

The family right next to us had a little girl just about Kasi's age named Keo. There was just enough light for them to see each other after the last stop before our destination. The noise of the boat's engine made it safe for us to talk, and Kasi and Keo began to play games together. I looked at them, and their youth and silliness brought a smile to my face. I only intervened when they began to tickle each other, and I didn't want Kasi—or Keo—to fall on the filthy floor. We would be dirty soon enough when we jumped into that Mekong River that was carrying us away from Laos.

Being much older than Kasi, Chansy was much more mature and understanding of the whole escape plan, and she handled herself very well. Most of the time, she just kept quiet and followed my leads.

It certainly seemed like a very long time that we were rushing through the waters of the Mekong River like a knife through butter. We were all uneasy. There was nothing we could do but wait. The children were no less nervous than the adults. There was no longer any light coming in from outside, because it was near dusk. It was better for us to swim to the shore when there was less light. Darkness would not be good, because it would be hard to find each other. We were lucky tonight, because there was a bright, nearly full moon and the sky was cloudless.

Suddenly, the engine's screams turned into the gargling that we were familiar with. Unfortunately, the boat would not be able to stop for us to jump overboard. We would have only a few seconds each to jump into the turbid Mekong River water while the boat was still moving. The rocking of the boat was noticeable again. I squeezed Kasi and prayed silently for our safety. I wiped the tears from my eyes quickly so that she would not notice. They opened the hatch, and everyone seemed to come to attention as if we were an army about to go on a dangerous march. And so, we were. We began to move as one toward the light that the hatch revealed. We took our children and the life preservers. We bumped against each other and steadied one another as we made progress toward the hatch. As each passenger arrived at the hatch, he or she would begin crawling through the tiny hatch again trying not to tear the inner-tube life preservers that we had been given. When it was our turn, I passed Kasi through first. Then, I passed her the inner tubes and finally crawled through myself.

Once on the main deck, we all gathered under a tarp for the signal to leap into the river. Khamphet came up behind me with Huck and squeezed my hand surreptitiously to let me know he was with us. Despite all his faults, he was a good man.

We didn't have much time, so we wiggled into the tubes while we hugged each other. I could see that Khamphet had been crying, too. He was too proud to admit it though or let anyone see. I caught him only once in a glance of mutual understanding.

"I will go last," I told him. He just nodded in acknowledgement.

As the lookout gave the silent signal for the passengers to jump into the river, I finally could envision what was really happening here from God's point of view. *Humanity was suddenly divided into three groups: those who fled the country, those stayed to help others, and those who joined the Communist Party. You were a refugee, an altruist, or a puppet.*

As the first of the passengers ran and jumped off the side of the boat, I knew we were the refugees. Now, all of the other passengers were throwing their children—with their inner tubes secured— over the side of the boat and into the river. The fathers and mothers threw their children into the river from the moving boat and jumped in immediately afterward to save them. It was crucial where and how far in the water they should be thrown. Some would make mistakes and those mistakes could be fatal.

As the last of them was approaching the edge of the boat, Seng came toward me, and I knew we were very close to the most dangerous part. He came over and said clearly, twice, "28. 28." That number was our only way to know if we all made it when we got to shore. He hugged me and quickly pushed me forward and toward the edge. I lifted Kasi onto the ledge and threw her as hard as I could. I saw Khamphet throwing Huck the same way. Neither of us took our eyes off of the children. We climbed onto the edge of the boat and launched ourselves toward our children with prayers and hope.

As I jumped, I thought of my brother and the crew of his ship. They were the altruists. They had everything to lose and only the consolation of having done the right thing by their fellow human beings to account for it. Grateful is too small a word to carry the emotions I felt toward them.

I hit the water hard and could not see for an instant. I thought I had lost track of Kasi, and then I saw her again and began to swim toward her as quickly as I could in the clumsy inner tube. When I got to her I asked if she was okay, and she looked at me with those fearless eyes of hers and said, "Yes, Mai, I am fine." We swam as fast as we could toward the shoreline.

There was no way for us to try to find Khamphet and Huck in the water. The Mekong River runs pretty fast and we had to get to shore before we drifted too far away from the place he had selected for our disembarking. As we began to swim the thirty feet toward the shore, I focused on the soldiers-of-honor and the soldiers-of-fortune that sought to prevent us from escaping from terror and reaching our land of liberty. They were the puppets who followed the orders of the state hierarchy without consulting their conscience. What, I wondered, did God think of them?

Finally, we reached land and climbed up the murky river bank to a place that seemed safe. I looked at my jewel, Kasi, and wondered if she would grow up to be just a refugee or an altruist. I shuddered to think if she was to become a puppet.

Although we were in Thailand, not Laos now, our escape was not complete. We were vulnerable to ruthless entrepreneurs as well as "honorable" soldiers. The first wanted to make a profit from us and the second wanted to curry favor with the military hierarchy. Sometimes the honorable soldiers would be corrupt and either use the power of their guns to get personal gratification or personal gain. I knew that this was another dangerous part of our journey. I was holding on tight to Kasi's hand, while looking around for Chansy, Khamphet and Huck.

Now, I permitted myself to look back toward the water and along the bank of the river to my right where Khamphet had been when we were still on the boat. I didn't see them. "Mai!" Kasi shouted. "The pocket in my shoulder strap is unzipped, and my journal is gone!" Suddenly, I remembered when I had unzipped her pocket to take out the little flashlight to signal to Chansy when she was getting on the boat. In the darkness, I never zipped it back up! I didn't know what to say to Kasi. I was the one that had bought her that journal, and I had encouraged her to write in it. Now it was gone, forever. That hurt badly. Still, I didn't have the courage to tell her it was my fault. I let it seem to be an act of fate. I hugged her and told her that I loved her and that it would be okay. We had other more pressing concern at hand.

"Look for your father and brother, Kasi. Use those sharp eyes to find them." I said to distract her. We both scanned the waters and the shoreline. Now, the boat was departing at full speed, and from here the engines seemed to roar rather than scream. The high frequency sounds were gradually muted by the distance and the water.

"Mai, there, there they are!" she shouted, tugging on my arm and pointing. Yes, I saw them, and we began to move toward them.

It was only then, once we found them alive and making their way toward us, that I realized how wet and cold I was. Perhaps because it was such a clear night, there was a brisk breeze and the evaporation of the water in the wind left our skin—and the clothes that touched our skin—very cold. I looked at Kasi as we were running now toward Khamphet and Huck, and I realized that she was shivering. The persistent feeling of being cold and wet wasn't a feeling that you could just simply shake off. There was nothing I could do to warm my daughter or my son. We had nothing.

We met close to where most of the others had gathered, and I finally had an opportunity to look, in the moonlight, at my fellow travelers. Everyone was wet and cold. I knew that I had to get everyone together and get a count.

Still holding Kasi by the hand, I spoke to all of the families and encouraged them to stick together so that we could all make it to the refugee camp alive and unharmed.

"Hey, everybody!" I shouted. "Gather together over here. Let's stick together. Are we all here? Is anyone missing?" They were grateful for my leadership. I knew that Kasi was watching and learning what a woman could do.

All of the refugees—that's what we were now—began to move toward the Champa family. Now, I could see that some were crying. One woman fell to her knees and buried her face in her arms. I ran over to her with Kasi in tow, to see if I could help. When she uncovered her face, I realized that it was the mother of Keo, the little girl that Kasi had befriended. My heart began to beat very hard from the adrenalin.

"Please, don't let it be Keo who was lost," I said to a God that I hoped was listening.

"Where is Keo?" Kasi asked.

The woman just covered her face again and wailed. I didn't know where to put myself. Kasi broke down and started to cry. She instinctively hugged the woman to lessen her grief. First, she lost her journal, and now, this. I tried to stop crying. I had a job to do. Everyone was close to us now, and I began to count. One, two, … fourteen, fifteen, … twenty-two, twenty-three, twenty-four. I looked around. I had counted everyone. I did it again. Twenty-four. We had lost four people and one of them was Keo.

I went around talking to everyone who had lost someone. Keo must have drowned. So did two others. But one child was drawn under the boat by the engines and met the most horrible death any of us could imagine. That tragedy did something to me inside, something permanent. That child had not lived long enough to have done anything wrong. That child died because of man's inhumanity to man. It was an unnecessary and innocent death, and it made me curse the men that had orchestrated our exodus. My anger almost reached on high. How could a just and righteous God permit such a travesty?

The bonds that united all of us on the boat — the bonds that were welded in the terrible loss of life that was borne most by the families that had lost loved ones, but that traumatized us all — those bonds meant that each family would **not** have to find its way to the refugee camp alone. There was safety in numbers. Atrocities are harder to commit when there are more witnesses.

I didn't have much time to ponder or question God. We were all mortified by the struggles of the escape, but we all knew that we would have to scramble to get to the nearby refugee camp. Our fate lied in the hands of the next human beings that we met. Would they be puppets or altruists?

We would have to make our way to the nearest road, I thought. There, we could begin to walk to the refugee camp. What would happen to us next depended on the nature of the people that found us first, and whether they had guns.

The boat had left quickly and probably drawn the attention of the coastal guard ships. They would be in radio contact with troops that might come to intercept us. If those troops arrived before any of the enterprising "guides" found us, then we would only be at the mercy of their honor. We marched toward the road, not far from the landing place, and I waited to see what kind of people or authorities we would encounter.

I looked down at Kasi and realized that our situation was life in its extreme. In every situation under those circumstances, we were at the mercy of those with guns, money, or power. We all must choose our own weapons, too. Some chose guns, some chose money, and some power. Refugees didn't have power to begin with and couldn't choose guns. And without guns to protect you, having money was more a liability than a protection. The last weapon of self-defense was God. At a powerless point, when you had no guns, and money was a liability, an appeal to God for protection was a natural response. That was all we had.

As we were all there walking toward the road and consoling those that had lost loved ones, the soldiers found us. They lined the road that we had been walking toward. One of them, who appeared to be in command, pointed his automatic rifle in the air and shot a warning round. He ordered us to come up the bank to where he and his soldiers were waiting with rifles at the ready.

We all knew there was nothing to do but obey. We all began moving up the bank toward the soldiers. My mind began racing. What did they want? Money or sex? I was worried for Kasi's cousin, Chansy. She was just fifteen and very attractive. Of course, I knew that the callous indifference that lay at the root of rape made no distinctions on esthetic grounds. It was too base for that.

"Everyone—strip down to your undergarments!" the commander said. I had the feeling that this was going to end badly.

47

I told Kasi to take her clothes off but to stand very close to her father. I told Chansy to do the same but to stand next to me. My poor son Huck was all confused and trembling with fear. I held my hand over his head as he was clinging tight to one of my legs. Never had I felt so powerless.

"Line up!" shouted the commander. We formed ourselves into four lines with six people in each. The soldiers came through the line looking at us. We were all really cold now, because the sun had set and the wind had picked up. The soldiers touched the girls as they passed by. They would make them bend over and would pull down their underwear or rip their shirts to see their bodies. One came near us. I looked at him with such daring that he just passed by without touching either of our girls. None of the others were seriously hurt or molested either. They just seemed to want a little entertainment at our expense.

The commander was using his walkie-talkie to communicate with others elsewhere. We were permitted to get dressed, but it didn't make much difference for our comfort. We were all still shivering from the cold. Even as the *tuk-tuks* arrived to take us to the refugee camp, we were still suffering from exposure.

If you have never been to India or other parts of Asia, you may not know what a *tuk-tuk* is. If you have been, you will recognize it as one of the most common modes of transportation there. It is like a rickshaw—it is sometimes called a trishaw because many have just three wheels—but the driver steers the *tuk-tuk* from the seat of a motorized tricycle with an enclosed cockpit. Some have powerful engines, but others are just motors with three wheels. Many are colorfully painted in the cities where they serve as taxis for hire. The ones that took us to the Nong Khai Refugee Camp were drab green or camouflaged. We were just glad to get a ride. The sooner we could get warm again, the better.

I am not sure how many *tuk-tuks* they called to get us all, but our whole family fit in one with some room left over. Two others came with us. So, I suppose they could have taken all twenty-four of us in just four *tuk-tuks*. The compartments that they put us in were covered, and we were a bit warmer by the time we got to the Nong Khai Refugee Camp.

Being a refugee is certainly a state of mind. If we all considered ourselves to be citizens of the world or just members of a global humanity, we would not consider ourselves to be refugees. However, even if we could think of ourselves in that way, we still can't simply choose to escape. Being a refugee is a state of mind that is enforced by others. The most significant part of that state is the feeling of vulnerability.

When we arrived at the camp, it was early morning, the day after our escape from Laos. We had boarded the boat at dawn and the whole trip had taken about eight hours. We had spent several dark and cold hours exposed to the wind and the elements, scantily clad in wet clothes. We were exhausted, shivering, and disheveled by the time we reached the camp. We had nothing but the clothes on our backs and our shoulder bags. Our clothes were mostly just an impediment to getting warm. Some of us had lost irreplaceable reminders of Laos or precious loved ones. Some of us had suffered indignities at the hands of armed soldiers. Our consolation prize was that we were alive.

We were five now. Chansy was under the protection of the Champa family and we took that quite seriously. That meant that she stayed with us while we were being processed.

I have three sisters. I am the oldest. At that time, my second younger one was in France and my youngest was already at the U.S. My next younger sister, Lai, was already in the Nong Khai Refugee Camp in Thailand, where we would soon be reunited. Lai had seven children. Every one of those children was precious to her. She had to hire trustworthy people to bring her children to

Thailand, one or two at a time. There were no phones at all for the refugees in the refugee camp. She had to rely on people she knew and the mail to make all of the arrangements. It was almost as difficult and time consuming as it was risky. Chansy was the last of her children, and if we could bring her to my sister healthy and whole, she would be beyond ecstatic.

Dawn had broken as we were standing in the first of the many lines for food, water, and relocation to the campsite that morning. By the time we were released to go to my sister's place, our clothes had finally dried. Still, we all wished for a bath more than anything, except for some food and water. Being a refugee is focusing on the bare necessities. We rarely thought about those things when we were living in a nice house in the capital city. Now, these necessities were our constant focus.

When we finally met my sister in the camp of Nong Khai, our emotions just boiled over, but Kasi was forlorn and tearful. She didn't cry the way most of us did. She stared and let herself be hugged, but there was little passion in her hugs. I went to her after the greetings were done and just wrapped my arms around her. I rocked her and whispered in her ear, "I am so sorry. It'll be okay, I promise."

First Freedom ~ Thailand

"Better to die fighting for freedom than be a prisoner all the days of your life." ~Bob Marley

Our first freedom was from the threats that were burgeoning in Laos. Those threats drove us to Thailand like the wind blows leaves against a hill. This first freedom included the Nong Khai Refugee Camp, where my sister and her family were already residing. It was where Kasi began keeping her diary and recording her adventures.

Some of those adventures were life threatening, others were sad. Some were uplifting. All were tinged with the context of uncertainty and violence that engulfs every lawless society.

Haven to Heaven

Refugee Camp

"Good evening, folks! This is your Friendly Fred Fry disc jockey and newsman. I will have news and rock tunes for you from now till midnight, right here at WTWR 99.3 FM Seattle, Washington. We are going to start a new segment tonight that we are calling the 'Monthly Roundup'. We will cover events in the United States and the World. We want you to be the best-informed radio audience in the U.S.! So here is the Monthly Roundup for the first half of December of 1975.

In world news: Sisavang Vatthana abdicated his throne as King of Laos and Laos came under full communist control when Vientiane fell to the Pathet Lao. Prince Souphanouvong became the first President of the People's Democratic Republic of Laos.

In other global news today: the United Nations General Assembly voted to approve the Declaration on the Rights of Disabled Persons and the Declaration on the Protection of All Persons from Being Subjected to Torture and Other Cruel, Inhuman or Degrading Treatment or Punishment.

More to come on the Monthly Roundup..."

"I know what it's like when you are a refugee, living on the mercy of others and having to adjust." ~Martti Ahtisaari

For the Champa family, joining the Nong Khai Refugee Camp was like starting a new job, but not the kind of job where you enter an office building on your first day and an office or cubicle awaits you with a desk, a chair, a telephone and so on. When we came into the crowded and packed Nong Khai Refugee Camp, there was no place for us to live. We had no shelter at all. All we had was an empty space and that was very small, indeed. Our situation was not unique. Although there may have been ready-made huts for some families, perhaps when the camp was first opened, none of the families that we arrived with were given huts. We were only provided with the barest minimum of materials to build a hut and were expected to find the rest of what we would need ourselves.

So, after escaping from a ruthless and tyrannical regime in Laos, crossing the storied Mekong River, and landing wet and cold in Thailand, our welcome from our fellow human beings was a small plot of land that we could use temporarily to build ourselves a shelter out of unclaimed scraps of material lying about.

We were a numerous, able-bodied, and healthy family. Naturally, we rose to the occasion. We scrounged materials from anywhere we could. Thankfully, we had the help of other family members who had been in the camp for a while. We also had the help of the other refugees with whom we arrived. We depended on each other to help build the seven huts that housed the 24 of us on the plots of land permitted by the authorities. Together, we relied on the solidarity and mutual aid of all the refugees.

However, what if we had not had available family members? What if we had not arrived in a group of 24? What if we had not been able-bodied and healthy? What then? Many refugees, not only the ones in our camp, die as a consequence of a pervasive indifference to the plight of the helpless. Despite the harsh conditions in the camp, one of the first things I noticed as we arrived was that people helped their fellow refugees — who were, after all, fellow human beings. Sometimes, those with the least were the ones that were willing to give the most. Most importantly, we didn't forget those feelings of helplessness and abandonment. We have to try to have integrity. That trying is what we call our will to integrity. It isn't difficult, really. Everyone, not just refugees, can adopt that will to integrity.

Refugee Camp

Lacking shelter, we stayed with my sister that first day and night at the crowded camp. The number of the Lao refugees in Nong Khai camp at that time reached about 23,000, including adults and children. We shared stories and meals. Those who had never met got to know each other and those of us who had known each other for a long time—and who were separated by events—were able to renew our bonds and our commitments. Then, the work began.

Imagine the situation in the Nong Khai Refugee Camp when we arrived. If you flew over the camp in an airplane that was too high up to permit you to see any details, the camp would look like it was made up of blocks of buildings with narrow dirt roads running between the buildings. If you spiraled down to get a closer look, though, you would realize that the roofs of the buildings were a ramshackle affair, a patchwork quilt of aluminum, bamboo, wood, and a variety of other materials in a hodge-podge of improvised construction. If you landed and began to walk along any one of the dirt roads, you would see that each block was made up of semi-open, pavilion-style structures. Within the structures, the huts were separated from each other by walls that each family had to put up for privacy. To say the walls were built would be an exaggeration. Most were made of cloth or pieces of bamboo woven together. They provided only a modicum of visual privacy, but everybody could hear most everything that their neighbors discussed. Under these conditions, arguments in the family became public affairs.

The other characteristic of life in Nong Khai was its smell. All of the huts had at least two levels. The first level was completely open to allow the flood waters to pass beneath the hut. There were only the stilts made of bamboo poles that held up the rest of the hut. It was under the huts, in the area reserved for the flood waters, where the families cooked and ate their meals. Just as you could overhear the conversations of the family next door, so you could smell their meals. That was not usually bad, but it was always present. All of the odors of the community wafted up from under the huts and became another shared source of good and bad memories.

Over the next few days, with the help of family, friends, and those we met on our escape journey, we built a little hut that would shelter us and give us a tiny bit of privacy in this sprawling Nong Khai camp. Our next task was to find a way to make it feel like a home, even if a temporary one. Khamphet worked all day and night with other members in the refugee community to build a "home" for all of us. Little Huck jumped in to help with what he could do, even though he should be playing like any seven-year-old. In addition to building a place to live, I focused on feeding the family, meal after meal, with what we had. I first had to figure out a way to build our own "stove" and cooking area.

Being a refugee means being housed, but homeless. We were determined to make our shelter a home. However, we had voluntarily given up practically every resource we had ever had in exchange for our lives beyond the reach of the Lao communists. Now, we had to depend on the charity of family and strangers for everything that we needed. That was hard for a proud family, and we did suffer it as an indignity.

Kasi suffered in a different way, though. She was too young to have to deal with the emotional effects of the death of someone she knew. I realized that she was traumatized by the death of Keo. She often seemed to be staring off into the distance. She seemed to prefer solitude to company. Her laughter, when she let herself laugh, was no longer that lively celebration of life that it had been. It was inhibited, stunted. This made me sad, and I would often go to her and just hug her silently. I really didn't know what to say. So, I said nothing and let my simple presence be her comfort. I had no idea if that was even helpful, let alone appropriate or sufficient.

On our first trip to the market, I found a way to help Kasi. A trip to the market was a big deal. Each family was permitted to go to the market only twice a month. It had to be scheduled and approved. If, for any reason, it had to be cancelled (either by the camp authorities or by the family) many dependent events would come crashing down. Birthday celebrations would have to be rescheduled, for example, and much more. We were very lucky to get a slot to go to the market just two days after we arrived. I had to borrow money from my sister, but I told her that I had an idea for a little business that would help us to earn some money. The first visit was not that ambitious, though. I took Kasi with me and we just bought the barest of necessities. I had to learn where things were and which merchants I could trust. Fortunately, Thai is not too difficult for a Laotian to understand. The Lao language, however, is not so easy for the Thai to understand; but in some places I was able to use French or Chinese to make myself understood. With those tools, a little curiosity, and holding Kasi tightly by the hand, I sought out the gift I had imagined for her.

At last, inside a shop of office supplies, I found the perfect diary for Kasi. It was small enough for her little hands, and it had a little lock with a pair of keys. While buying it, I asked the merchant to give me the keys. Kasi was distracted by all of the commotion outside the shop, in any case, so I separated the keys and put one in my pocket. I told her nothing about the gift while we were there. I left the market that day with a big smile.

After we got back to the camp and everything had been put away, I found Kasi alone, looking out over all the activities of the camp.

"Kasi, I have something for you," I said.

She turned slowly toward me, and I realized that she was crying. I hugged her and wiped away her tears. I started crying too.

"Here," I said as I presented her with the diary. "This is a new diary. You should keep it in a safe place and whenever you feel strong emotions, you can always open it and write a letter to yourself in the future to remind you of your present. You can make friends with yourself here and then, you will never be lonely. Okay? Do you understand?"

"Yes, Mai," she replied. Then, after a pause, she looked up from the diary and into my eyes. I saw the eyes that I remembered when I scolded her the day she was born. They were looking at me from beneath a pool of sadness, but I recognized those Kasi eyes, irreverent and proud. Now, those qualities were tempered with something else.

"Thank you, Mai," she said. I hugged her hard. I wiped the tears from my eyes before I let her go.

"This is a key that locks it so that no one else can read it. That is what privacy means. You are a big girl now and you deserve privacy, okay?" She looked at the diary and the key. Then, when she looked at me again, she was smiling silently. I knew that I had done the right thing.

The next day—our third day at the camp—we had our first visitor. I learned that Brother Seng often visited the camp because he wanted to be sure that the refugees that he had transported actually made it to the camp. I thought that must be very risky, but he took it as just a part of his charity work. He always had a business reason for coming to Thailand, and he had the means to get around. He did not want to call attention to our family or his relation to us. Still, he managed to sneak some rice, flour, and canned goods to both our families. He had communicated with my sister, Lai, and she knew when to expect him. As he passed the section of the housing where we were, he looked up and paused. "28?" he asked.

"Only 24," I replied. "Our family is all here, though." I added.

He just nodded and continued on his way. I saw him take a note in his notepad. People mattered to us.

December 1975: First Interview

Bureaucracies have no hearts. Just because you (or your family, or your community) think something is important or urgent doesn't mean that the authorities—those that make command-and-control decisions about who is to do what, and which resources are to be applied where—will take action on your concern in any reasonable timeframe. They don't and probably won't.

We arrived at the camp in early December. It was now late December, and we had not gotten our first interview. Kasi had been writing in her journal for two weeks before the Thai authorities got around to granting us our first slot to the interview. I had set up my vendor's stand and had been supplementing our food and drink by selling small necessities purchased from the market – drinks, soaps, shampoo, salt, spices, candles, and paper products – to the other refugees. We were always hungry and thirsty and everyone in the family had been losing weight. Still, there was no appointment chance for our first interview.

Perhaps I should back up a bit and explain how the interview system worked. Most Lao refugees would become permanent residents or even citizens of Thailand, France, Australia, or the United States. We refer to France, Australia, and the United States as "Third Countries" when they are the place of permanent settlement for refugees from Laos who escape to Thailand. To be accepted by any one of these Third Countries, the refugees had to be interviewed. The accepting countries then examined the records of the family and either offered them entry or not. However, we—each refugee family—didn't endure just one interview. No. Each family would be interviewed up to three times. All of these interviews were conducted by the Thai authorities. Then, if your family was called by one of the Third Countries, you would endure a so-called vis-à-vis interview by that country.

The obvious question is: "Why are there three interviews?" Why not four? Why not two? There may be many answers to that question, but there was at least one answer that I knew to be true. The United States required there to be three interviews on record for each family that wanted to apply for immigration into the country. It was widely believed that the United States was more discriminating and wanted to know more about the particular refugees before permitting them to enter. I didn't believe that explanation for a second. As far as I could see, the reason for the difficult process of enduring three interviews was simply to get the families to give up and go elsewhere.

The conditions in the camp were horrendous. Every member of every family was anxious to leave. I had seen for myself, with my own eyes, that some families had been accepted by France or Australia after only one interview. Consequently, it was easy to imagine that the purpose of the United States insistence on three interviews was because many families would opt out of waiting and would accept invitations from Australia or France, for example. Given that reasoning—which I was committed to—it appeared that enduring the wait for all three interviews was a pre-condition for going to the United States. Additionally, if you were offered entry to another country, you would have to turn that offer down if you wanted to go to the United States. Isn't it the home of the free and the brave? It seemed to me that we would have to be brave to be free. It also seemed likely that—if you endured the wait—you were quite likely to be accepted because there would not be much competition at that point. Naturally — if in addition to having waited — you could show that you were well-educated and hard-working, then your chances would be even greater, and the United States would look favorably on your petition.

That was the reasoning that motivated me to endure the waits that the Thai authorities and their bureaucracy imposed. But let me tell you the stories of our Champa family wait so that you can understand how Kasi was formed by that period in Thailand.

A week after our arrival at the camp, we were informed of an application slot for an interview. A Thai "runner" came to see us. He wore a Thai military uniform with a red cloth band around his upper left arm, and a distinctive cap. There was probably no good reason for a cap, but it was part of the uniform, and the runners always wore them regardless of the season or weather. The runners got their name from the fact that they - from house to house - went on foot to deliver the interview papers. The absence of a car or a *tuk-tuk* was because of security concerns. If they were driven around, it would be an opportunity for refugees to steal the transport to escape from the camp. The likelihood of that was minuscule, but they avoided even those probabilities by sending them out on foot.

The runner had to climb the steps that everyone else did to reach our habitat on stilts. We could always feel when someone was climbing the steps because the whole house would sway. I looked at Khamphet, and he quickly understood that I meant for him to be the face of the family. He went to the entranceway and greeted the runner there.

"Welcome Sir! Please come into our humble abode," he said. We all said the same greeting to the runners. They all knew that we didn't mean it, and they had no time to accept anyway. It was just a courtesy that meant nothing, really.

This runner was different. He was taller than most and more robust, almost fat in a land where food was a perpetual problem. He accepted the invitation and entered the house. I remained in the bedroom with Kasi and Chansy. Chansy was still asleep, and I woke her and told her in no uncertain terms to dress quickly. I peered into the main living area and saw the runner walking around the room scoping out our possessions. I noticed the pistol at his hip. He hadn't said a word to Khamphet, and it was clear that Khamphet wasn't sure of the runner's intentions.

I decided that it was not safe for Kasi and Chansy to remain there. We had agreed several weeks before on a special signal for an escape: I would kneel down as if to pray. I turned my back to the bedroom entrance and kneeled to pray. I reached into the nearby storage box, which we used as a dresser, and retrieved my disguise. Kasi, that sharp little one, saw me and understood immediately. I put the disguise on. Chansy was still waking up. I made a subtle head nod toward the window and Kasi understood. She grabbed Chansy's hand and led her to the window. Her cousin finally understood and climbed down right behind Kasi. They knew exactly where to go and how to get there. Soon they would be at my sister's house where they would hide and be protected.

As I rose up from my prayer and turned to the bedroom entrance, the runner came in. Khamphet was close behind him, and Huck was looking around his father to see what was happening. It seemed to me a shameful thing that human beings would put each other in such situations. Khamphet and I had rehearsed this situation many times, although he was never a willing participant. Now, I had to depend on his having understood those practices.

My disguise was simple enough. On one of my shopping trips, I found an ulcer sticker. It had a suction cup that you could use to stick on to yourself. I put it on my forehead where it was sure to stay and was easily seen. Venereal diseases were rumored to be rampant among the Lao refugees. We had started the rumor to protect ourselves. We had conspired to find different ways to make our infection obvious. The runners rarely saw any of us, so they did not know whether we had had the indicator yesterday in the marketplace or not. I knelt again, drew a translucent veil over my face, and pretended to pray again. I recited a well-known Buddhist mantra for the healing of the sick.

Now it was Khamphet's turn.

"Sir, please have mercy on our family. My wife, as you can see, has contracted a terrible disease. Sir, I think you understand. Perhaps we could offer you something to eat. We have some freshly picked mangoes if you would like one, Sir," he said obsequiously.

The fat runner took the bait and turned back toward the kitchen and sat at the table waiting to be served. I wished that we could have murdered that man as he sat there indulging himself in the sweet juicy mango, that represented a week of my work. I had to work selling things to other refugees for a week to earn the money we used to buy that mango. I wish we could have poisoned him or stabbed him with a knife or taken his gun and shot him. All those fantasies were useless. Our whole family and many others as well would have been rounded up and summarily executed if we had done such a thing. Only foolishly emotional people would act on such thoughts. Still, such thoughts occurred to many people in the camp. Violence begets thoughts of violence. When the authorities beat a refugee, the refugee would think about revenge and retaliation. That was true, even if those thoughts must be repressed. I was just glad that Kasi and Chansy were safe.

After he had eaten his fill and washed his hands in our precious water, he finally delivered the interview slot paper and left. I went to hug Khamphet who was still trembling from suppressed rage and fear. Then, I saw Huck. He was so confused and could barely understand the words that we spoke to console and reassure him. I left him crying, but to be comforted in his father's arms. I had to go get Kasi and Chansy at my sister's.

"Thank you, Kasi, for your quick understanding and action. You saved your cousin and yourself from harm. Do you understand that?" I asked Kasi as soon as I saw her.

"Yes, Mai. I understand. That man was not a good one. Why was he wearing a uniform?" she asked.

"You can't blame the uniform for the man," I replied.

"I know, Mai. But the ones in uniform who protect us from bad men must not have done their job," she replied immediately. She was not a child anymore. My sister and I exchanged knowing glances. Chansy was not quite so attuned to the dangers.

"Why did we have to leave that way?" Chansy asked. Kasi didn't wait for the adults to answer.

"Chansy, you should know by now after what happened when we first arrived. Boys and men can hurt girls like us. They can hurt us very badly. They are not all like that, but you have to be able to tell the ones who are kind from the ones who are not. Sometimes, even the ones that seem kind can turn on you if you are not careful about where you go with them." She looked at her cousin with an intensity that I had to admire. There was nothing that I could really add to that. I would not underestimate my Kasi again.

When we got back to our hut, I watched Kasi more carefully than I had before. She seemed to follow a careful routine. I had not realized that she was capable of such care. When she entered our house, and I had not noticed before, she bowed her head and mumbled something that I could not hear. Then, she went directly to the wash basin and—with as little water as possible—she washed her hands carefully. Then, she dried them and arranged the towel as though she had never touched it. She came to me and asked, as she had many other times, if she could go to her lookout to write in her diary. Naturally, I gave her permission to do so. This time, though, I crept up the stairs after her and watched what she actually did. First, she took out her diary and unlocked it. She was very careful with the key, and I had never been able to find where she hid it. Then, she looked through the holes from our hut and scanned the camp carefully. I stayed watching her for just a few minutes, but the pattern was clear. She would observe and then record. She would observe again and record again. I concluded that it was through her diary that she had become so mature so quickly. She obviously thought about her feelings just as much as she thought and wrote about her surroundings. I was right that she would surpass me one day. She kept to her patient and meticulous routine. I went downstairs very quietly.

That night, we had to prepare to go sign up for the interview request, and even rehearsed what we would tell and what we would not tell the interviewers when that time came. We would not tell them about our political opinions or about our means of escape. We would tell them about our education and our languages. We would show our gratefulness to the Thai government. The children would be clean and polite. We would keep our dignity. We would have to share with them what and how we plan to contribute to our new home country. That was how we had to prepare ourselves, at all times.

Haven to Heaven

Vantage Point

"Life is like a landscape. You live in the midst of it but can describe it only from the vantage point of distance." ~Charles Lindbergh

Much of what I will recount about our time in the refugee camp comes from Kasi's personal journal. These diary entries establish her perspective, her vantage point on the events and people of the camp. These are her entries between the 9th and the 17th of December 1975.

Kasi's Diary 9-Dec-1975

I lost my diary that had all my memories of Laos. I think I lost it when we jumped overboard and swam to the shore of Thailand. I was so sad because you can't just buy the words you use to describe your memories.

I am so happy, now. Yesterday, Mai got me this diary when we went to the town and marketplace. I didn't ask her for it or anything. Maybe it is wrong, but I was glad that Chansy didn't come with us. Mai might not have gotten me my diary if she were there. Mai always tries to be fair. But I am her daughter, not Chansy! I know I shouldn't say stuff like that, but it is true. That is why I am glad that I have a diary. Now, I don't have to say what I think and then get punished for it. Pa is very mean to me sometimes.

But Mai can be mean, too. I remember very well

67

when I asked her where I came from. It must have been after Huck was born. She told me that she found me on a garbage dump, and that they cleaned me up so that I would not disgrace the family. I always felt that I needed to keep myself clean and work extra hard to be sure that I didn't disgrace the family. When I found out where babies really come from, I was sad that Mai had told me that. I can't stop myself from trying extra hard to do well though. That is part of me already.

Now, when I get bored or when Huck gets on my nerves, I can come here to the attic. I can write whatever I want, no matter how mean it is. I just want to speak the truth, that's all.

This attic is where we store things that we are collecting for our trip to the United States. I don't really know what the United States is, but Mai says it is a wonderful place.

Anyway, for me, this attic is the best place in the whole camp. I can come up here when no one is around, and I can write about everything that happens and everything that I want to say but can't say out loud without punishment.

Right now, being a refugee means not having things from the past. I wish I still had my other diary, the one from before we became refugees, when we were still in Laos. Then, I would be able to read about life there. I didn't think it was very good. But, then, I didn't know what it would be like here. I like to pretend that I am writing to myself in the future.

When I look back to read what I wrote, I won't be sorry that I have nothing from the past like I am now.

One thing is for sure. Whenever Mai wants to go to the town and the marketplace, I will go too. She will make me carry heavy things, but I have to help out.

Another thing that I like about this attic is the big window that lets light in. It's no good at night or when it is raining, but if I get up early or after lunch if I come up here, I can see the whole area behind the house. I call it the square because that is what it looks like. It's nothing special, really. It's just huts and dirt paths and weeds. There are 3 porta potties for the 12 huts around the square.

Sometimes, I see people in the huts or on the paths. When I look out I can see three huts on the other side. They are pretty far away, but I can see a lot. I see the two dirt paths that separate our hut from those on our left and right. They run across the square and past the three houses on the other side to connect to the road behind them. The roads are all just made of dirt. I remember that many of the roads in Laos were different. They were hard and smooth. Then, there are six houses on each side of the square. Those houses also have two dirt paths between them. So, there are four dirt paths that cross the square, so it looks sort of like a window frame with nine panes!

We don't have any running water like we used to have in Laos. We have to go get the community water *every day. Mai does that.*

10-Dec-1975

I almost forgot to write about the visit from Uncle Seng. He made a surprise visit just to make sure that we were all okay.

I like to write in the morning. After I wrote yesterday, Mai asked me to help her get ready to start selling things. She made me work all day until dinner time. I thought we were going to have lunch, but she said we didn't have enough so we would have to wait till dinner to eat. It was really hot, and I was sweating. Mai let me wear the only hat we have until Chansy came. Then, she got to wear the hat. And Huck was inside all day with Pa. I think that is so unfair. They were making slingshots, and arrows for a bow to go hunting. Making arrows is easy compared to peeling vegetables, cooking, and cleaning all the cans of food to sell. He always gets to do the fun stuff.

11-Dec-1975

Last night, I had a dream about Keo. She was alive and in the camp with us. She lived right next door. We were playing hop-scotch together and laughing a lot. Then, she suddenly stopped and there was the river right behind her. She said "Sorry, I have to drown now." Then, she just waded out into the water and disappeared. I started crying in the dream and my crying woke me up. My face was wet with the tears. I miss her so much.

I wish every day there were things I could depend on. Let me tell you (me in the future!) about a day in my life in this camp. We live in a good-sized hut. It is really just one big room, but we have divided it with bamboo curtains.

But Mai always changes some of the things that we do. Sometimes we all eat lunch and sometimes only some of us do. Sometimes, I get to sit in my favorite place for dinner, and sometimes Chansy or Huck does. Yesterday, Chansy sat in my favorite place. Then, instead of getting my favorite chopsticks, I got a different kind. I complained when I didn't get my chopsticks because I didn't even get to sit where I wanted. Mai looked at Pa and he got up and scolded me. He said that if I didn't like my chopsticks, then I didn't have to eat. He held my shoulders really hard and looked right at me. I started crying. He yelled at me for that, too, and I had to stop because I was hungry. He said that I could go to sleep without dinner if I couldn't stop crying. I was so mad. But I thought that I could write about it here and that made me feel a little bit better.

12-Dec-1975

I have a lot to write about this morning. I forgot to say that yesterday afternoon was the first time that we set up the stand to sell vegetables and food and some other stuff. Mai made me stay near the stand but wouldn't let me talk to anybody. "Just watch," she said "and learn." I learn better when I do something. I liked to watch Mai make change, though. Money is neat.

Then, last night, before I went to sleep, Chansy

came to talk to me. She said she was sorry about what Pa did to me. I said thank you. Then, I asked her if she minded if I sat in my favorite place at dinner. She said she didn't mind at all. She didn't know that it was my favorite place. I hugged her and told her that I would do something for her sometime. She asked if I would give her my meat, just once because she was always hungry. I had to think for a minute about that because I really like the piece of meat that we get sometimes. We don't get it very often, either. But then, I looked at her. She was a lot taller than me and very skinny. So, I told her that I would give her half of my meat twice instead of giving her all of it once. She started crying and thanked me and gave me a big hug. I like her more now.

13-Dec-1975

Yesterday, I got a big surprise. We all did. Our Aunt in France sent us a package. When Pa brought it to the hut, Mai said that we were lucky that the guards let it through. Just then, Uncle Seng walked into our hut for a second visit. I could see that he was very happy to see us. We got the package because he brought it to us. Uncle Seng said that Mai was right not to trust the guards. He and Mai had a long talk.

Anyway, I got two things. I got a really cool tee-shirt and a gold necklace! Mai said that it isn't real gold, but I don't care. It is very beautiful, and it makes me feel beautiful and important when I wear it.

Mai didn't seem very happy about me getting that necklace. Later, when she came to say good night, she gave me a really nice ring. She told me to be very careful with the ring because it was real gold. She told me not to show it off or even wear it outside of the house because people would think I was pretentious. I didn't understand that word. She told me it means when somebody thinks they are better than other people.

Mai sometimes just comes over to me and hugs me without saying anything. It is hard to be mad at her when she does that. I know she loves me.

14-Dec-1975

Yesterday, I forgot to tell something else that happened. Mai made us all write letters to our Aunt in France. She said that each letter had to say different things. She wouldn't let me write a practice letter either. She said that paper was too expensive. I really like to make things perfect. I wrote my letter very carefully, but I made one mistake. I asked Mai if I could write it over and she said "No". She made me cross out my mistake and write the correct word after it. I was so embarrassed that I cried secretly afterword. I hate making mistakes.

Yesterday, Mai got the whole family to have a serious talk over dinner. She wants us to begin practicing for our interviews. I didn't understand about the interviews. I know that when I don't ask questions, I don't get to know the answers. Then, the grown-ups always know more than me. I don't like that. So, I asked my questions. Here is what I found out.

Everyone that goes to the United States must have three interviews. The Americans don't usually do the interviews. The Thai men in uniforms do the interviews. Mai called them bureaucrats. She said that is a French word that comes from the fact that they work behind a desk. That made it easy for me to remember. I call men that wear uniforms and work behind a desk "Crats". Anyway, these Crats have to interview us three times before the Americans will call us to go with them. Mai wants us to go to the United States. She wants to be sure that we say the right things in our interviews. Last night was the first time that she got us to practice interviews.

The way the interviews work is that a Crat will ask us questions and we have to answer that right way. Mai says that sometimes the Crats will ask a family member separately, instead of only asking Pa. They do that to try to trick us into telling them things that will make the Americans pass over us. Our job is not to let them trick us. That is why we have to practice answering questions. That way, no matter who they ask, we will tell then the same correct answer. I don't know how Mai knows the correct answer, but she does.

15-Dec-1975

Mai did it again. She made me work all day and skip lunch! By the time dinner came, I was really hungry. Luckily, I saw that we were each getting a little piece of meat. When I got mine, I saw Chansy look at me and I remembered my promise. Tears came into my eyes because I really didn't want to share my meat. But I was sitting in my favorite place just like every night since we made our agreement. I hid my tears from everybody and cut the little piece of meat in half. Chansy always sat right next to me so I just had to wait until Mai went to get something and Pa was paying attention to his own food to pass her the meat. Chansy gave me a look of such gratitude that the sacrifice was worth it.

Anyway, this morning, I am looking out at the square and it worries me a little. It is raining pretty hard. All the dirt paths are just little rivers of mud. The weeds are blowing back and forth like crazy. I had to move away from the window so that I didn't get wet. I see that there is a leak in the roof, too.

I wonder if Mai is going to put up the stand in this weather. I hope not. But if we can't sell anything today, we may not get much meat when we go to the market this Monday.

There is a girl about my age that lives in the hut exactly across the square from us. Sometimes, I see her in their attic, but I don't think she is writing. It looks like she is folding clothes. Sometimes, it looks like she is reading. Other times, I see her changing the diapers on her baby sister or brother. I can't tell if the baby is a boy or a girl, because it is too far away. I wish I could see better over there.

Haven to Heaven

Grrr! I am so angry and frustrated! Last night, I
was helping Mai with the stand until late. We were
selling by flashlight. When I got inside, Huck was
sitting in my place! I was about to say something
when Pa gave me the look that he would give me to
warn me not to do whatever I was thinking about
doing. I was really tired from working all day and
hungry, because I had only some fruit for lunch. Huck
was clueless. He didn't care where he sat. I think Pa
put him there just to bother me. He doesn't like it
when I am "pretentious". I felt the lump forming in
my throat, you know, the one that comes just before
you start crying. Then, I thought of my diary. I
counted to 10 silently. Mai had taught me to do that
because she didn't want me to get angry at the
customers when they acted stupid. Now, I used it to
keep control of my emotions so that Pa would not
take my meat portion away. He's not like Mai.
Sometimes he will do things just for spite.

Anyway, when I thought of my diary and all the
nasty things I could write about how they treated
me, I started to laugh. I sat down in Huck's place and
ate dinner without any commotion. Oh, wasn't Pa
angry! His little ploy hadn't worked. I don't even need
to write all the nasty things I thought of saying
because I won't. He couldn't deny me my meat
portion. This complicated things a bit. I got up and
went over to Chansy. I couldn't very well cut my
meat and take it to her, so I did the next best thing. I
whispered in her ear that I would share my meat

with her again the next time I was sitting in my
special seat.

17-Dec-1975

I am up early again because I want to see what
that girl in the other house is doing. No matter how
early I get up, I always find her awake and doing
something. Doesn't she ever sleep?

This morning, she left the house all by herself with
the water canisters. It's a pretty long walk to the
water spouts. Mai always says it is dangerous, too.
That girl doesn't look scared, just determined. She
walks fast. It almost looks like she is telling people to
get out of her way or else. Of course, she may be very
scared inside but just doesn't show it on the outside.
Chansy is like that, sometimes. Maybe that is what
happens when you get older.

I figured, if I could talk to her, we might be able
to walk together. That would be safer and less scary
for both of us. Maybe Mai would let me collect the
water if I tell her that I am going to go with Chansy.
Mai hates to go get the water because after you walk
all the way there, you have to wait on a long line
because everybody can only get their water at 9 in
the morning and 5 at night.

Haven to Heaven

Helicopter

"Good evening, folks! This is your Friendly Fred Fry disc jockey and newsman. I will have news and rock tunes for you from now till midnight, right here at WTWR 99.3 FM Seattle, Washington. As promised, we would be updating you with the Monthly Roundup for the last half of December 1975.

The 1961 Convention on the Reduction of Statelessness became effective, having taken 14 years to be ratified by at least six nations.

The observation deck at 2 World Trade Center opened, giving visitors a chance to see New York City from the 111th floor of the nation's tallest building.

In one of the most eagerly anticipated events of the 1975-76, U.S. television season, Joey Stivic was born on *All in the Family*, which finished No. 1 in the Nielsen ratings that week with the episode, which attracted the Monday night viewing audience.

Soviet Union's supersonic transport jet airplane, the Tupolev Tu-144, began regular service a month before the British and French Concorde began scheduled flights.

After the French pornographic film *Emmanuelle* became the most popular film in the nation, and the hardcore Jean-François Davy film *Exhibition* became a hit, France passed a law increasing the taxes on the production and showing of porn films.

The U.S. Postal Service increased the price of a postage stamp from 10 cents to 13 cents.

And that's what happened in the last half of December of 1975!"

In the beginning, I said that you would have to understand our culture to understand why I chose to turn our family into refugees to give Kasi a better life in the United States. Now that we are refugees, I want to be sure that I explain just what that means. I don't want you to imagine it from the outside looking in. I want you to imagine it from the inside looking out. I want to help you to see it from Kasi's point of view. As a child, she must watch her parents assume the role of beggars. By that, I mean, they must seek the charity of benefactors—whether it is for the day-to-day necessities or for permission to go anywhere. In particular, beggars don't threaten or demand. If you are a refugee who is powerless and dispossessed—but your pride makes you appear to be dangerous—well, then you may be categorized as a threat. That is not where you want to be. It would be far worse for your children than if they were to see you beg.

The Lao culture values humility—that comes from the inside. Our humility is a response to a situation—like being a refugee—in which it is coerced, forced by an outside power. Our humility makes the behavior that others see as begging relatively easy for us. Still, we have our pride, and we neither forget nor forgive. Lao refugees who make it to a third country as their permanent home may be forgiven, if they fail to distinguish between the government of Thailand and the Thai bureaucrats who were the face of that government in the refugee camps. The Thai taxpayers who bore part of the burden of the salaries of those bureaucrats—because another part was certainly born by the taxpayers in the third countries who gave the Thai government foreign aid—were just as powerless as the refugees. They had to pay the taxes; yet they rarely knew how their money was spent. So, the Lao refugees in third countries have no ill will toward the Thai people. However, when they meet a Thai person in any of the third countries, they have no way of knowing whether they were one of the bureaucrats in the refugee camps or an innocent taxpayer. Trust is lacking until they know. There's no other way.

We had to walk a fine line between begging the authorities and maintaining our dignity in the eyes of our children. Kasi will look back on what happened in that refugee camp and see that it was an important ingredient in her faith.

Helicopter

Kasi changed after I gave her the diary. She was sometimes still withdrawn, because of the death of her friend Keo. However, she was no longer sullen. She was resilient, and with time, would come to terms with the loss.

There was a bit of sibling rivalry between Kasi and Chansy, just as there was between Kasi and Huck. Kasi was always ready to come with me when I went to the market. However, when we were working at the shop, she wasn't very happy to share things with Chansy. One day, it was about wearing the only hat we had. Then, she got it into her head that she had to sit at a certain place or eat with a certain pair of chopsticks when we had dinner. I didn't know where that came from. We didn't have any special chopsticks or places. We all just shared and sat wherever there was a place. She really needed to learn some humility. She is not special. There is no special place in the world that is just for her. She needs to fight for her place under the sun just like the rest of us. She will not dominate in our home, though. Khamphet and I are in agreement about that.

Brother Seng came for another visit the other day. He brought a package from my sister in France. Kasi got a tee shirt and a fake gold necklace. I was not very happy about the latter. That was not what we needed at all. She wanted to go around in a refugee camp wearing what looked like a gold necklace. The fact that she thought that was a good idea just indicated to me that I had not explained our situation to her well enough. I had worked so hard. I just wanted our family to be seen by others as humble and hard-working. Now, she wanted to show off that she was better than others by wearing that fake necklace. I won't stand for it! If she was not still grieving the loss of her friend Keo, I would just find it and throw it away. My sister was certainly going to hear about this. How could she send such a thing without my permission?

I didn't want Kasi to have more regard for my sister than she did for me. I also wanted her to understand the difference between real things and fake things. So, I gave her a real gold ring that I had been saving for her. This gave me the opportunity I needed to give her the lecture that she needed to hear.

I also made all of the kids sit down and write thank you notes to my sister. Those notes were not just formalities. They were part of what made us different from the Communists. A thank you note tells the person that he or she matters. It shows that you noticed that the person made an effort to do something nice for you and that you acknowledge that effort. I despise people who are ungrateful.

By the 10th of December, as much as I disliked it, I decided that we needed to apply to France. I hadn't changed my mind—although Khamphet may have gotten the impression that I had—about going to the United States. I just wanted to have a fallback position. I also wanted to see just what it would be like to be interviewed. The only way to get an interview was to apply. So, I applied. Everyone, for the moment, was very happy. I knew, however, there would be disappointments to come.

By the middle of December, without receiving any answer to our application, I decided that we had better practice answering the kinds of questions that the Thai authorities would likely ask us during the interviews. I structured it as a role-playing game. It went like this:

"Kasi, I want you to play yourself, and I am going to play the questioning bureaucrat," I began.

"What is a bureaucrat, Mai?" Kasi asked. I explained and then continued.

I tried to get Khamphet to join us, but he was making arrows and slingshots with Huck because he wanted to take him hunting the next day.

"Do your parents teach you about France?" I asked. Kasi paused and thought. Then, she seemed to understand and spoke confidently.

"Yes. My mother taught us that the word 'bureaucrat' is from the French and it means that the person sits behind a desk." I couldn't stop myself from laughing. Oh, what would they have thought if my sweet little daughter had said that to them? Of course, she had understood my explanation perfectly and reflected it right back to me. She was a smart one, alright. This was the fine line that I described. I was trying to appear to my daughter as a competent and educated person. When she mimicked that, she appeared dangerously smart.

Of course, that would never do. They must not even suspect that we are smarter than they are. They must not suspect that we could outsmart them or that we thought we were better than they were. I didn't know exactly how to explain these subtleties to Kasi. It convinced me that I really would have to start some lessons. I would have to teach Kasi about France, of course. However, I would also have to teach her about Australia. I would have to teach her French, but I would also have to do my best to teach her a little English. Actually, the English was more important than the French, but it is hard to teach someone a language that you yourself don't know. I was determined to teach myself a little English, and then to teach her. It wasn't until later that I learned there were French and English classes taught by the Thai government.

These realizations were all against a background of hunger and exhaustion. We could never seem to get enough to eat. Sometimes I had to make the kids work through lunch so that we would have enough for dinner. That was really difficult, and I know that Kasi took it pretty hard. Children need food to grow up strong.

On the 22nd of December, we went to the market just a few miles from the camp. As usual, we were escorted by the camp authorities, and bought things that we could sell in the camp. On that trip, I broke down and bought Kasi a very nice hand-held toy telescope (actually, it is more a spyglass) that she really wanted. She said that she wanted to be an astronomer, and I reprimanded her for that. What kind of aspiration is that for a Lao immigrant? Of course, I couldn't help wishing that she could actually aspire, realistically, to such an occupation. I bought her the telescope, just in case.

Here are some of the entries that I discovered in Kasi's Diary.

Sunday 21-Dec-1975

I am always hungry. Mai and Pa always give me and Huck the best part of the food that we get but it isn't enough. Sometimes, Huck tries to steal food from me when Mai and Pa aren't looking. Last night when he did that I protested, and Mai yelled at him. He deserved it.

Monday 22-Dec-1975

Today was really boring, except for one thing. I had to go with Mai to shop in the village. It is a long walk, and she made me carry a heavy portion of the rice. She carried some too, but I am just little. When we were in the store, I saw a little telescope. I really wanted the telescope! I thought for a little while after I saw it and then told Mai that I wanted to become an astronomer and asked if she could buy me that little telescope. At first, she scolded me, but then later she must have changed her mind; she smiled at me and bought me the telescope.

Helicopter

Life in the camp was not easy for the kids, either. Sometimes, just a sight or sound of something around the camp would spark excitement. Most of those kids probably had never been in an airplane or any form of sophisticated transportation vehicles in their lives. When the helicopter came one day, Kasi was playing outside. I was singing and preparing sticky rice for our meal when I heard the helicopter. At first, I was not sure what it was. Then, I heard the distinctive cadence of the rotors and the background roar of the engine. When I went out to get Kasi, who was playing in front of the hut, she was nowhere in sight. I was frantic with fear and anger.

I shook Khamphet from his nap and told him that I was going to find Kasi and that he should stay and take care of Huck. I ran out the door and toward the field where the helicopter was landing. I saw several rivers of people streaming toward the helicopter in the field from different parts of the camp. Where was Kasi? I could not see her. I stopped and began to call her name. I turned around and looked in every direction. People were moving toward the helicopter with excitement but there was no way for me to find Kasi. By now, I realized that she must be ahead of me. I began to run toward the helicopter, frantically calling her name and stopping occasionally to survey the area for her bright yellow shirt and pony tail. Even after I got closer to the helicopter, I could not find her. I began to cry. I was sure that I would never see her again. I decided to turn back. Perhaps she had come to her senses before it was too late and made her way back safely to the house. I hurried in that direction.

When I got back to the house, though, she was not there. Khamphet and Huck were inside the house, calm, as if nothing had happened. I went to Khamphet to tell him the bad news.

"I think Kasi is lost," I told him with tears in my eyes.

"Lost?" he looked up from what he was doing and said in disbelief.

"Yes, I am sure that she ran to the field where that helicopter was landing. All the kids in our area went there. But there were too many people streaming toward the helicopter for me to find Kasi. I was calling her name, over and over. I never heard her and never saw her. We may never see her again!"

I couldn't contain my grief. It spilled over onto Khamphet and he reacted, too. Of course, he could not cry. He became silently angry. He gave me Huck to watch, and he went off into the bedroom. He emerged with a flashlight. It was approaching dusk and soon it would be dark. I supposed it was his intention to go out in search of Kasi.

"Stay here," he ordered in his authoritarian way.

Just before he was heading out, he stopped and turned to me. "How could she do such a thing to us after we told her over and over about the dangers of getting out of our sight?"

"Stay here," he repeated.

He opened the door, and there was Kasi with a neighbor! I pushed Huck aside and ran to the door to embrace her. Khamphet interceded. He ordered her into the house and thanked the neighbor profusely.

After the door closed, he immediately began to take off his belt. I began my lecture. I criticized her for having left the yard. I told her that her irresponsible behavior would have to be punished. Then, Khamphet, with a relaxed and confident manner, began his lecture. It had all the same themes that I had used to reprimand her, but it obviously stood as if it were a deposition against her in court. Then, as he had never done before, he glanced at me and gave me a look that I was sure was an offer for me to help him with the punishment. As much as it broke my heart to see her being punished, I knew it was the only way to impress upon her that there were and always will be times when you must say the bare minimum.

It wasn't until I read her diary entry that the truth of what had happened became clear.

Kasi's Diary 23-Dec-1975

A helicopter landed near our camp this morning. I heard the chop, chop, chop, of the rotor (my new word for the day) even before I could see it, while I was playing outside our home. When it got close to the ground, though, I could see it and all the other kids who were playing outside their yards could see it too. I didn't remember to think about anything my parents had told me. I just followed all of the other kids toward the field where it was landing.

As I left the buildings of the camp and followed the other children out to the helicopter, they got further and further ahead of me, because I couldn't run as fast as them. Suddenly, I was alone, running toward the helicopter and I noticed four older boys coming toward me instead of running to the helicopter. I was afraid of them. I tried to run around them, but they were faster than I was and soon caught up to me. The bigger boy threw me to the ground and held me down. He ripped open the front of my blouse and saw the imitation gold necklace that my aunt in France gave me. He ripped the necklace off of me and then saw that I had the ring that my mother had given me, too. He held my arm against the ground and took the ring off from my right pinky. He hurt my finger, and I cried out for help. The younger boy was keeping watch, and he started warning the older boy that people were coming. That older boy lifted my skirt, so I started pushing him away and kicking to get free. I could hear the others in the distance yelling at the boys to leave me alone. Just as suddenly as they had attacked me, they ran away. I was dirty and hurt and crying when the group of adults found me. They were kind and helped me back to camp. I looked over my shoulder one last time and I saw the helicopter taking off.

Only then did I realize what was in store for me. I had broken Mai's rule not to leave her sight. She always told me that if I could not see her, then she could not see me, and that I should always stop to find her. Besides that, I had worn the golden ring and the necklace outside the house. When I ran to the helicopter, I broke all of Mai's rules. I knew that she would be mad. I knew that she would tell Pa. I knew that he would hit me. It was much worse than I thought, though. Mai and Pa both yelled at me for a long time. They reminded me of all of the times that they had warned me. They reminded me of the shame I brought to the family by my disobedience.

Why couldn't I be more like the daughter of our neighbors across the square? She was always helping her parents. She would work every morning cleaning and preparing food for her parents. She never left the house to go anywhere. She always obeyed them and never brought dishonor to her family. Then, they

started talking about what could have happened.
They told me that I could have gotten pregnant like
the dishonorable girl across the way. Or, that I might
never have come home like the girl that everyone told
stories about.

I was crying and saying that I was sorry, but they
wouldn't stop yelling at me. They said more and more
bad things that could happen to me. They were very
upset. Then, Pa took off his belt and Mai held me
while he hit me many times, at least three. They sent
me to my room without dinner and that is where I
am now, still crying.

I just wanted to put all of that behind me. It was a terrible feeling. I was afraid that I had lost my precious Kasi, and that was a feeling that haunted me forever. It could happen at any time. I became more aware of how precious she was to me and how difficult it was to protect anyone from the ravages of the world.

The dynamics of the family changed considerably after the helicopter incident. Everyone was more quiet and cautious about everything every day. Even managing the shop required more than two sets of eyes and hands at every moment. Khamphet and Huck would act as security guards at the stand.

The new year found us toiling at making ends meet. Kasi was so careful and watchful that she was able to prevent me from making a mistake that would have cost us quite a bit of money. Clever girl!

Haven to Heaven

Kasi's Diary 2-Jan-1976

We have started a new year! I am looking out on the square with all the porta potties and the dirt paths. They are all dry again. The girl across the square came out of her house and stood in line for the porta potty. Maybe I could talk to her if I timed my trip to the porta potty just right.

A blind and toothless old lady, and a man with one leg came by the stand today. I saw Mai giving them some coconut rice and bananas, but they didn't have to pay. Mai said they didn't have any money to pay, and we had to help them.

Yesterday, when Mai was counting change for a customer, she counted wrong. I know that money is very important to her and to us. If we lose money, we can't get food. I was afraid to interrupt Mai in front of the customer, but I didn't want Mai to make that mistake. "Mai, you gave her too much!" I said. She looked at me and seemed like she was about to scold me. Then, she asked the customer to show the money and realized that I was right. She apologized to the customer and corrected her error.

When we were alone, I thought she was going to yell at me for correcting her in public. Instead, she hugged me and promised that soon I would be able to take care of the money and make change for the customers. That made me really proud!

Health Clinic

Kasi's Diary 4-Jan-1976

There is something very wrong with me. My left hand is all swollen and it is very hard for me to use it to do anything. It has been getting worse ever since I first noticed it on Friday.

The Health Clinic was just outside of the camp. To get a pass to go there, one of the officials would have to examine Kasi to decide about the necessity of the visit. Can you imagine that? A parent has a sick child. The parent knows the child intimately. She knows the child is sick, just as I knew that Kasi was sick. Now, imagine that an outsider—a bureaucrat—has the power to deny you access to a doctor for your child! The fact that a bureaucrat determines a child's access to medical attention is odious. For refugees, it was just one more indignity that we had to endure because we had no rights.

I was not sure what made Kasi sick. The first symptom that I noticed was a swelling in her hand. She thought that she had cut herself on a tin can that she opened when we were working in our shop. I suspected that it might have been an insect bite. It was already late on that Friday when I discovered her injury—she was afraid to tell me right away for some reason—so the office that gave passes was already closed when we got there.

That weekend, Kasi was sick with a very high fever. By the time we got to see the official on Monday, she had been vomiting and had diarrhea for days. I was frantic with worry. As it turned out, it was fortunate that she had a fever, because it was an objective criterion that permitted the official to give us a pass. I don't know what I would have done if an official had denied us the pass.

I told Kasi a little white lie about her Uncle Seng recommending the clinic because I wanted her to be confident that it was a good place no matter what it looked like.

Kasi's Diary 9-Jan-1976

It started on the 3rd of January. I know that because I wrote it in my diary. I was helping Mai with the stand. I think it was because I got a little cut from a tin can lid. Anyway, it was so small that I didn't bother telling anyone about it. By the time we were closing up the stand, though, it started to really hurt. When I looked down at my hand, I was shocked to see how swollen it was. That is when I told Mai. She got a really worried look on her face. She took me to the place that they call the infirmary, but it was closed. We went home, and she put me to sleep with a towel around my hand.

She went to all of our relatives and neighbors to find medicine. Somebody had something called Benadryl, and she brought that back and told me to drink some. It was yucky, but the swelling did start to go down.

The next day, I was not feeling well enough to write because I was getting a fever and throwing up and stuff. Mai said I would have to stay in the hut and not help at the stand. I was not much good for anything, actually. They gave me more of that medicine and then let me sleep. I felt a little better *the next morning. Mai said that I had to go with her to the Marketplace because there is a doctor in the town that she thought could help me. Uncle Seng recommended him. Uncle Seng always saves us.*

Writing all this stuff that happened so many days ago is not as fun as writing it as happens. But I want to be able to read about what really happened, because I won't be able remember all of the details. I will write more tomorrow.

As it turned out, it was probably some kind of a bacterial infection compounded by the fact that Kasi was dehydrated. I scrambled to get some antihistamine for her that Saturday because I was concerned about the swelling in her hand. However, that may just have been coincidental to the real cause of her illness.

The trip to the health clinic that Monday was the first time that I saw the clinic. It was quite dirty, because the roads leading to the clinic were unpaved dirt. Inside, the old building was well lit, but the old fluorescent lights cast a harsh light. When we went in to the waiting room, it smelled like penicillin and antiseptic cleaner, because it also had a pharmacy inside. The floor was just hard concrete but mostly covered with dirt. The waiting room had just a few chairs for parents to sit on, with their children in their laps. The next room was just one undivided space with many beds, examining chairs, and tables. These were separated by movable partitions that really didn't afford much privacy.

The patients were people with all sorts of illnesses. There was a man who was having epileptic seizures and a pregnant woman with complications. As I was sitting in the waiting room with Kasi in my lap, we saw something that I wished we hadn't seen. The child across from us had a worm coming out of her mouth. It was at least a foot long and as thick as your thumb. These were some of the most terrifying scenes I had ever seen, and Kasi actually threw up watching this.

Kasi's Diary 10-Jan-1976

After a few days of the terrible swelling in my hand, I am able to write again! I am finally feeling like I used to. The swelling is gone, and Mai says that I can go back to work at the stand tomorrow.

I learned one very important lesson from being sick like that. Don't get sick! I was just lucky that what I had was pretty easy to fix. Some of the people that I saw in the health clinic were not as lucky as me.

The health clinic was not easy to get to. After we got to the marketplace, we still had a long walk, up and down stairs, and along crowded streets with too much traffic. There was a lot of smoke in the air. I think it came from the big trucks, and from the vendor's stands where they were cooking food to sell.

The health clinic was at the top of steep stairs and it was all white. When we opened the door, I got scared. There was only one waiting room and it was already crowded with all kinds of people. There were lots of children with their parents, but there were old people and teenagers, too. There was a funny smell that made me hold my nose and snuggle into Mai's clothes.

Mai looked the place over and then decided on the

best place for us to go to sit. The good thing was that there were chairs. The bad thing was that they were very old and wobbly.

Many of the other people there were much worse than I was. I had a swollen hand and a fever, but one woman had a swollen leg. There was a baby that was so skinny and weak, and he couldn't even lift his own head. There was a teenage girl who looked fine, but she was all alone and crying a lot. When I asked Mai about her in a whisper, she replied, "I will tell you on the way home."

There was a little kid not far from us who looked very sick. Suddenly, he leaned over and vomited all over the floor. I felt really bad for the boy, but I felt really bad for all of us, because you could smell it all over the room. Three people in uniform – maybe they were nurses – came out and asked everyone to move away from the mess. They had masks on, and they took the boy and his mother away. It was hard for them to clean up because the floor was just dirt. They put the dirty dirt in a wheelbarrow and brought in clean dirt to fill in the hole they dug.

When it was my turn to be seen, the doctor talked to Mai in Thai and French. Mai got some medicine and thanked the doctor. She also gave the doctor some money. Then, we left.

I asked Mai again about the teenage girl who was crying. She thought a little bit before she answered me. Her answer was sort of strange at first. She asked me if I remembered when I was little, and she used to brush my hair. I said I remembered that. She asked me if I liked it. I told her that I did, because I knew that she was trying to make me look beautiful. Then, she asked me if I remembered the time that she spanked me with the hair brush. I did remember that time. I thought that she was really mean.

Then, she asked me a question that I didn't expect. She asked me if I knew what a penis was. I told her that I did. Huck has a penis, I said. I wanted to prove that I knew. She seemed relieved. Then, she said that grown up men sometimes use their penis to please their wives just like I pleased you when I brushed your hair. But sometimes, men use their penis to hurt their wives or other women just like when I hit you with the hair brush. I was a little confused by this, but I didn't want Mai to think that I didn't understand. So, I just nodded my head.

Anyway, she said that the teenage girl that was there was hurt by a man in that way. She taught me a new word: rape. She said that I needed to be careful when I was around strange men and not under the protection of a parent. I asked about the helicopter. She said, yes, and that I could have been raped, and that I was lucky. I asked her if the teenage girl would be okay. That is when she explained to me that when men use their penis to please a woman, they sometimes make babies. That's what it means to get pregnant. But sometimes, when a man uses his penis to hurt a woman, to rape her, she still can get pregnant. That teenage girl was probably there to take a test to see if her rape made her pregnant.

This was a lot for me to learn. I had to think about it for a long time. So, I was quiet for the rest of the trip. As we got close to the camp Mai asked me if I had any questions. I told her that I didn't, but I asked if I could talk to her if I did. She said that was what mothers are for. That makes me feel better. I feel closer to her.

On the way home, I talked to Kasi a bit about women's issues. I don't like talking about those things, and I could tell that my story about the hair brush didn't really help her that much. I didn't think it really matters, though. She would eventually learn by herself. I didn't need to tell her everything.

Haven to Heaven

Refugee Neighborhood

It is easy to forget how essential electricity is to modern life. There was no electricity in the camp, so we used an oil lantern for light at night. Kasi would read and write until the lantern ran out of oil and went out by itself.

We had limited access to clean water. Most people in the U.S. take that access and its unlimited availability for granted. As refugees in that camp, we were only allowed to shower once a day in the late afternoon for fifteen minutes. People had to take turns using the water. Because there were so many of us, the process of showering and washing clothes was like an assembly line, with people moving through. The community water room had a huge, rectangular, cement tub that was about 30 feet long by 5 feet wide by 3 feet deep. Water was scarce, so they rationed it. Each person was allowed to bring a bucket back for household use. Good hygiene was difficult to attend to in the camp. None of us brushed our teeth thoroughly until we came to the United States. We gargled with salt and warm water every morning, because salt is cheap. Sometimes Kasi and Huck used their fingers like a toothbrush.

I did laundry every few days with the water we fetched from the community water room. Kasi would help sometimes. To hang up clothes to dry, we just made a clothes line where ever we could.

Kasi also helped with the shop by doing the mundane things that had to be done every day. Laos and Thailand were certainly not the only places where child labor was used to support a family on the economic borders. (Picture the society as a circle, where the most well-to-do are at the center, and the poorest are on the borders of the circle.) But here, in this Thai refugee camp, you can be sure that most of the children of a certain age were recruited to do real work.

When I said that Kasi was "helping with the shop" I actually meant that she was working. She was washing dishes, pots and pans. She was making drinks (lemonade, sugarcane drink, coffee, Milo and Ribena); and packaging things (salt, sugar, spices, soap, detergents, and candles) to sell. She had to label things with prices, and she also had to keep track of the money. Keeping track of the money meant counting it throughout the day and hiding some of it under a rock in the ground or in pots and pans or rice baskets. The rationale was, if we got robbed, all the money wouldn't be in the same place, so we wouldn't lose all of it. When it was time to hide the money, Khamphet would make sure there was no one in sight. That was the system I taught Kasi.

The camp had a school for learning French and English. The teachers were usually French and American missionaries. They were incredibly nice and friendly people. By school, I mean a field under a pavilion—sometimes on a bench or a dirt floor—with banana leaves or bamboo mats to sit on. Of course, I wanted both of my children to learn English, so they went to school a few times a week for a few hours. Kasi came back to our hut soon after she began and proudly told me that the first English words she learned were "apples" and "bananas" with the help of the teacher's visual aids. They learned to sing and write the alphabet. They learned phrases like "hello," "goodbye," "I'm hungry," and "I need to go to the bathroom." Of course, that's about all they learned the entire time she took those classes. Sometimes, they would have some children books that they would lend to us. The kids would take turns each week borrowing them. Khamphet and I would try to read them with Kasi as a way of learning English too. Khamphet was very frustrated and wished that we would just stick with the language we already knew: French.

With all these issues – the lack of food, hygiene, and opportunities to learn – Kasi was focused on the little things that she could control and in making friends in the new neighborhood.

After we had been at the camp for a little over five weeks, she wrote:

Kasi's Diary 11-Jan-1976

I got a chance to talk to my brother about our seating during dinner. All he wanted was for me to promise to play with him sometimes. That seemed like a good deal to be made.

Today, I am going to ask Chansy if she will come with me to the porta potty to talk to that girl that lives across the square. Of course, I will have to explain to her my idea of going to get water in a group instead of letting Mai do it all the time. If she agrees to go with me, I think that will be a big change for our family. Mai will be very proud of us.

12-Jan-1976

Wow! I am so happy that Chansy decided to come with me to talk to our neighbor across the way. Of course, you can't just go up to someone and start asking questions. We decided that my plan was a good one. We would try to get in line with her at the porta potty and strike up a conversation. It worked!

We introduced ourselves and found out that her name is Phoemkhun. She is a Hmong and speaks in a different accent from ours. So, I asked her why she seems to be working all the time. She seemed very uncomfortable when she answered the question. She just said that her family had a lot of work to do and she wanted to help. She asked us about the store that she saw us working in often. We told her that we had to work in the store to help the family. We asked her if she would like us to go with her to get water in the morning. She looked terrified! She said that her parents did not want her to have any friends and that they watched her carefully whenever she left the house.

Then, she started crying! She quickly wiped the tears from her face and said that she would really like to have company to go get water, but we would have to meet beyond the square so that we would not be seen by her parents. That was all we were able to talk about. Now, Chansy and I will have to talk to Mai to see if we can get her permission to take her place on the trip to get water.

13-Jan -1976

Today, I was able to keep my promise to Huck. Last year in Laos, Mai and Pa had shown me how to make bottle-cap spinner toys. I asked him if he would like to learn how. He said, "yes." I asked him if he would be able to show me how to make arrows and slingshots. He said he could, because he had gotten very good at it. Pa would teach him, but not me — because I am a girl. Huck didn't know why Pa didn't teach me, and I wasn't going to talk about it. So, we were able to spend some time together. I taught him how to make the bottle-cap spinner toy, and he taught me how to make arrows. We figured out how to make a slingshot together. We used whatever we could find around us: tree branches for the body and the rubber part of an old flip-flop for the string.

Before he went away very happy with his self-made spinner toy, I reminded him of his promise to let me sit in my favorite place. He said that was fine with him. We had so much fun!

The weather was nice yesterday, so Pa made a kite with us using newspaper, some bamboo sticks, sticky rice, and water or saliva. I didn't like the saliva part, but it really worked!

Of course, I will still have to worry about Pa forcing Huck to sit in my place. But at least I won't have to fight them both.

14-Jan-1976

Everything went fine yesterday. Everything was orderly all-day long. I got to sit in my place at mealtimes, I helped Mai by making change at the stand, and my tee-shirt was folded nicely in its place. I felt so calm and in control!

15-Jan-1976

Chansy and I worked all day with Mai at the stand, yesterday. When there weren't any customers, we talked to Mai about going to get the water. She was not against the idea. In fact, she liked it, but she wanted to be sure we understood all of the possible dangers. She used the word rape again. Chansy seemed to understand, and I was glad that Mai had explained it to me when we were in the Health Clinic. She told us to stay within sight of each other. She even wanted us to hold hands. We had to talk her out of that because we would not be able to carry as much water if we were holding our hands. She finally

gave up on that idea. Then she told us how we should
dress, and how not to look at people in the eyes, and
on and on. Chansy and I were both exhausted after
the talk, but tomorrow she is going to go with us to
be sure we understand what will have to be done.
That is progress!

I was glad that Kasi was seeking out friends despite the
destitution of the refugee camp. There must be some good kids
here. The one she had chosen, Phoemkhun, was the one that
Khamphet and I had noticed because she behaved so well. We had
lauded her as a model, and now Kasi was actually going to meet
her. It seemed like she had taken our approval to heart.

She was also realizing that life in the camp was difficult and
that the easy life she had in Laos was no longer possible. We would
have to fight our way back to that standard of living from the lowly
status of refugees.

Kasi's Diary 16-Jan-1976

I am only a kid, but so many things are happening
to me and to our family. It is always hard to get
enough to eat. That means that I have to fight with
Chansy and Huck sometimes to get my fair share.
That never happened in Laos.

Everything is more difficult here in Thailand,
because we don't have electricity and running water
like we did in Laos. It seems to me that we live closer
to the ground than we did in Laos. We sit on the
ground to eat. We sleep on the same thin bamboo
mats that we sit on. Only our hut is higher. It is on

stilts – that is to save it from flooding.

All the refugees are suspicious of each other. We need to hide any money we make, because everybody has so little. Even the children are like that. If one child shows some toy or piece of clothing or anything that makes them feel good about themselves, the others want it and even try to take it sometimes. And there's nothing you can do about it. That is what happened to me during the helicopter incident. Since I write about these things, I must be thinking about them even more than others are. Maybe I have more questions than answers.

My relations with the other members of my family are very important. But, they are difficult, too. Mai is always in charge, and I always want to help her and go to the market with her, but sometimes she treats me bad. Pa usually treats me bad. If I try to speak up, he always punishes me. He always wants to have the last word. I know that what I say is sometimes right, but he doesn't listen to me. And when Pa says something, Mai never defends me. She will defend me against anyone else, but not against him.

So, I really hope that I will be able to make friends with Phoemkhun. I put a lot of hope on her now.

On the 16th of January, we went to see the USCC (U.S. Catholic Charities) people for the first time. I believe that they are somewhat different now than they were then. However, at that time—and in our interactions with them—they were models of Christian charity. Actually, it might be more fair to say that they were models of human charity. It was quite notable that they did not explicitly mention their Catholic, or even Christian, affiliation. They gave us the things that we needed and did so without any requirement. We did not have to sit through their lectures or accept their literature, their Bible, or their God. They gave in pure response to our expressed need, and we knew that they did not expect us to be ashamed of that need, either. For refugees like us, that was a refreshing reprieve.

Kasi noticed this and that made me happy, but she was also focused on our domestic situation:

Kasi's Diary 17-Jan-1976

Yesterday, we went to the stand where a very nice group of people give us food and clothes. I don't know who they are or why they are doing it, but it is so nice to see their smiling faces. They never make you feel ashamed, because you depend on their charity. I really like them. They come every week, I think.

When I read over my last entry, I realized that I have not described where I sleep. We don't have much space, so we have to put our bedding down every night, and then roll it up and put it away every morning. It isn't very comfortable, either. We don't have beds or mattresses like in Laos. Instead, we just lie on the same bamboo mats that we use to sit on for mealtimes. They are very thin.

As usual, it was hard to get to sleep last night. If you want to sleep before anyone else, it is almost impossible because they are all moving around and talking. So, it is sometimes hard to sleep until the last person lies down. That is usually Mai, because she always waits until Pa is asleep before she lies down near him. Pa always seems to be able to sleep no matter what. Lucky him. I sleep in the corner, Chansy sleeps next to me, and then Huck. Chansy snores a little.

Mai and Pa have been fighting a lot. It is grown-up stuff, but I can understand some of it. I understand that Mai wants to go to the United States, and Pa wants to go to France. Where do I want to go? I don't even know how to answer that question. I want to go somewhere else, and I want to go there soon. I want to be in school like I used to be. I want to have electricity and running water. I want to be able to read books. I think they speak English in the United States, and they speak French in France. But I just speak Lao. That makes me feel very small. How can I survive in this big world when I can't even understand what other people say? Mai says that she is going to begin to teach us basic English. But she doesn't even speak English!

I have to go have breakfast and start the day.

She was right about the fights that Khamphet and I were having. Without any privacy, it was very difficult to keep our arguments to ourselves. Khamphet's reason for wanting to go to France was not only because he spoke French and not English. It was also because he had a "friend" there. His friend was a woman, and she was a threat to the unity of our family. My insistence on going to the United States was, admittedly, in part, to prevent

Khamphet and his "friend" from destroying this family that I had worked so hard to nourish. I was not able to explain that to Kasi. Maybe someday.

Certainly, it is possible that some of our frustrations with each other were taken out on the kids. I realized this when I read this diary entry:

Kasi's Diary 18-Jan-1976

Yesterday I was punished by Pa again. I wish I was as big as he is so that he could not treat me the way he does. The whole thing started over the fruit juice. Mai made some juice from oranges and mangoes that would soon have gone bad. Everybody wanted some, because it is very good. I got the last bit, and I didn't get nearly as much as Huck who was sitting right next to me. I asked him if he could share a little bit of his with me. He said "Okay." Pa overheard us. "No!" he shouted. I don't know what I was thinking, but I told him that it was none of his business! I know that was a bad thing to say. What did I think his reaction would be?

Anyway, he reacted pretty much the way you would expect. He got up from the table and came over to me. He picked up the switch that he keeps near the table and when he got to me he grabbed me by the arm and said, "What did you say?" I wouldn't answer him. That only made him angrier. He took my pants down in front of everyone, and he hit me with the switch while he was holding my arm so that I couldn't get away. I looked at Mai, and she just looked away. I looked at Chansy and she was crying, but I could see that she was afraid to say anything. Then, he let me go and told me to pull up my pants and to go to sleep. I hadn't finished my dinner. But I couldn't even get back down to sit near my food because it hurt so badly. I really wanted to get back at him for embarrassing me and hurting me, but I knew there was nothing that I could do. Anything I did would only have made it worse. I just went to my sleeping mat and cried.

Our family, like most, is not a democracy. Khamphet and I are the leaders, and the children must obey or at least show respect. In time, I believe they will come to understand why we have done the things that we are doing now. Until then, we simply have to do what has to be done and hope for the best. Kasi's angry and hurt diary entry, however, gave me a more balanced perspective. Of course, Khamphet did not have the benefit of Kasi's perspective, because I was not able to tell him that I was spying on my own daughter.

Our life as refugees did not stop as a consequence of the domestic focus of our daughter. I continued to take the kids with me to check the list on the Interview Building to see if France had responded to our application. As usual, it hadn't. France was a backup plan. America was still our first choice. We also continued our daily trek to the market to get necessities and the things that we wanted to sell. Getting meat, because it was expensive, was always a problem.

Haven to Heaven

Kasi's Diary 19-Jan-1976

Today, Mai and I will be going to the market. Last night we had a little meat with our meal before the fight. Mai and Pa know that Mai and I will need the strength to bring back the heavy bundles. We have to buy rice for ourselves, but Mai thinks that we should buy some extra to make some sweet rice cakes to sell to customers. I think that I helped to convince her, because I used my math skills to figure out how much we could profit.

Mai is beginning to depend on me more and more, now. And I feel good. She let me deal with the money and with customers, too. She even trusts me to hide the money. She always tells me that people might try to steal it, but nobody ever does. I can't imagine the kind of person that would do that!

It is still hard for me to walk because of the beating that I got from Pa yesterday. I won't let him see that I am in pain, though. Sometimes I hate him!

I suppose, while any refugee still has hope, our dreams reveal a lot about the nature of that hope, if we are willing to listen. I hadn't been able to remember my dreams for a long time. I don't think it was because I had lost hope; I was still determined to get to the United States. Still, I slept so little each night, that I guess I may not have had time for dreams or for remembering them. But Kasi could dream, and she wrote about them. Her dreams told me a lot about her, and in a strange way, about all of us.

Refugee Neighborhood

Kasi's Diary 20-Jan-1976

I was so tired when we got back from the market last night that I almost went to sleep without dinner! I finally dragged myself to the eating area and had some sticky rice and broth, but that was it. It still hurts when I sit. I went straight to sleep afterwards.

When I fell asleep, I dreamt for the first time in a long time. In my dream, I was paddling a canoe in the Mekong River. Swimming next to me were several elephants! They were very friendly at first, but then they seemed to get mad. I started paddling faster to get away from them, because they were not very fast. When I looked back, they seemed far away, but I heard someone calling my name. It was Keo! She was riding on the back of one of the elephants and calling my name. I slowed down to try to let her get into my canoe. She jumped from the elephant but missed the boat and fell into the water. I pushed my oar into the water where she had sunk, and I thought I saw her face and one hand reaching for the oar. But then she was gone, and I was crying.

Normally, when I dream like that with so much emotion, I wake up. This time, I kept on dreaming. Suddenly, I was Keo and I could see the sky above me, and the elephant legs moving next to me. I thought that the only way that I could save myself was by getting inside the elephant. I was holding my breath, and I climbed inside the elephant's mouth and into his stomach. Much to my surprise, there was a swimming pool inside! It reminded me of that very rich friend I had in Laos in the capital city. Then, suddenly, I was

on the shore of the Mekong River again. We had all
just gotten to land, and I could see Uncle Seng's boat
leaving and going into the fog. Then, I heard Mai
calling my name, and it was really her. I was late for
breakfast. What does my dream mean?

What does it mean? That is a good question, my bright-eyed one! For me, the metaphor of the elephant's mouth as a gateway to a world with swimming pools is about the gateway of the application to the United States, and the interview that would grant us entry. To me, the loss of Keo represents the many other losses that are a consequence of the war that has driven us from our native land and into the unknown. Kasi is a deep dreamer, for sure.

Reading Kasi's description of her dream made me realize that we are all living between the dream-world and the physical-world. Without the dream-world it is hard to imagine how the physical world would make any sense. I think we carry the dream-world with us as we go through our day. We are dreaming-while-awake. That is how we impose meaning on the physical world.

I'm glad to see Kasi forging ahead in making friends with Phoemkhun:

Kasi's Diary 21-Jan-1976

I finally got a chance to fetch water with
Phoemkhun. She's 13. She is even stranger than I
thought! She is really quiet and doesn't laugh easily. In
fact, she usually laughs only long after you would
expect. I don't know how to explain it, exactly.
Anyway, she doesn't talk much either. I don't mind
that because it gives me more of a chance to talk. I

really need to talk to a friend. But when she does talk, she talks so softly. You have to listen really hard to hear her.

When we walk, it's always Chansy on the right, Phoemkhun in the middle, and me on the left. That is tallest to shortest (also oldest to youngest) right to left. Like me, Chansy is pretty talkative. But, she is a good listener when she wants to be. After we were walking and joking for a while, we got to the water place and had to wait in line. That gave us a chance to talk a bit more.

Then, on the way back, we were all pretty relaxed and comfortable. Phoemkhun finally had the courage to tell us what is going on with her. Her parents basically treat her like a slave. That is why she looks like she is such a good daughter from the outside. She told us some of the punishments her father has for her. Sometimes, he locks her in the storage area. She is afraid of the dark and of closed places, so that would be the worst thing that could happen to her. She would do anything to avoid having to go back in there. So, she does all of the work that has to be done around the house. We both told her that we have it pretty bad too. But, we recognized that she has it worse. I think we are comforting to her.

We agreed to try to help each other and vowed to continue to see each other every third day on the water trip. Mai doesn't want us to go every day. Besides the whole family goes to the Interview Building every day in the afternoon to check if we are

listed to go to another country. I wouldn't want to go
to get water everyday anyway.

Sometimes, my family thinks that I am slightly paranoid,
because I am too suspicious of outsiders. Kasi, I knew from her
diary entries, was not at all convinced that the kind of people that
would rob us actually existed. If you don't believe such people
exist, there is little I can do or say to convince you. Unfortunately,
only life experience will convince you in a way my words can't.
Here is how Kasi became convinced:

Kasi's Diary 22-Jan-1976

Well, it finally happened. We were robbed
yesterday! It is hard for me to even remember how it
happened, even though it was just yesterday.

Mai was selling things to an older couple. I don't
remember what she was selling. I was putting things
in order, because it was almost time to close shop. I
think the robbers were waiting till the end of the day
when they expected us to have the most money. Of
course, we stash the money every few hours, so we
never have much. That time, I hadn't been able to
stash the money for a while, so we had more than
usual. When the older couple left, I went up front to
collect and stash the money. That is when the robbers
came from the side. They must have been hiding
there, just waiting for the old couple to leave.
Anyway, they came from both sides. One of them
grabbed me, and the other one grabbed Mai. The one
who grabbed me had a cloth over his face so that I

couldn't see what he looked like. He smelled like lemon juice, though. I will always remember that. Anyway, he grabbed the money that I had in my hand, and then he grabbed me by the neck and told me that if I said anything to anyone he would be back to do what he wanted with me. Then, he put his hand on my chest and threw me to the ground. The other one had done the same thing to Mai. I was so scared for Mai. Pa and Huck were not there to protect us.

They found the money that we used to make change, and they took it. They even stole some of the stuff we had for sale. Then, they turned over the stand and ran away. It was just dusk so that it was hard to see them, and we were too concerned about saving the stuff at the stand to worry about going after them.

Refugees are disillusioned by these kinds of encounters. Many people in the United States that I have met are naive like Kasi was before the robbery. They can't fathom that that anyone would have such evil intentions. They seem fearless, because they have never encountered the predators. Those of us who have encountered those predators never forget our encounters, and we are not the same afterward.

The real challenge is to be fearless despite your recognition that fear is reasonable. Unless you are able to cultivate your own fearlessness, the predators can control you. The predator's actions have a powerful effect on their victims. And, enraging. It hurt me when I read Kasi's words.

Haven to Heaven

Kasi's Diary 23-Jan-1976

As usual, we were not on any list at the Interview Building yesterday.

The effects of the robbery were worse than the robbery itself. I had a nightmare last night. Pa took the robbery very hard. He blames himself for not having been there to protect us. He had been out hunting with Huck. Of course, he also blames Mai for having the stand at all. Mai had a very cold response to Pa's suggestion that she stop doing the stand. She suggested, instead, that he stop hunting since he rarely gets anything while she constantly makes money with the shop. Pa went to his corner and began writing a letter to someone.

But it gets worse. When Chansy's mother learned of the robbery, she asked Chansy to come back and stay with her. But she has 6 other children! There is less privacy and space, and peace of mind in Chansy's mother's hut than there is in ours. And besides, Chansy and I are good friends now. We don't want to be split up by this stupid event.

Huck is very confused about everything that is happening. He doesn't really like to go hunting with Pa, because he doesn't like killing. Still, he likes the fact that Pa pays attention to him, because the rest of us are too busy to spend much time with him. I will play one of his games with him sometimes, but it is just too much trouble, really.

Like Kasi, I felt bad for Khamphet. He really did take it hard. However, it was completely irrational for him to suggest that I ought to stop selling things at the shop and shutdown the business. That I would not stand for.

I also opposed my sister's plan to take Chansy back. Just when the cousins had gotten to this good point in their relationship, it would have been a terrible punishment to separate them. Of course, I was thankful for the help that Chansy gave to us at the shop. However, we were the ones that were feeding and housing her. So, there was mutual benefit. It was not as if we were taking advantage of her. Anyway, she wanted to stay, and she ended up staying.

I am well aware of our difficulty in discussing violence. Violence is a terrible thing. But, we all know that it is everywhere. The robbery just brought it to the surface of our awareness. But we seem to carry the dream world around with us to help give meaning to the world. That dream world can reveal much about our desire to defend ourselves from others. Listen to Kasi:

Kasi's Diary 24-Jan-1976

I had another nightmare about the robbery last night. They were the same guys. I recognized the lemon smell before they even came closer. I held back my fear and decided to do something. This time, I had a stick of some kind, and I saw the robbers coming. I hit the one that was coming at me in the head with the stick, and he fell down. The one that was attacking Mai saw me coming at him with the stick, and he ran away. Mai was terrified. She hugged me afterward, and we cried. Then, I woke up.

Haven to Heaven

By the end of January, Kasi, Chansy, and Phoemkhun were beginning to form the bonds of friendship that forged from loneliness, deprivation and violence.

Kasi's Diary 25-Jan-1976

The nightmares about the robbery continue, but I can't remember the one that I had last night. Chansy and I got a chance to get the water again and to meet Phoemkhun. We told her about the robbery, and she told us about what was going on between her mother and father.

Phoemkhun is a slave in her house. But her mother is also a slave. She said that her father abuses them both. I didn't really understand what she meant, so I just asked. She looked very uncomfortable, but then she told us. His way to abuse her mother is what Mai told me about. Rape. His way to abuse Phoemkhun is to beat her. I told her what Pa had done to me. She said she was sorry to hear that. She paused and then she said that what her father does is different. He doesn't beat her to punish her. He just beats her because he enjoys it. Chansy and I didn't know what to say about that. I just couldn't understand how someone could enjoy beating someone else. Chansy acted sort of uncomfortable. Because she is older than us, she knows some words that we don't know. She told us that it is called sadism. That is the first time I ever heard that word. Anyway, her father is a sadist.

I am back at home, and the arguments continue.

Mai has started our English lessons. Pa wanted no part of it, and he just went to the corner to write letters. We learned all of the pronouns and the verb "go". I go, you go, and he goes. The spelling is the funniest part. The word "rough" is so strange!

When Mai and Pa are not fighting, they are silent. It gets very awkward. I want to say something, but the only sounds are of everyone eating sticky rice and drinking water. After the silent dinner, I was so tired that I just lay down on my mat and went to sleep.

After being in the refugee camp for almost two months, my nine-year-old beautiful, pristine Kasi has now encountered human perversity. I suppose that is not surprising. Human perversity is probably much more common than we think. But, I reserve the word "perverse" for those that do things against the will of others. Coercion is a necessary component of perversion. Who cares what consenting adults do? What Kasi was hearing about from Phoemkhun was about abusive power, not simply sexual deviance.

Kasi and I were experiencing very similar symptoms of trauma survivors. The robbery had affected both of our sleep cycles. From her writings at the end of January, Kasi seemed to be refocusing from the loss of Keo and the robbery to the more salient issue of the safety of her new friend, Phoemkhun.

The rest of the family members carried on with their day-to-day activities. Khamphet was finally successful in bringing home some protein from his hunting expeditions with Huck. We had boundaries that we were allowed to go out and hunt for food. If lucky, he would be able to come home with squirrels, turtles, wild cats, birds, or snakes. Pretty much anything that moved was edible.

Haven to Heaven

Kasi's Diary 26-Jan-1976

Still having nightmares! This morning I woke up crying but not knowing why. It is as if part of me wants to protect the other part from the pain. So, I can't remember the nightmares even though they make me cry.

Tomorrow, I will get to see Phoemkhun again. I can't wait. I want to tell her what has been happening at our house and ask her what is happening at hers.

I am using my telescope to look out on the square this morning. I can see Phoemkhun's house, and now I can even see inside! She is not near the opening. So, I can't see her. There are lines of people at each of the three porta-potties. I can look at each person and imagine their life story. There is a Chinese woman holding the hand of her little daughter who is squirming, because she has to go so badly. In another line, there is a boy next to his father. He is probably bored, because he is picking up stones and throwing them in the gutter behind the toilets.

The sun is just coming up, and it looks like it will be a nice day.

27-Jan-1976

More forgotten nightmares! I am not getting much sleep. I repeatedly wake up, and then fall asleep briefly, only to wake up again. I can hear Mai moving around, and I guess she is having the same trouble sleeping. I am very angry at the people that robbed us. I wish there were some way to make them pay for all the pain and suffering that they have caused my family!

28-Jan-1976

I saw Phoemkhun yesterday with Chansy, and I asked her if she wakes up early like me. Phoemkhun said that she does. I told her about my telescope. (I know it's a spyglass, like what the pirates use, but I think it's more cool to call it a telescope.) I asked if she would wave to me. I just saw her waving, and I waved back. I am going to find a way to get her a telescope so that she can see me, too. The next time I see her, I am going to try to work out some signals that she can use to communicate with me, especially in an emergency.

30-Jan-1976

Today, Pa declared that he and Huck would be going out hunting using the bows and arrows that they have been making this past week. I hope that they are able to get something so that we can have some meat before we go to market. I really hope it is not a monkey, though. There is something about eating a monkey that I don't like.

31-Jan-1976

Yesterday, when I saw Phoemkhun, we agreed on several signals that she could use to let me know how she is. Both arms up pointing at the sky means that both she and her mother are okay. The right arm refers to Phoemkhun and the left to her mother. If the arm is at an angle, it means that person is ok now, but was hurt earlier. If the arm is straight out to the side, it means that the person is in immediate danger.

We don't have a plan about what we will do if we see those signs, but at least we have a means of communication. We agreed to reserve the time slot between 6 and 6:30 AM for our communications, because it must be light out for us to be able to see.

I don't know how they did it, but Pa and Huck were able to get a bird when they were hunting! I am pretty sure that it was Pa that shot it. Huck is only seven and not that good yet. Pa prepared it last night, and we will cook it today at the stand.

Feb 1976: First Call of Acceptance – France

> "Good evening, folks! This is your Friendly Fred Fry, disc jockey and newsman extraordinaire. I will have news and rock tunes for you from now till midnight, right here at WTWR 99.3 FM Seattle, Washington. We want you to be the best-informed radio audience in the United States! So here is one important news item from February 1976.
>
> The film *Taxi Driver* starring Robert De Niro was released. It depicts a lonely and depressed Marine who is a Vietnam War veteran that can't fit in to the society that he fought for.
>
> In music news, the Eagles just released their *Greatest Hits (1971-1975)* album and it is selling like hot cakes!
>
> And that's what happened in February of 1976!"

After that first interview, we expected to be called to our second interview soon. Still, we had to carry on with our life in the meantime. We were allowed to go to the market every other week. It was a long walk to get there and it was a back-breaking walk to get back with the purchases. Kasi was dressed and ready to go every market morning. Sometimes Chansy would come with us.

When we got back from the market, there was always much to do to ensure that all of the purchases were stored appropriately and undamaged. It mattered because damaged goods would be difficult to sell. Kasi was my constant companion. She worked tirelessly and without complaint.

On all of the other days, Kasi helped me with the vendor stall. Khamphet acted as our security guard. Even so, we were robbed several times. Once, I was sure that it was the soldiers that had orchestrated the robbery. After that, I found a place to hide all of the money we collected as well as any goods that did not need to be displayed immediately. Kasi watched and learned all of the tricks of the trade. Whenever we established a routine, she memorized it and would complain if I skipped a step or even did one out of order. This was comforting to me. I knew that if I couldn't be there for part of the day—not that I would ever let that happen—she would be able to run the shop without me. If Chansy had been a bit more interested, I really might have been able to scale back my efforts. However, when I let them run it themselves for a few hours, I noticed that many more Lao boys of a certain age came around, but rarely bought anything. I doubted if they were interested in the spices, rice and flour. I determined that it would not be safe to leave them alone at the store for any substantial time.

As time went by, the business slowly grew, and we were able to afford some clothes. I focused on those that would make us look good at the interviews. Also, I wanted to be sure that they were easy to take care of. I even found a western-style jacket for Khamphet who looked like he had just come from a corporate outing when he put it on. It was to be worn only for interviews, I admonished him.

Weeks passed, and we got no further call to an interview. I wondered if I was going to have to bribe someone to make it happen. I was on the verge of doing that when we got our first call of acceptance.

Unfortunately, it was a call to go to France. Khamphet, Huck, and Kasi all just wanted to get out of that camp. They wanted to settle for anywhere. I did, too, of course. But I was still aiming for the USA. Honestly, it would have been much easier if they hadn't called us. When the call came to go to France, it brought great conflict to our family. I was not going to change my mind. Each of my family members tried to get me to change though.

You can imagine what it was like. My shop permitted us a few luxuries, but it couldn't change the fact that we were living in squalor. We still had to use the communal bathrooms for showers. We could only use them in groups for safety. The streets were unpaved and often clogged with mud when it rained. When anyone got sick, if it was contagious, we were all afraid it would affect all of us. Going to the hospital was like taking your life in your hands. Many went in and never came out.

So, this happened. One day, a big chartered bus arrived to deliver some supplies and to take away some families that had been selected to go to France. They also posted the list and announced all the people approved for the next round. The French had offered us the option to go to France and to the surprise and consternation of Khamphet, I refused. He was very angry with me, and we argued heatedly.

"Why did I apply if we had no intention of accepting the offer?" he shouted. He tried to persuade me that we should go to France because we both speak French, and we have my sister there.

"Life would be much easier for us there than it is for us here. We speak French. How easy it would be for us to settle in France!" He continued to convince me that we would have an easy way to earn a living in France because I had been teaching the French language and French literature in Laos.

That was ridiculous, of course, and I told him so.

"Just because I can teach the French language to Lao people does not mean that I could earn a living in France teaching French! The French people already speak French, and better than I do. And there are plenty of native French speakers that can teach French literature, too. Why would they want to take a course in French literature from a Lao teacher when they could take it from a native French teacher?" Ridiculous! Sometimes, Khamphet has no common sense.

I continued on. "Besides, I want my children to grow up in the United States. That is the land of liberty. They will learn to speak English fluently. There, they will have a better life than anywhere else. They deserve that. I want to wait for the Americans to call us. We are well-educated, and the Americans prefer people like us. The odds are in our favor. We will wait."

"Kim, we have been here for three long months. This place is like hell! Anywhere is better than this!" he exclaimed.

"Khamphet, you know what it is like in France for Lao immigrants," I argued back. "You know that the good jobs and the good houses are all beyond the reach of immigrants. France is a traditional society. They have their national cuisine and their Champagne. We are just good to be waiters and dancers. Do you want me to be a dancer in some sleazy French Club? How will you protect your daughter from unemployment when she comes of age? I don't think that is the kind of life you want for us," I admonished him.

He looked at me, disheartened and disappointed. He was just hoping to sway me further now that we had a concrete offer.

"They won't make another offer if we refuse, you know. There are plenty of other families that would be glad to get out of this God-forsaken place and start their life. How long do you think we are going to have to wait? We haven't even been called for a second interview to Australia. I think this is a very risky venture, Kim," he warned.

He was right. It was a very risky venture. But every venture has its risks and its rewards. I had already done the risk-benefit analysis.

Next was Chansy.

"Please, Aunt Kim. I will return to my family soon, and we don't know when we will be selected. But Kasi can't do this anymore. Go somewhere that they want you. France is offering you a place. Take it and get out of here!" She was on the brink of tears. Her reasons were very altruistic but still adolescent. I couldn't tell her that, but that is what I thought. Instead, I appealed to her vanity.

"Chansy, haven't you seen any of the movies? France has porn movies like *Emmanuelle* while the United States has Hollywood's *It's a Wonderful Life*. There is opportunity in the United States, and there is degradation in France. The French are proud and nationalistic, but that means they are provincial and chauvinistic, too. We should wait a little longer. The United States will welcome us with open arms. Kasi's children will grow up speaking English and living in the land of liberty that even has a statue to represent it." She turned and left without putting up any further resistance.

Huck was indifferent, and too young to understand all this. Kasi was different. Surprisingly, she didn't want to convince me of anything. She just gave me the look of assurance that whatever I decided for the family would be the safest place to go.

Kasi's Diary 1-Feb-1976

When I looked at Phoemkhun's house at 6 this morning I saw her smiling with both arms up over her head. Our communication works, and I am so happy that she is safe.

Yesterday, we found out that our family has been called to France! This is actually the first good news we have gotten since we left Laos.

We were all together at the Interview Building where they had posted the list. We were the very last ones listed. Pa, Huck and I were all thrilled, until I saw Mai's reaction. Then, it became awkward.

Everyone around us was hugging and cheering. Only Mai was silent. She didn't even smile. I didn't know what to think.

Of course, this caused a huge fight between Mai and Pa when we got home. Pa is desperate to get out of this camp. We all are, actually. I sort of agree with Pa about that. But Mai is insistent that we not go to France. It is as if she has something against France or thinks that France has something against us. I just can't understand her thinking. She alone thinks that we would be no better off in France than we are here. That just can't be true! We would have beds, electricity, running water, and much better food. How can Mai not see that?

But her belief that the United States is our destiny is unshakeable. She refuses to go to France and told Pa that if he chooses to go, it will be without the family. Pa went back to writing letters after she said that. Who on earth is he always writing to?

Tomorrow we will go to market in the late morning after I see Phoemkhun again to get water.

Kasi had developed an elaborate arm signaling system for Phoemkhun that allowed her to communicate with Kasi at a distance using her telescope. Of course, since Phoemkhun did not have a telescope, the communication channel was only one way. When we went to the market, Kasi asked me to buy another telescope for her friend.

Refugee Neighborhood

Kasi's Diary 2-Feb-1976

I saw Phoemkhun in her house this morning with my telescope. She had her right arm up but her left arm at an angle of 2 o'clock. That means that her mother is okay but hurt. I think I am going to have to tell Mai, at least about my new friend and our communication channel. I will see if she is willing to buy another telescope so that Phoemkhun can see me, too.

Today, I don't think there is anything that we can do about her mother's distress. I hope that Mai will be understanding. I am still having nightmares about the robbery and Keo. I would not be able to bear it if anything happened to Phoemkhun's mother. I will write more tomorrow when I know more.

Since we need to get water and go to the market, we will not be opening the stand today. It will be too late by the time we get back. Mai may use that loss of income against us and may not want to buy the telescope for Phoemkhun.

I relented and bought another telescope for Kasi to share with her friend. I wouldn't be able to live with myself if anything happened to Phoemkhun, and I had refused to lift a finger to help. On the other hand, I didn't want Kasi to think that we could afford to stick our necks out to help her. There is no law here, and so there can be no legitimate law enforcement. Justice is out of reach for us refugees in the lawless camp. I had to be sure Kasi understood the limits to her family's ability to protect anyone outside the family. It was basically impossible, or at least very risky.

Haven to Heaven

Kasi's Diary 3-Feb-1976

Phoemkhun had both arms up this morning!

Mai was very understanding about her situation, and even decided to buy the telescope at the market. She says that women must stick together for protection. I asked her how we might be able to protect Phoemkhun and her mother. Mai's response disappointed me, but I understood. She said that we couldn't really help her, because we just couldn't risk getting involved.

Tomorrow is the day that we have to go to the pre-departure meeting for the trip to France if we are going to go. Mai was like an unmovable rock when Pa pleaded with her (almost in tears) to go with him to the meeting. She will not go. We will not go. If Pa decides to go, he will go alone. I feel sorry for him, but I really trust Mai. I know that she needs me to be dependable, and I don't want to fail her.

Reading that diary entry made me so happy and proud! Kasi was expressing her true opinion, and she trusted me. A mother could ask for nothing more from a child. Now, I just had to be sure that I deserved her trust. I wanted to try to make her friendship with Phoemkhun possible. I began to monitor her diary a bit more frequently.

Kasi's Diary 4-Feb-1976

Phoemkhun had both arms up again today and that is a relief. Pa decided not to go to the meeting for the trip to France. Mai was very grateful and was very nice to him all day. Still, he didn't stay with us at the stand. He took off with Huck and just went around the neighborhood, maybe flying kites or hunting for food.

As usual, there were no other postings on the board outside the Interview Building. We are back to waiting and practicing for our next interview. Mai is still sending us to the English classes. We learned words for colors: purple, blue, green, yellow, orange, red, black, and white. And the word "flower".

5-Feb-1976

Finally, I will get to see Phoemkhun again today and give her the telescope! She looked happy with her arms up straight again. I guess things are going better there now.

Mai is still treating Pa very well. She has been cutting him extra fruits and paying more attention to him. She even smiles more. His spirits are better than they have been. He decided to go out hunting with Huck again.

6-Feb-1976

Phoemkhun was not there this morning! I waited as long as I could, but Mai wanted to open the stand, so I had to go and eat breakfast.

When we saw each other yesterday, everything was fine. I gave her the telescope, and she hid it in her underclothes. That was a little bit shocking. She said that if her father saw it, he would take it and

131

beat her. I hope that is not what happened! This is crazy! I am worried sick. I can't wait till tomorrow morning to see if she shows up. I wish we had talked more about what we will do in an emergency.

This time, Pa brought back a dead monkey. I couldn't stand the sight of it, and I decided that I would not eat any of it. I told Mai, and she said that I was being foolish. I asked her please to give others more, and me none. Everyone else likes it so that was fine with Mai.

Paupers can't be too picky. Honestly, I didn't particularly like the idea of eating monkey meat, either, but I realized that we were all very thin and getting thinner as a consequence of our poor diet here. Khamphet was doing his part by teaching Huck to hunt – making the bows and arrows with him and going hunting to provide us with extra protein. What was there to complain about? I wanted Kasi to show some appreciation for her father's contribution as well as that of Huck who was very proud to be part of the hunting party. I thought Kasi was being snobbish and selfish with her pickiness. On the other hand, if she really felt that strongly about it, that would just mean there was more for the rest of us. I let it go at that.

Kasi's Diary 7-Feb-1976

Phoemkhun was back this morning, but she signaled 10 o'clock which means that she is okay but hurt. She had her telescope though, and I gave her both arms up. I definitely need to talk to Mai and Chansy today about what we can do for Phoemkhun

and her mother if they really need us. We may need
to create more codes to cover more situations. I can't
wait to see Phoemkhun again tomorrow.

8-Feb-1976

Phoemkhun signaled a quarter to three. That
means that both she and her mother need immediate
help and are not okay. I can't write more now,
because I really should talk to the whole family.

These are the kinds of events that force people to make hard
choices. When Kasi came to talk to the whole family, I had to be
careful not to reveal how much I already knew from reading her
diary. It was quite clear to me that we might be able to save that
girl's life and perhaps that of her mother, too. It is true that there
were risks, but I actually felt safer than before, now that Khamphet
was hunting and had some bows and arrows as self-made weapons.
So, I encouraged Kasi and Chansy to go and meet their friend. I
told Kasi that I would watch Phoemkhun's house and send Pa out
after them if her father came out.

Kasi's Diary 9-Feb-1976

Phoemkhun was in a terrible state when we met
her just beyond where her father could see us. Her
mouth was all swollen, and she walked funny. At the
next square, we took her into one of the porta-
potties by cutting in line. They didn't mind because
they could see that she was in bad shape. She had a
cloth wrapped around her privates, so that she would
not drip blood. She was bleeding internally. Chansy
and I looked at each other, and we knew. We had to

get her to the infirmary. Phoemkhun would not allow that. She said that her father would go there to find her if she didn't come home right away. We told her that she couldn't go back, because he would just keep doing this. What if she got pregnant? There was no way for a refugee girl of such trouble to get out of trouble. She would have to have her own father's child. That didn't seem right to any of us.

Phoemkhun was agitated and wanted to get the water and go straight back to her mother. She was afraid that he would do something to her mother. We had to reason with her. If he did anything to her mother, we would try to form a community and fight him back. He wouldn't do anything to her, because he would be afraid of what the community would do to him.

She asked us what we were proposing. We said that she should go first to Chansy's mother's hut, and then, under cover of darkness, come to hide at our hut. She was crying and bleeding. We changed her cloth and got her dressed. We took her to Chansy's mother's hut and I stayed with her there until Chansy was able to get the water and bring it back. Then, we waited until it was dusk and started back to our hut. I went first because I had the telescope. I scouted the place from between the buildings. I made sure we were unseen. I went inside first and got a blanket. We covered her with a blanket and took her into the hut as if she was a package.

I wished that we had running water so that we

*could have cleaned her up. We had to make do with
whatever we had.*

When that poor girl arrived in our hut, I refused to let my emotions overcome me. I told Phoemkhun that I was a nurse, to Kasi's surprise, and that I needed to examine her. I wanted to know the full extent of her injuries and just what had happened to her. Her injuries were obvious, and she was so distraught that she told her story willingly to me, the nurse.

After the examination and her storytelling, I finally let myself feel. What I felt was a red-hot fury that I thought could burn through even the most robust excuses. The man that did this to his own daughter was unworthy of our selfish fears. My fear of what he could do to us vanished in my knowledge of what I could do to him.

After I came to my senses and remembered our lawless state and the fragility of our defenses, I realized that the best we could do would be to hide the girl and remain hidden ourselves. It must appear to her father that his daughter had run away or been abducted. I used all of my strategic intelligence to be sure that our tricks could not be discovered, and her stay here would be a closely held secret.

There was no reason for her father to suspect us any more than any other of the neighbors in the neighborhood. He knew nothing of the trips to fetch water with Kasi and Chansy, or of their friendship. We were protected by the extensive anonymity that pervaded the camp. Kasi took care of many of the details. I just had to watch over the operations.

Haven to Heaven

Kasi's Diary 10-Feb-1976

AM

The problem with hiding Phoemkhun is that she is afraid of dark and confined places. Last night, we had to figure out ways to hide her in plain sight. She had to appear as if she were someone else. We decided that she would take my place. My job was to use my telescope to scout. We needed to be sure that her mother was okay. Phoemkhun was beside herself with guilt about leaving her mother alone with her abusive father. I also needed to look out for her father. I took that job very seriously. While I was scouting, she could appear in the house in my clothes. We arranged a small space for both of us to sleep in the attic under the eaves of the roof. We hung bamboo mats from the roof to give us privacy and covered the opening of the square. We found a long rope and a bell. We put the bell near the stand and strung the rope up to where I was scouting under the roof. We agreed that I would ring the bell if I saw Phoemkhun's mother or father.

Pa was changed by seeing Phoemkhun and hearing her story. He took more initiatives. He said that he would try to recruit two of his hunting buddies to act as guards at the stand. He would tell them that it was because of the robbery. In reality, it was to protect the whole family from Phoemkhun's father.

Refugee Neighborhood

Until we know better what we will do to save her mother, Chansy will take my place at the stand.

PM

Phoemkhun's parents came out of their hut together before the water place closed. I rang the bell and Pa and his hunter-guard friend were alerted to be especially watchful about robbers.

Phoemkhun crouched behind me with her telescope. It was just as we had suspected. They walked right by our stand, which convinced us that they had no knowledge of our connection to Phoemkhun. They went straight to get water. Phoemkhun's father needed her mother now more than ever. She was wearing an obviously improvised veil so that nobody could see her face. Phoemkhun went behind the bamboo curtain, and I could hear her sobbing, while I continued to scout for their return. As soon as I saw them returning, I rang the bell again, and we all were on high alert.

After her parents returned to their hut and the sun was setting, Mai and Chansy put away the stand, and Mai paid the guard. He left. We usually ate outside under the hut, unless the weather was bad, and we didn't want to change our routines. Chansy left to eat at her mother's house; and Phoemkhun dressed as Chansy and ate with us *with her back to the square.*

It was a great source of comfort to me to see Phoemkhun's parents walking together. Hopefully, that meant that the parents were reconciled and united by grief over the loss of their daughter. In addition, it was clear to me that the mother had knowledge that the father needed her to survive. I had to go to Kasi's diary more than once a day now to keep up with all that was happening.

Kasi's Diary 11-Feb-1976

AM

Today, Mai will accompany Chansy and me to get water. Phoemkhun will stay in the scout's nest and ring the bell to alert Pa if her parents come out of the hut.

As we slept next to each other under the roof of our hut, Phoemkhun and I talked, and she cried a lot. She misses her mother and is very worried about her. I am still just a kid, but it seems very clear to me that the problem is that there is no help from authorities for the refugees. I can only imagine a different world where we would all look out for each other, ringing a bell if we saw someone abusing someone else. We would all act together against the abusers. We would act quickly in time to save the victim.

That is not the world that we live in, though. In this world, everybody is afraid of everybody else.

When we are afraid to help the abused, it only
empowers the abusers. It only makes things worse. I
can see this, but I feel helpless to change it. I will talk
with Mai and Chansy when we go to get water today.

PM

Mai and Chansy both thought that it was very
mature of me to tell my observations and ask
questions. Chansy really didn't know what to say. Mai
said that there are some questions that just can't be
answered or even understood. All we can do, she said,
is meditate.

I just nodded my head as if I understood, but I
didn't. The strength in numbers seems like a solution
for us refugees. I still can't imagine how to solve it
though.

Yes, that was what I said to Kasi. As Buddhist refugees, all we
could do was meditate. She was only a kid! How could she even
think of a way to bring the community together for a common
purpose? I didn't believe it until I read her diary entry, and by then
it was too late. I would have lost face if I had agreed that some sort
of a crime prevention or intervention group could be organized
within the refugee committee. That's just not the way things
worked at that given time.

I focused on making sure that we had security at the stand. The
neighborhood young men were always looking for ways to make
extra money, or at least, for a meal. We were selling the basic
commodities such as salt, sugar, spices, soap, sugarcane drinks,
iced coffee, rice – those basic necessities became valuable
commodities when scarcity and hunger were always present.

Sometimes I had the girls help me make sticky rice snacks or fried banana desserts. Business was getting better and better, and that made me very happy. Also, it would make us look good in our application to the United States. They seemed to like good business people.

Kasi's Diary 12-Feb-1976

Now that we have a guard, customers seem to feel safer, too. Yesterday, we had the longest lines we have had yet. Mai is happy because all of the extra business helps to pay for the guard. Last night, at dinner, Mai said that we ought to get another table so that we can have two lines. Chansy and I would have our own table and Mai would have our traditional table. We would sell the same things, though.

I was on the lookout most of the day, but we never saw either of Phoemkhun's parents. Phoemkhun says that her father probably killed her mother because she never came back. We all told her that would be a stupid thing for him to do. It didn't seem to help her though. She keeps asking what we are going to do to save her mother.

Pa said that he would ask if any of his fellow hunters would be willing to go to her parent's hut to ask about her mother. Mai told him to be very careful to ask only people that he can trust.

That made me think a lot. How do you know whether you can trust someone?

Tomorrow we will be able to go to the nice people

that give us food and clothing. We want to get something for Phoemkhun to wear.

Kasi had hit upon another deep question, the question of the origin of trust. We trust some people and not others. Why? Sometimes we don't even know why. Sometimes, we don't even ask. Reading Kasi's words made me think about my relationship to Khamphet. Do I trust him? Should I?

Khamphet and I had known each other for at least fifteen years. We had to negotiate our marriage with our respective parents. I won't go into the details, but the point is that we developed a certain trust as a consequence of that process. We began a life together, and we decided together that we would have children. That was a big step in a trusting relationship. You can't take children back. We bought a house together. That was a big investment and a serious commitment for our future. These things all resulted from a growing trust.

However, after the birth of our son, Khamphet changed. Perhaps the stresses of married life with children were too much for him. He strayed with that woman who is now in France. His desire to go to France instead of the United States is a factor in the degree to which I feel I could trust him. However, unrealistically, he wanted everything. But he didn't want to make any sacrifice. He would be willing to go to France and have two families, I suppose. Any woman would think that is a terrible thing and declare him untrustworthy.

I don't deny that he is untrustworthy in certain respects. However, I also realize that I can trust his selfishness. He values his life with me and our children. He does not want to give that up. He wants more, not something else. It is that that I could trust.

Of course, all that could change at any time. He might decide that the other woman would be enough for him and that going to her would be worth betraying and abandoning his family. I can also trust that he is not in denial about that. I know he would recognize his fault and suffer as a consequence. There is a certain kind of trust that flows from knowing that, too.

When I consider whether I trust Khamphet or not, I consider probabilities. It is not a black or white situation that he is or isn't trustworthy. In certain situations, he is 100% trustworthy—while in another situation he is, perhaps, 75% trustworthy. For now, the probabilities are enough for me to carry on as if he were completely trustworthy. There will come a day of reckoning when he will have to choose definitively. I am constantly trying to figure out how I can make that decision swing in favor of our family. Trust is a practical thing for me.

On the 13th of February, everything changed. Here is how Kasi reported it:

Kasi's Diary 13-Feb-1976

Last night, I heard something unusual in the square. It was dark, but I tried to see with my telescope anyway. There was someone at the far end of the square—near Phoemkhun's hut—digging. He seemed to be planting flowers or herbs. At first, he was working in candlelight. Then, he put out the candle, and I really couldn't see what was going on. This did not look good. I was terrified. Phoemkhun was fast asleep, because we had given her some cough medicine to help her sleep better. I didn't really sleep much at all after that. I couldn't wait for morning to come.

Refugee Neighborhood

14-Feb-1976

AM

When I looked at the square this morning, I could see the newly exposed earth. There were a few flowers planted there but not many. I have a bad feeling about it.

PM

When Phoemkhun got up and saw the flower garden, she immediately began sobbing. She said those were the flowers that her mother had been growing in the hut. I could see that all hope of ever seeing her mother again just melted away.

Of course, we still had to go to get water. Pa stayed with Phoemkhun while the rest of us went to get water. We also checked the Interview Building to see if we were listed again. We weren't. I had gotten so discouraged, that I often wondered why we even bothered going anymore.

Pa and his hunter friends will visit Phoemkhun's parents' hut tomorrow. Crying, Phoemkhun told us it would be too late and no use.

15-Feb-1976

Phoemkhun and I watched as the hunter group, led by Pa, went over to Phoemkhun's parents' hut. There were no doors on the huts, so they waited at the entrance way asking to enter. After a bit, the whole group entered. We couldn't see what happened inside, so we just had to wait. Phoemkhun was inconsolable, so I put down my telescope to hug her.

I imagined how I would feel if anything happened to Mai. Soon we were both crying without regard for the outside world. Then, Phoemkhun pointed through her tears and sobs without saying anything. I turned around to look. I picked up the telescope, and I saw the hunters carrying her father's body across the square. We didn't know if the hunters had killed him, or if he had killed himself. They brought the body to our side of the square just outside our hut. They wanted Phoemkhun to go down to identify the body. I went with her.

I had never been with a friend who lost a parent. All I could do was hold her and steady her as she walked.

Phoemkhun didn't spend much time with her father's body. She identified it and then spat on it. We were so shocked! We didn't expect it, but we certainly understood it. Phoemkhun ran across the square toward the flower garden, and the hunters grabbed some sticks and followed her.

They found her mother's body buried there, and Phoemkhun just fell apart. I knew she felt responsible for her mother's death. I felt responsible for her mother's death, too. I was sure that Phoemkhun would soon blame me and Chansy, too. Why wouldn't she? We had convinced her to escape. Certainly, that had saved her life. But we had told her that her father would not hurt her mother because he needed her now that Phoemkhun was gone. Obviously, that was not true. The hunters had not killed him. He had killed himself. I need to take care of Phoemkhun and myself now. I can't write.

18-Feb-1976

Looking out at the square, everything seems different now. A new refugee family has already moved into Phoemkhun's family's hut. The raw earth covered her mother's grave is just as it was when the hunters unearthed her. The earth on opposite sides of the path from our hut is charred from the cremations that we did for each of her parents.

I have spent the last two days as if I were a ghost. I am not really here, not really living all of this just observing it. I am living everything through the eyes, ears, and skin of Phoemkhun. I know that she will never be the same. She will never forget this, and she will probably never recover from it. At least I don't think I would be able to recover if I were her.

And yet, life must go on. We all went to the market together even though Phoemkhun had no desire to go and was crying most of the time. Still, she helped us to bring the supplies back.

We went to get the water as we had before, just the three of us girls. It was very hard work, but it reminded us of our strength in numbers. Two lives have been lost, but together at least we had been able to save one — Phoemkhun's.

Mar 1976: Second Interview

"Good evening, folks! This is your Friendly Fred Fry disc jockey and newsman. I will have news and rock tunes for you from now till midnight, right here at WTWR 99.3 FM Seattle, Washington. We want you to be the best-informed radio audience in the United States! So here is the Monthly Roundup for March of 1976.

In the first week of March: The costliest ice storm on record struck a large section of western New York. Ice was reported to be four inches thick in some spots. Erie, Chautauqua, Genesee, and Wyoming counties were declared major disaster areas by President Ford as a result of the ice storm and localized flooding. The two-day storm left more than 100,000 families without power, 5000 without telephone service, and at least 10,000 without water.

In the last week of March: Argentina's new military government has moved swiftly to consolidate power, banning all political activities, replacing elected officials and slapping censorship regulations on the press. Former President Isabel Peron was under military arrest in a tiny Andean mountain resort 720 miles southwest of Buenos Aires. There was speculation she may be exiled or tried on corruption charges. The nation of 25 million appeared calm, with the armed forces in firm control. Peron was arrested at gunpoint and forced to leave the capital. Elected officials, ranging from cabinet ministers to municipal functionaries, were replaced by military officers. Censorship was imposed on Argentine newspapers.

And that's what happened in March of 1976!"

Kasi was definitely dependable. I was depending on her more and more, and she never failed me.

However, our situation was more complicated now. Back in December, when Kasi was still mourning from the death of Keo, I was sure that she would recover because I recognized her resilience. However, clearly there are some experiences that you can just never overcome. I thought that the murder of her friend's mother and the suicide of her friend's father would qualify as just such an experience. I had seen a lot in my life, but nothing like this. I just didn't know what effect this would have on Kasi at her young and tender age.

We needed to decide whether Phoemkhun would be our adopted daughter or somebody else's problem. No matter what I think, I would have to convince Kasi and Khamphet. Huck would have to be included in the family decision, too, even though he was very young and had been indifferent about everything that was happening. In a way, that was good.

My only concern was whether Phoemkhun's status would improve or harm our family's chances of being called to the United States. Would the Americans care whether our family is altruistic? I doubted it. If, however, we were able to show that we could create a business that could employ others, that would count for a lot. I hope you will not judge me harshly for this, either. If putting Phoemkhun to work—even if that work is a bit of exploitation— would help our family to get to the United States, I would do it. I had come too far to stop now. I did not come this far, to only come this far.

I felt great sympathy for Phoemkhun. Who wouldn't? But, I was much more interested in Kasi's reaction to the new situation. I decided that I would take a look at her personal journal. I didn't have much time. So, I only read the parts in February. After the 18th, she wrote no more. I wondered why? I had to assume that it was because she was living these events immediately and was not able to draw back and describe them objectively. Of course, I understand that. I don't keep a personal journal for just that reason. I am too busy surviving to write. All of my reflections are in my conversations and in my letters. I just happen to have a very good memory, thank heavens.

147

We all know that successful businesses sell products or services that appeal to the emotional part of customers, not to the calculator in our brains. Business is business, whether it's a big entrepreneurship in the U.S. or a tiny stand in the refugee camp. The success behind that business philosophy is still the same. The murder-suicide affair shocked the entire village, and instinctively everyone felt sorry for Phoemkhun. The story quickly got around about how Phoemkhun had been saved through the use of the telescope. That planted the seed in me. Kasi's journal entries made me realize that the events of February could help us to create a new line of business, using the second table that we bought last time. The emotional response of the whole community to the violation of one of our children could be a powerful motivation for parents to spend money for their children.

On the first of March, we took another trip to the market. Phoemkhun came with us for the first time since the middle of February

"Phoemkhun," I inquired, "What would you and Kasi have done without your telescopes?"

"We would not have been able to communicate with each other," she replied. She spoke so softly that I had to move closer to her to hear. "They were almost like a telephone for us."

"Do you think other children would want to have one?" I wondered.

"Oh yes. Well, at least the girls. Maybe the boys would be shy about it. Maybe not."

To my ears, that sounded like an opportunity for sales. The question that was haunting me was whether I could depend on Kasi to understand how important it was for us to make a living, and to convince the American interviewers that we were the type of entrepreneurs they wanted.

Refugee Neighborhood

If I was going to hire Phoemkhun, I would have to be sure that her participation would boost sales more than it would cost me to pay her. It was obvious to me that her primary benefit was being the protagonist in the affair of the murder and suicide of her parents. Having the victim helping to sell telescopes to the children of others who might be affected was perfect. Still, was it too soon after the event to take economic advantage of it? I didn't think so. Phoemkhun was easy because she was still confused and just being polite to the mother of her best friend. But, I didn't know how to approach Kasi about it. Kasi would certainly be more skeptical, and very likely be protective of her friend.

Still, I had to make a decision about how to allocate resources and time. If I didn't purchase the telescopes right away, I might not have the money later, and I would have lost all of the time between now and the next visit to the market for sales. In addition, we would soon apply for refuge in Australia. I knew that would be the next challenge. I wanted to be ready with the story of entrepreneurship when we got that next interview.

I decided to purchase the telescopes but didn't say anything to Kasi about my ideas of employing Phoemkhun at the stand to help sell the telescopes. I would do that later after I had a bit more time to consider how to approach her.

I frankly do not believe in complete transparency in the context of the family. If not in that context—you may ask—then when? Well, I am not sure. I tend to believe taking the time to carefully consider the information that you reveal to others, in any context, is wise and certainly prudent. You can't take back an impromptu revelation of an important secret. I'd say, keep it until you are sure it will not harm you or others. Unless, of course, they are your enemies. Similarly, I also believe in a certain restrained transparency in business. Some business people are cooperative. Others only pretend to be so and are actually better considered to be enemies.

149

Kasi hovered next to Phoemkhun the whole way to the market and back. Kasi was very helpful with the physical things that I asked her to do, but her mind was clearly on Phoemkhun. I mostly left them to their own devices on the way back. I listened carefully to their conversation, but I said very little. I concluded that Phoemkhun was as quiet and reserved as she had always been. Kasi was careful and respectful but a constant verbal presence in her friend's life. We would not go back to the market again until the 15th of March. In the meantime, we continued our weekly routine. We would go for water on Wednesday and visit the USCC again on Friday.

The sooner we put in the application for Australia, the sooner we would get our interview, and the closer we would be to being able to apply, with confidence, to the United States. From my point of view though, it would be better to have hired Phoemkhun and have the numbers to show that the enterprise was successful than to apply prematurely to Australia. Of course, I fully expected Khamphet to want to apply as soon as possible.

"I put in the application for Australia today," he said in a sort of offhanded way as soon as I finished putting the stuff away from the market trip. I couldn't believe it.

"How could you do that without consulting me?" I asked angrily.

"Kim, I know that you would just try to delay it. I don't want to stay here anymore, and that is all there is to it. I have two generous and caring nieces who live in Australia. They will sponsor us, and we can be there much sooner than we would be able to be in the United States," he said sternly.

Khamphet was right about my trying to delay it. But I never expected him to take that kind of initiative by himself. It didn't really matter, though. I was not going to fight with him about it now. I would save my energy for the fight that would come when I refused to go. Which I was sure to do, and he knew it. Instead, I would just arrange for Kasi and Phoemkhun to start selling the telescopes. I went to my sleeping place immediately because I was too tired to argue further.

The next morning was a Tuesday. The early dawn was a spectacular sight to behold. Everything was calm and no one else was up yet. I savored this time alone. As was my habit, I used it to meditate and just bask in peace and silence, sitting on my bamboo mat, thinking about what it all meant. I think it is important to do that every once in a while. You have to just stop everything and ask yourself: What is really important?

When I asked myself that question as the sun was rising and the metaphor of a new dawn hugged my lonely consciousness, the answer I got was simple: ask Kasi. That was how I should approach her. I should ask her what she thinks is important. I sat there watching the sunrise for some time after that without moving, almost without breathing. It was really quite sacred.

Kasi had gone up to her writing place as soon as she got up. I didn't want to interrupt her, so I called up to her before I went up.

"Kasi, could I talk to you?" I asked.

"Sure, Mai. Do you want to come up or should I come down?" she replied.

"I can come up. It's nice up there in the morning."

"I know," she said as I popped my head into her space. She had her diary on her lap, but she didn't seem to feel any need to put it away just because I was coming up. As I sat close to her, she closed her diary and set it aside. She looked at me directly and attentively. I knew she was listening and that she understood, because it was such a rare event, that this talk was important.

151

"I just wanted to ask you what you think is important, now, Kasi?"

She looked at me in that Kasi way and was thoughtfully silent for a few seconds.

"I was just writing about that, Mai. Why do you ask, though?" she replied. I could sense that she was a bit wary of my motivation. That was understandable.

"Well," I began, "I think there are some important decisions to be made, and I want to understand what your concerns might be before I make any decisions. How are you after all that happened to your friend, Phoemkhun?"

She looked out toward the square silently for a while before she turned to me and replied.

"I feel like I have seen too much. I can't believe that people like her father really exist. It seems hard not to think that there is a whole kind of human being—like the ones that robbed us—that are different on the inside than I am. I think that they are different from you and Phoemkhun and all of our family. It worries me that I don't know when I might run into someone like that again. I don't know how to tell what kind of person is beneath the faces of the new people that I meet," she admitted.

Again, silence encroached on our conversation, because I did not want to speak too soon after such a heartfelt expression. That seemed to me to be the most important lesson we could learn: how to identify a predator. It is also an impossible task because the predators have as many disguises as there were elephants in the ancient regime. All we can do is try, and as we get older, we do get better.

"Part of what I wanted to talk to you about was Phoemkhun and what will become of her." I held her gaze without flinching.

"What do we have to do with what will become of her?" she wondered.

"Well, we could adopt her, I suppose. What do you think about that?" I asked with curiosity.

"I would love it. But, I have talked to her about that. She has some relatives in France that she really likes. I think it would put her in a difficult position if we were to ask her if she wanted us to adopt her. I wish that she could stay with us wherever we go. She is a very good friend—really the best that I think I have ever had. But I really want what is best for her, and she seems to think that going to her relatives in France is the best thing that could happen to her. She went with Pa today and put in an application to France. I cried a bit, but I am committed to supporting her in whatever she needs," she said quickly and confidently. She knew her friend well, and she knew herself, too.

"Oh!" I acted surprised but was secretly relieved. It didn't matter. All I wanted to know was if Kasi would talk to Phoemkhun about selling the telescopes to customers at our shop.

"Well, let's make the best of it, then," I continued, "I have been thinking that I might offer to pay her to work with us at the stand. How do you think that would go over with her?"

"You mean, that you would offer to pay her?" she asked, with eyes wide open.

"Yes. Of course, it would have to be a commission," I clarified.

"A commission? What is that?" She still had her big eyes filled with curiosity.

I explained. I offered her the same deal. Her eyes got even bigger. Now, I just had to make the conditions clear.

"Now, you understand that I can only make this offer to her—I mean, to both of you—if you will agree to talk to her about it. I don't really know her that well and..." I was going to say that she might not trust me, but I didn't want to reveal more than was absolutely necessary. "...I mean, selling the telescopes will mean that she will have to answer questions from customers that may make her uncomfortable, you understand?"

"Well, maybe I could answer the questions for her. She would be there, and she could answer if she wanted, but I would be willing to answer the questions if they made her uncomfortable. I will talk to her," she replied.

Then, Kasi looked at me as if our conversation were over. I liked that about her. She didn't like to just talk for the sake of talking. She had a lot that she wanted to record in her diary which she had reopened and set on her lap. I knew it was time to leave. I had planted the seed, and now I had to wait until the harvest to see if the crop would be good.

The month of March wrapped up with an interview for Australia, which we all attended as a family. I just went along to show some cooperation to Khamphet, knowing that I would need the same from him when it was time for the USA interview. The interview procedure was not much different from the one we had with France. They asked us basic questions - first separately, then together. Separately to make sure our answers were consistent, since refugees could not prove their previous occupation, educational background, or age, as no one carried with them any official documents when they escaped. There's a simple reason for this – in case the escapees did not survive the escape, they wouldn't want to be identified and traced back to their family or relatives in Laos and putting them in harm's way.

Apr 1976: Second Call of Acceptance – Australia

> "Good evening, folks! This is your Friendly Fred Fry disc jockey and newsman. I will have news and rock tunes for you from now till midnight, right here at WTWR 99.3 FM Seattle, Washington. We want you to be the best-informed radio audience in the United States! So here is the Monthly Roundup for April 1976.
>
> USSR performs nuclear test at Eastern Kazakh/Semipalitinsk, USSR.
>
> Apple Computer Company is formed by Steve Jobs, Steve Wozniak and Ronald Wayne, in Cupertino, California.
>
> Norodom Sihanouk resigns as Cambodia's head of state, having been kept under house arrest by the Khmer Rouge, after witnessing conditions in the countryside.
>
> And that's what happened in April of 1976!"

By April of 1976, Phoemkhun had settled into selling telescopes to other refugees. She was quite good at it, actually. She believed in the product and knew how to explain how to put it to good use. Even her quiet voice turned out to be helpful. The customers were forced to be quiet and listen to her instead of trying to overpower her and get a better deal. She gradually came to understand that and used it to her advantage.

Of course, Kasi was her constant companion. She was nearby, listening and ready to help whenever Phoemkhun faltered. She did, sometimes, falter. There were angry fathers whose wives had come with their daughters to buy the telescope. The husband didn't like the fact that the women had made economic decisions without them and even ones that might affect their domestic relations.

Kasi would rise to the occasion. She was not afraid to challenge the men and other customers, sometimes. She was not above shaming them, publicly, if the situation called for it. Sometimes, I

155

would have to step in to smooth over the situation. Once, I even took a man aside and refunded his money just to get rid of him. However, that was the only time that was necessary.

From my perspective, of course, the big benefit was that my strategy was a success. We increased overall sales by about 20%. The expenses associated with the commissions that I paid the two of them only amounted to less than half of that. The remainder went toward our savings for our trip to the USA. I had never been surer that it would happen. I wrote a little presentation and rehearsed it with Kasi. My plan was to present it during our next interview. All of this gratified me greatly.

The second of April was a special day. It just happened that it was a day for us to go get water and also a day to get some necessities at the USCC tent. The USCC's generosity constantly renewed our faith in the essential goodness of humanity.

"Kasi, could you and Phoemkhun get the water today?" I asked that morning.

"Yes, Mai," she answered immediately. I knew that she was happy to do that because she would have a chance to talk to Phoemkhun alone and uninterrupted.

My goal was to find out what was happening with them by reading her diary after the trip.

Kasi's Diary 1-April-1976

Finally, P and I got a chance to talk! We have both been working so hard since Mai gave us a chance to make money on the commissions from the telescopes that we hardly ever talk. I asked her how she was and if she had heard anything from her relatives. As usual, she hesitated and then talked really softly. She told

me that she got a letter from her aunt in France.
Then she stopped. I had to shake her and ask her
what the aunt said. I guess she didn't want to tell me,
or Mai, because she is afraid if she tells anyone that it
won't come true. I don't know if I believe in that stuff.
But, anyway, she said that her aunt would like her to
come to France and that she has some way to make
that happen quickly.

I really wish the best for her, but that would
mean that I would lose my best friend. I didn't really
know how to react to that news. I mostly sort of
pretended to be really happy for her. I hugged her
and smiled and everything, but she didn't believe any
of it. She just stood there and started crying. That
made me stop pretending. I told her that I was really
going to miss her, and I hoped that she didn't have to
leave very soon.

She said that she felt the same way. She said that
she was really afraid of going somewhere to be with
someone new. She has grown to be more skeptical.
How could she even be sure it was the person that she
is saying she is?

P is like that now. She really doesn't trust anyone.
I have to say, I understand why she is like that.
People are pretty untrustworthy, sometimes. But you
can't go through life like that! We have to be able to
find a way to tell whether or not a person is actually
trustworthy or not. I am afraid it takes a long time.
Sometimes, the untrustworthy people just pretend to
be your friend when they actually aren't. I don't yet

know how you can protect yourself from those kinds
of people.

That, basically, told me everything that I needed to know. Even though P (as Kasi called her) was selling more than what I paid her, she was still an issue that needed to be resolved. I was hoping hard that she would find a good home soon.

Fortunately, we didn't really have to wait too long. By the end of April, Phoemkhun had been interviewed by France. Given her unusual circumstance, the process was expedited. So, by the first week of May, she already had a date to leave. She would only talk with Kasi about these things though.

At the same time, by the end of April, for our family, we were notified that we got accepted to go to Australia. This would be a day of disappointments that I had been expecting. It created much tension between me and Khamphet. He continued to be angry with me, and again, we argued heatedly. Again, he tried to persuade me that we should take this offer and get out of this place. He was running out of patience, I could see, but I was not going to change my mind.

"Kim, please be reasonable. We have been here for five months and look at all we have had to endure. How close have our daughter and her cousin come to harm? Even you, Kim, even you! What would I do if something were to happen to you? If we were citizens in a normal society, I could protect you, or we would be protected by the police. Here, if I were to protect you, you know well what would happen. That situation does something to a man. I can't live like this," he pleaded.

He looked at me disheartened and disappointed. I was sympathetic. I really was. But I knew that I couldn't give in. So, I had to find some words that would protect me from his judgements.

"Listen. We have discussed this before. We are exactly the kind of people that the United States needs and wants. We are well educated. We can teach others. The U.S. society is open and there is good social mobility. You can be born poor and become the President! You just have to be willing to work hard. They love new ideas, and they welcome immigrants. They are a nation of immigrants and Asians are respected there. Just think of the Statue of Liberty. France gave it to the United States, but the U.S. is now a much better representative of that," I opined.

Of course, I knew I was taking some liberty with the truth. I knew the history of the Chinese in the West during the time that the railroads were being built. But, I was sure that Khamphet did not know that history. I was right. With the mention of the Statue of Liberty, he relented.

Kasi overheard our heated exchange. She was not going to convince me of anything, but this time, she had the look of puzzlement – or rather, curiosity.

She wanted me to explain myself. She had good questions, and they made me doubt myself even more than the others had.

"What makes one place better than another, really?" she asked with an inquiring mind.

Of course, that is easily answered if you know about two concrete places, and you have some criteria to use for the comparison. But that is not what she was asking, I realized. She knew that we did not have any concrete experience of any of the places that we might go. We could not even say that the bread in U.S. is better than it is in France or Australia; or that the neighborhood we would be living in in California would be safer and cleaner than the neighborhood we would be living in in France. None of us had any direct experience of these things. And we didn't even know what our situation would be like in any of the possible countries. So, I was forced to wonder, what was the real basis for our decision, for my decision?

I couldn't – wouldn't – admit this to Kasi, but we were – I was – making this decision based on a myth that I believed in. It was the myth of the United States – to me, as "the Land of Opportunity" where dreams come true – that seemed to be better than the myth of France or Australia. But what is a myth, really? It is something repeated over and over until we believe it. But did it have any relation to reality? How could we know without going there and finding out? We couldn't. We could only dive head first into the mythical world and swim in it. We would have to swim in the socio-economic and cultural sea of the United States for years before we would be able to judge the veracity of the myth. That, ultimately, was what I decided we all had to do and why we had to do it. So, I told Kasi what I wanted to believe was true, not what I knew to be true.

"I just know it will be better for us in the United States. I can feel it in my bones, but I can't really explain it. Can you trust your mother in this adventure?" I replied.

Kasi looked at me and hesitated just long enough to make me uncomfortable. Then she said, "I guess we will have to go there to find out for sure. I trust you, Mai."

November 1976: Third Interview – U.S.A.

"Good evening, folks! This is your Friendly Fred Fry disc jockey and newsman. I will have news and rock tunes for you from now till midnight, right here at WTWR 99.3 FM Seattle, Washington. We want you to be the best-informed radio audience in the United States! So here is the Monthly Roundup for May 1976.

In the first week: *1600 Pennsylvania Avenue* Broadway Musical opened at Mark Hellinger NYC for seven performances.

In the second week: the first LAGEOS (Laser Geodynamics Satellite) was launched and an earthquake hit the Friuli area in Italy, killing more than 900 people and making another 100,000 homeless.

In the third week: Ulrike Meinhof of the Red Army Faction was found hanged in an apparent suicide, in her Stuttgart-Stammheim Prison cell. Also, in this week, the U.S. President Gerald Ford signed the amended Federal Election Campaign Act.

In the fourth week: Washington D.C. Concorde service began. U.S. President Gerald Ford defeated challenger Ronald Reagan in the Republican presidential primaries in Kentucky, Tennessee and Oregon.

And that's what happened in May of 1976!"

Approval for Phoemkhun to emigrate to France all happened very quickly by Nong Khai Refugee Camp standards. Apparently, Phoemkhun's aunt in France was well connected, and that, in combination with Phoemkhun's situation at the camp, seemed to convince the whole bureaucracy to act quickly. I knew that Kasi would be grief-stricken if Phoemkhun were to leave without having a chance to say goodbye, so I had to intervene to permit that to happen.

As we all know, the left hand of a bureaucracy often knows not what the right hand is doing. That was certainly true of the bureaucracy that oversaw the camp. Standard operating procedures were skipped because some powerful person demanded immediate action.

So, the part of the administration that approves requests to go to the market did not communicate with the part of the administration that transports departing emigrants. We had gotten permission to go to the market on the 10th of May. I had decided that it was Khamphet's turn to go and that he should take Kasi and Phoemkhun with him. The administration approved that request. So, when a group of men came to my stand to pick up Phoemkhun to send her to France immediately, she was not with me. I told them that they should come back the next day at the same time and she would be ready to go.

That night, while we were working together to put away the items from the market, I told Phoemkhun and Kasi what had happened, and that they would have to be ready for Phoemkhun to go that next day.

Kasi's Diary 12-May-1976

Yesterday, I said goodbye to Phoemkhun for the last time. She gave me her address in France. It was only a post-office box, but it gave me a little hope that we would be able to stay in touch.

Neither of us had a lot to say. All the experiences that we shared together were so closely tied to her parents' deaths that even the happy times had a certain tint of sadness. Mostly, we just hugged each other and cried. We both realized that hugs would soon be impossible and that we may never be able to see each other face to face again.

> I learn that people matter regardless of our ability
> to keep them in our immediate world. That is what I
> learned from Mom when she counted the survivors
> from our boat trip, and this is the lesson of my
> separation from Phoemkhun, too.

A few months later at the end of August, my sister Lai and her children, including Chansy, were called to the U.S. and we were so happy for them. It was also a good indication that we would be next, as they would want to keep families together as much as possible. So, that was another goodbye for Kasi within just a few months. My gut feeling was that we would be reunited sooner than we anticipated.

I had been working on my presentation for the third interview for months – six months to be exact. Of course, a presentation during an immigration interview in a refugee camp is not like a presentation in a business meeting. I had to memorize the whole script and be ready to be interrupted at any point and to be questioned by the interviewer. These constraints meant that my presentation was extremely brief and to the point.

Our whole family, all dressed up nicely, anxiously went in for the third interview on the 12th of November 1976, which covered our application for visas to the United States. The Thai interviewer addressed himself to Khamphet as the nominal head of our family.

"Mr. Champa, you have completed the application for entry into the United States, is that correct?" the official asked as a formality.

"Yes Sir. I did," Khamphet replied.

"The United States requires that both spouses agree about the application and the facts stated in the application. Do you, Mrs.

Champa, agree with all of the matters of fact stated in this application?" he turned to me.

"Yes, I do. I would like to make a statement that is very important to our application. May I?" I asked in my most polite Thai.

The official looked up from his paperwork and looked directly at me with surprise. I suppose no spouse – let alone wife – had ever been quite that forthright or audacious or fluent in Thai. He looked at Khamphet, who nodded his approval, and then turned back to me and gave his consent.

"Go ahead," he said and sat back in his chair with his arms folded skeptically.

"I just wanted to be sure that you and the United States government know how successful my little business has been. I have expanded to the point that I have been able to give an employment opportunity to an unfortunate girl – I think you know about the case of Phoemkhun whose parents were killed in a murder-suicide a while ago – and I hope that entrepreneurial success will be considered when our application is reviewed," I explained. That was it.

I didn't want to appear self-aggrandizing or pushy. I just wanted the facts to be known in the proper context. Because I was so brief, the official stayed with his arms folded and silent for a while before finally realizing that I was finished. Then, he took up his pen and made a notation in our file. That was the best that I could have expected from this interview.

Dec 1976: Third Call of Acceptance – U.S.A.

We had to wait thirty-six days after our third interview before we got the notification of our acceptance to the United States. Every one of those days was a new struggle to survive. It was another day at the little shop selling things or a day of travel to town to shop for things to eat and to sell. It was hundreds of trips to get water and just as many squabbles between the kids to settle. *Time is not your friend when daily life has so few rewards.*

Still, after having survived those hundreds of days, we had arrived at a successful conclusion of the project I had led to get our family from Laos to the United States.

This was a time of mending fences with Khamphet and Kasi, especially. They finally understood why I had been asking them to endure our suffering for a little while longer.

Kasi came up to me first, after we got the news.

"Mai," she said as she looked straight at me, "You were right to ask us to make the sacrifice to wait for our invitation to go to the United States." She continued on, "I am sorry that I doubted you."

That was such a sweet moment. I know that I had asked her— everyone, really—to make big sacrifices. None of us knew if we would ever be accepted. This acceptance was really only a first step. But it was a very big and obviously necessary first step.

The mending of fences with Khamphet was very different. He did not express himself to me in words. All he did was come over to me, hold me by my arms and look into my eyes with tears in his. Then, he hugged me for a long time. I knew that he meant this as an apology, but it was also a kind of resignation. I had won the battle of where we would go. I finally got the recognition that I had hoped for, and it was one of the greatest reliefs of my life.

It was time to bid farewell to those we had come to know in the camp. As we had led our lives in the camp, we had come to know some of the other residents. I had some customers who were regulars and whose names I knew. I decided to close the shop each afternoon instead of working all day. Word soon got around that there was a sale at the shop, and all of the regular customers came in to see what bargains they could find and to say goodbye.

I also made a special point of going to the USCC table and giving our thanks for all that they had done for us. To my surprise, they were not done giving. They asked about our destination, and they gave us contacts in the USCC in California. I was overcome with an incredible sense of gratitude and warmth.

Finally, I was able to take one last trip to the marketplace. There, I got a chance to say goodbye and thank each of the merchants that I had dealt with and had come to know. While I was there, I also went to the clinic that had seen Kasi when she was so sick, and I thanked them.

All that was left to do was to get ready. We had just four days to do that. We needed to get ready for another evacuation. This time, it was an evacuation from Nong Khai of Thailand to San Francisco in the United States.

Airplane Ride

> "Good evening, folks! This is your Friendly Fred Fry disc jockey and great newsman. I will have news and rock tunes for you from now till midnight, right here at WTWR 99.3 FM Seattle, Washington. We want you to be the best-informed radio audience in the United States! Just for a change, let's review some economic statistics of 1976:
>
> Yearly Inflation Rate USA 5.76%,
> Year End Close Dow Jones Industrial Average 1004.65,
> Interest Rates Year End Federal Reserve 6.25%,
> Average Cost of new house $43,400,
> Average Income per year $16,000,
> Average Monthly Rent $220,
> Cost of a gallon of Gas 59 cents."

It was the evening of the 23rd of December 1976 when we almost reached U.S. soil, after our twenty-four-hour flight.

As we got closer to our destination, Kasi became increasingly excited. She was looking forward to seeing what the Americans looked like. I couldn't help her much there. I only knew one American – Mr. John – from the USCC in the camp. The very nice and friendly Mr. John was a Caucasian who spoke fluent Lao. There was actually a song about him, describing the well-dressed Laotians that come before Mr. John. I told Kasi that he was tall, bald, and white, but I cautioned her not to generalize from just one individual. "There are probably many kinds of Americans," I told her.

Once we had arrived at our cruising altitude, we – all of us were Lao refugees – were given some papers that had English expressions on one side and Lao expressions on the other side. They were to be used whenever we needed something in the airplane or during our flight connection. Clearly, there were no stewardesses on board that spoke Lao. We would have to use English if we wanted to communicate.

Some of the expressions were: Please show us the nearest restroom; we are lost, please help us get to the next flight; we don't speak English, but we can speak French, Lao, Thai, two dialects of Chinese; this is my relative, please call her for us; new in the United States, please help us contact our family.

When the plane finally landed in San Francisco of California, we were not allowed to get off immediately. Instead, the captain made an announcement. Of course, since we didn't speak English, we did not understand it. So, it came as a complete surprise when the plane door suddenly opened and five big, fat, old, white men with big bellies – all seemingly jolly – came striding down the aisle. They were dressed in red and white suits and hats and were carrying bags over their shoulders. When they began shouting "Ho Ho Ho," we were terrified!

Kasi asked me, "Mai, what is happening? This is the United States?"

Khamphet had always been fearful and skeptical. After all the events of the refugee camp, he was traumatized. His first emotion when the red-suited men with sacks arrived was great unease. My whole body was on high alert. I actually thought these costumed men might be high-jacking the airplane for some political purpose. We were certainly not prepared for this and were in a state of shock and confusion. Then, they started giving out gifts, not only to all the children, but even to the adults! The gifts were all nicely wrapped up in beautiful boxes and bows. We finally understood that this must be some peculiar cultural tradition, and we relaxed. We had never experienced anything so nice. So, our first impression of Americans was that they are such generous and kind people. Is it like this every day?

After they left the plane, we were directed out and to the waiting area right outside of the plane, where my two sisters and all their children were waiting. They threw their arms around us, all were with tears flowing down our faces, and we hugged each other for quite some time. Kasi and Chansy were beyond ecstatic to be reunited. We were just glad to be alive and together again.

When we got to the car, we were all excited to open our presents. Kasi was so happy that she got a music recorder. Huck got a basketball, and Khamphet and I each got a nice blanket and a set of towels.

Later, we learned that those Santas were sent from the USCC just to welcome us to our new country and wish us Merry Christmas. None of us understood what that meant at that time – Santa? Christmas? Gift giving? We were happy, but we knew we were in a completely different world – our second, and hopefully final freedom.

Haven to Heaven

Second Freedom ~ U.S.A.

"Freedom consists not in doing what we like, but in having the right to do what we ought." ~Pope John Paul II

Our airplane ride from Thailand to the San Francisco airport in the USA. took us from one kind of freedom to an entirely different kind of freedom. The freedom in Thailand was a freedom from the growing tyranny in Laos. However, a refugee camp was almost like a prison. We were not in Thailand to become citizens and to normalize our lives. The freedom in the USA was a freedom to act, participate, and change the very conditions of our lives. We would be able to find new homes, new schools, and Kasi and Huck would be able to grow up and start their own family. These new freedoms, however, came at the price of some disillusionment.

Haven to Heaven

Welcome

"Give me your tired, your poor, your huddled masses yearning to breathe free, the wretched refuse of your teeming shore. Send these, the homeless, tempest-tossed, to me, I lift my lamp beside the golden door." ~Emma Lazarus' sonnet, New Colossus, the Statue of Liberty poem

It took a while before we could return to what most Americans would consider a normal state of being.

There are certain unconscious assumptions you make when you are living in a lawless society. When you can depend on the rule of law, you are free to shed certain habits and ways of thinking. Those are ways of thinking that are embedded in your consciousness.

When you are a refugee living in a lawless land, you don't sleep well. You are constantly listening, constantly vigilant. When in Thailand, even some faint, distant sound would jolt me awake. It might have been the closing of a door on one of the porta-potties in the square. Who was that? When we arrived in San Francisco of California, the unfamiliar sounds seemed to set off alarm bells in my head all night. It took quite some time to get used to those new sounds, and to realize that if there were some criminal act outside our house, we could even call the police. That would not get us in trouble. That certainly took some getting used to.

The friendly police in California would sometimes walk in the community. We would often encounter them when we went shopping or to the park. In Laos, the Pathet Lao uniform was hated and feared. In Thailand, the uniformed officials were routinely corrupt and had the power of life and death over any Lao refugee in the camp. My reflexive fear reaction to uniformed people took quite some time to go away.

I was hesitant to wear any jewelry for the fear of being robbed. In our new homeland, I had to force myself to wear jewelry. It made me so nervous at first that it just wasn't worth it. I would divide my money into several wallets and put one in my purse and another in my pocket. I never wanted to wear a dress that had no pockets. And most often, those pockets were sewn inside the garment.

In Thailand, the shopkeepers were always suspicious of Lao people. So, I had developed the habit of looking down when I walked through a commercial area. Now, it was hard to look up. My sister, who had been living in the Bay Area five years longer, would often remind me that I could walk proudly. That is when you realize the rule of law exists. You can walk with your head up and feel proud to be who you are. You can look at the people in the eyes when you're talking to them. You can even greet and smile at strangers.

Finally, the rule of law affected how we felt when we took Kasi and Huck to the playground, where for the first time, they could play and simply be kids. We never did that at the camp. I was very uneasy when we first took the children to the park in the U.S. Gradually, I learned to relax. I did not need to watch the children's every move or suspiciously monitor the other adults. Believing in the rule of law meant that I, too, could enjoy the pleasure of the park. I could relax and let the children play. That took some time to learn and adjust.

It also took a while to appreciate that there would be no more violence. Violence was a normal part of camp life. Our family never had to inflict violence on others. We were all witnesses to violence, though. Phoemkhun's story was the closest we came to murder, but we were certainly traumatized by the violence of the robberies at our little shop in the camp. Now, my sister claimed we did not need to worry about that anymore, but I really did not believe her. Whenever I watched the TV news at night, I saw that there was violence in the United States, too. My sister would say that it was "only in the cities." Certainly, it was behind the TV screen, and therefore seemed far away. Nevertheless, there was an uneasiness that I never really let go of in the United States.

No more hunger! This was one of the greatest sources of relief. Knowing that Kasi and Huck would be able to eat as much as they wanted was an almost incredible relief. Of course, I am not saying that we could afford all of the good things in life. That was certainly far from the truth. However, we could afford the meat and fresh fruits and vegetables, which were so rare in Thailand. I was truly grateful for that.

We would not have to worry about exposure to dangerous diseases. Of course, that is a bit of an exaggeration. The kids got colds, even the flu. But there were no scenes like the tapeworm crawling out of a child's mouth we witnessed at the health clinic. The women in our family were delivered from the constant fear of rape, and the possibility of sexually transmitted diseases.

As a consequence, we lost our sense of vulnerability. Again, this may sound like an exaggeration, but it captured the way we felt. Sometimes, the way you feel is more important than the exact facts of the matter. It certainly was like that for us, even if it took us quite a while to appreciate it fully.

From now on, there will be law and order, fairness and kindness everywhere. My children will grow up, be educated, and become contributing members of this society.

My tears of joy when we arrived in the U.S. were uncountable – infinite, really – because they were not just my tears, or the tears of the Champa family – they were the tears of every immigrant who has left behind the oppressive conditions that they once endured. *Forever free, at last.* We took our first deep breath in the land of San Francisco, California of the USA, and we could exquisitely smell freedom. Our freedom and the freedom of all of the others that had come here. It was a good feeling. Still, I couldn't hold back those tears of joy, tears of freedom. My hopes and dreams had finally come true. *This was heaven.*

New Homes

"The strength of a nation derives from the integrity of the home." ~Confucius

My youngest sister Thanom, our co-sponsor with the USCC, had been living in a single-family, seven hundred square foot home in Antioch of California for five years prior to our arrival. While working with the U.S. utilities company in Laos, she had an opportunity to come to the USA as an interpreter. Her company later sponsored her, and she proudly became a U.S. Citizen, just five years before she sponsored us over. Because Thanom was able to co-sponsor us while we were in the Nong Khai Refugee Camp, the process went much faster. That's why we remained in the camp for only twelve months, although it felt like a decade. At that time, Thanom and her husband had two small boys – a two-year old, and an eleven-month old toddler.

My other sister Lai – a single mother, not by choice – and her family arrived in the U.S. just a few months before us. Lai had all seven of her children, including Chansy, with her. She was thankful that she had been able to gather her whole family in one place from the Nong Khai camp to the California home. So, when the Champa family of four arrived, we stayed at Thanom's house with her two sons and husband, along with Lai and her seven children. Yes, all sixteen of us in that seven hundred square foot home! It was, in some sense, worse than the Nong Khai camp, because it was so crowded.

Sixteen people were living in that house. Thanom did not own the house. She rented it. As newly arrived immigrants, we were in no position to help her, because we were all still unemployed and the majority of us were just children. Naturally, the children couldn't work because, in the United States, child labor is illegal. Shouldn't it be? Should we become more like those countries that treat children like slaves? Of course not. There is a simple and practical principle: Children are children!

We were all family, and we loved each other tremendously. We were all willing to help the others. That meant that those who had more at a particular time would help those who had less. Are those not family values? However, if all of the adults could have gotten jobs that paid well enough to rent their own house, we would have done that. And that arrangement would have benefited the surrounding community as well. We would have been paying rent and buying more than just the bare necessities in the shops of the local business owners.

It was clear that our circumstance came down to a matter of jobs. Why was there a scarcity of jobs? Why did employers feel that giving an immigrant a job necessarily took a job away from a citizen? Even though it was temporary, why were there sixteen of us in that 700 square foot house?

I was just a teacher. I had taught French and Lao in schools in Laos. My English was not that good. I came to the United States, because I wanted to be free of interference from an oppressive and undemocratic government. I came here expecting that I could work hard to better my condition. I wanted to start my own business. But starting a business requires an initial investment from savings or from credit. At the minimum wage jobs that I was able to get— even when I took more than one at a time—there was no way for me to save for a business investment.

In Thanom's house, we still had no beds. We slept and sat on the same bamboo mats that we slept and sat upon in Thailand. With sixteen people in the tiny space sucking up all the air, it was hard to breathe. Every so often we had to just sit outside the house for fresh air. Subsequently, the USCC helped throughout the first year with clothes, bedding, and so on. The United States government just provided food stamps. Although we didn't know it at the time, many Americans ascribed shame to using food stamps. We took it simply as it was probably intended by those who designed the system: It was as good as cash.

Whereas the USCC did everything that they could to help us get to a point where we could be contributing members of society, there were some in the community who took the opposite approach. For about ten months, in addition to the crowded living conditions, the lack of work, and learning a new language and new customs, we had to endure drive-by hecklers, mostly young men or teenagers. At all hours of the day and night, people would yell, beep their car horns, and throw eggs and trash in our front yard. While we were working – in just about any jobs we could find – and saving up for deposits and rents, those good "citizens' terrorized us and spread refuse around the community. This was the most troubling aspect of coming to the United States for me. I thought that I would find respect for the rule of law among everyone. I was disillusioned to discover that not all Americans respected the rule of law as a foundation for civil engagement. This was my first glimpse of the disturbing underbelly of the society I had decided to adopt. I suppose it was the same for my children.

At the end of that traumatic ten-month period, just on the last weekend in October 1977 when everyone around us was celebrating Halloween, we had saved enough money to finally manage to move into a 45-year old 1,200 square foot three-bedroom home that we rented from our landlord, Mr. Smouse, the same landlord that Thanom rented from. The home was more than enough space for the four of us, with each of the kids getting their own room. There was even an extra room for me to use as a study to begin writing this book. Our goal was to save up every dollar we had to purchase a permanent home. This was an exciting time for us, and we ended up staying in Mr. Smouse's rental home in

Haven to Heaven

Antioch for eight years, until we purchased our own home in Oakland when Kasi was a senior in high school.

Mr. Smouse was very influential in the Lao community. He was a landlord for many Lao people and a benefactor to all. I don't know if Mr. Smouse made a great deal of money from the houses that he rented to the members of the Lao community. However, I know that everyone that I spoke to was grateful to him for his beneficence. Of course, he was also humble. When you asked him why he was so nice, he would look at you and ask: why wouldn't I be?

A few years later in 1980, Thanom actually bought a decent three-bedroom home—her first home purchase in the U.S.—and she took pride in it. Thanom was a model for all of us, and we all aspired to own a house, just like her. When she and her husband moved in to their new home, everyone that we knew in the Lao community came to wish her well.

I don't mean to say that the U.S. as a country—or that the U.S. immigration policy itself—was anti-immigrant at that time. Those unfortunate incidents that we experienced were due to the behavior of a few groups of ignorant people, not the country as a whole.

To counter that impression, I keep in mind all of the positive experiences, too – like the Santa Claus greetings in the airplane, and the help of good and generous people in the United States, such as the USCC aid, which was crucial in our first years of settlement. They provided us with clothing and blankets; helped us apply for jobs, get a driver's license, register for schools and job training; and they were always available to help us if we needed an interpreter for anything in our early years.

Naturally, we struggled. But our situation was not unique. Many non-immigrants were struggling, too. What was more important was those challenges were overcome.

School Bullies

"Standing up to bullies is the hallmark of a civilized society."
~Robert Reich

When Kasi started 4th grade, her primary task was learning English. She and her brother were pulled out of class each day to take a special English class in 4th (Kasi) and 2nd (Huck) grades. While Khamphet and I seemed to be struggling with English, the children were much more adaptable, both in the language and culture. Learning a second language is difficult at any age. However, it is always easier to learn a language when you are young.

Obviously, it is easier to learn a second language that uses the same alphabet as your mother tongue. It is also easier to learn a second language if the spoken and written forms are complementary. Young Kasi learned English much more easily than I or Khamphet did. The alphabet that she learned to write in Laos was completely different from the alphabet that she had to learn for English (example: ສະບາຍດີ which means "hello".) Further, English is a difficult language to learn, just because the pronunciation of words sometimes has no relation to the way they are written. It is similar to French in that. For example, when I was learning French, I would often pronounce letters in the words that native speaking French people would not. The most well-known example is the word "Paris." It is written with a silent "s" at the end. English is like that, too. For example, the word "enough" has a final "f" sound that you would never expect when "ghost" is pronounced with an initial "g" sound.

Kasi had her work cut out for her. So did Huck. And the mountain that Khamphet and I had to climb was even higher. Of course, we knew we were completely on our own. That is why we basically had to teach ourselves by listening to TV, reading the newspapers, and talking with Kasi and Huck.

This effort also put me in a completely new relation to the Lao culture. Whereas I had been advocating the practical abandonment of the Lao language and culture as a means of embracing our new nation, I now became much more of an advocate of preserving them both. There is much to be proud of in the Lao language and culture. First of all, the Lao script is beautiful. I don't deny that beauty is a subjective judgement, but that is my judgement. I love beautiful things and the Lao script is a beautiful thing. It is also ancient. It connects modern day Laos to southern India and to the Buddhist religion. I did not want to lose those connections, and I did not want my children to ignore or forget them. This sometimes created tension between me and the children.

In any case, Kasi made friends quite easily despite her initial inability to speak English. I was certainly proud of her. I remembered when she was first born, and I had reprimanded her for thinking so highly of herself. I think it was related to that inner pride towards which, as a Lao person, I had a very ambivalent attitude. As her name implied, she was brilliant and colorful. These qualities shone through even without a mastery of the language. I knew how important it was for her to fit in if we were going to be successful as a family. So, I held my temper and did not reprimand her as much as I would have otherwise. Huck had always been a more mellow child and seemed to just take the most comfortable and neutral position in everything. In many ways, it was a much safer approach in life.

Kasi excelled in school even in those early years whenever language didn't get in her way. For example, she breezed through math, the only subject that was the same in every language. I noticed her grades, and they gave me hope that she might be able to attend university one day and bring the family into the American middle class proudly.

However, the kids also had their own share of being picked on and made fun of because they were "different".

The school that they attended was predominantly Caucasian, with only about 10% Hispanic and less than 5% being Asian.

Everyone could see that Kasi and Huck looked different and dressed differently. They looked different because they were Lao. Laotians are Asians, and they look like Asians. They dressed differently, simply because we were poor. As parents, we were just thankful for any clothes donated to us. It didn't matter to us if the clothes didn't match or looked weird. As long as the children were clothed and had food to eat every meal, we were happy. Naturally, we did not have to live with the consequences of those clothing gifts. Children can be cruel to non-conformists. Education strives to overcome those prejudices, and the mob mentality that is built upon them.

I didn't think their differences would be a problem. But, they were. I didn't know much about it until it had gotten far out of hand. Kasi suffered most for my ignorance.

Kasi often came home crying. She told us that she was often teased for being weird or not speaking English correctly. I thought it was a minor problem that would clear up by itself, and I did nothing. But I decided that I ought to look at her diary to see if I could find out more about it.

Kasi's Diary 15-Feb-1977

Yesterday was Valentine's Day. We celebrated at school by making Valentine's cards for our classmates. The teachers told us that we would not be able to choose who to give a valentine to. They said it was to avoid problems that had happened in the past, when they just let everyone choose their Valentine person. I don't know what happened in the past, but I didn't like what happened yesterday.

We all picked the name of another student out of one of two hats — either the hat with girls' names or the boys' names. I got Carrie. She got Debbie. Angela got me.

Carrie is pretty nice. Some of the kids tease her and call her a tomboy because she likes sports. I just think she is nice, because she never teases me. She is my height and size, and smart, too. She doesn't let anybody push her around. One day, I helped her to understand a math problem. Ever since then, she smiles at me whenever our eyes meet.

I don't know Debbie very well. She has long dark hair that her mother must braid. Carrie seems to like her. Angela is friends with Tommy. All the guys like Tommy, because he makes them laugh. I don't like Tommy because he makes the boys laugh at me. He has lots of names for me that I never understand. I just try to stay away from him. Angela has long blonde hair and very blue eyes. All the boys think that she is pretty. She always has name-brand clothes on. I didn't even know what that meant until they started teasing me about the brands that I wore. They asked me, "Are those K-Mart brand?" Tommy and Angela are part of the popular kids, and me and Carrie are not (I don't know about Debbie.)

School Bullies

When Angela realized that she had gotten me, she raised her hand and asked to go to the girls' room. She got permission, and when she was leaving, she dropped off my name and the card she was making on Tommy's desk. By the time she got back, he had already put all of those bad names in the card. But, Angela is very smart. She pretended that she hadn't gotten a card (or that it was lost) and asked the teacher for another one. Then, when we were all supposed to give each other the cards, I suddenly noticed that I had two. One was signed by Angela, and it was very plain. The other one was not signed, and it had lots of nasty names and a picture of an Asian face with small eyes.

I showed Carrie when the teacher wasn't looking. She can understand all of the English that people are talking, and she overheard Tommy whispering to another boy and laughing. She figured it all out. She put the bad card in her backpack and zipped it up. Then she asked to go to the bathroom. As Carrie was leaving, she whispered to me: "It's okay. This will never happen again." When she was leaving the room, she passed by Tommy's desk and said something to him.

The next period was recess. I was pretty scared, but you can't stay in from recess. Everybody had to go out. Carrie came over to me and thanked me in very slow English for the nice card that I made for her. I was sort of embarrassed, but I did my best to thank her for looking out for me. She told me not to worry and just to watch what happened.

Tommy was standing with Angela and the boys that were his fan club. She told me again to stay where I was and watch. I stayed, and I watched. She went walking right into the middle of the group of boys standing around Tommy and laughing. Like I said, Carrie is pretty athletic. She pushed Tommy and tripped him at the same time. He fell down in a muddy spot, and Carrie just started laughing at him. I heard her use the word "sissy" a few times. Tommy got up, and Carrie tripped him and put him down again. This time, she got on top of him and pretended to kiss him. Actually, she was whispering to him. She told me later that she told him if he ever bothered me again that she would tell Angela everything she knew about him. Then, she got up and walked over to me without the stupid teachers even noticing what had happened.

When I read that, I knew that I would have to get involved. I really wanted to defend my daughter, but I was not sure what I should do. I decided that I would go to talk with Mr. Smouse. He welcomed me into his house on the Saturday that same week.

"Please come in, Mr. and Mrs. Champa. My home is your home," he said at the door. That is what I liked about him. He was always welcoming even when he was very formal.

"We wanted to get your advice about a situation that has developed with my daughter in school," I began. "It seems that the other children are teasing her because of her Asian eyes and the way she dresses. I wouldn't bring it to your attention except it seems to be on the border of violence. Here was the Valentine's card that one of the boys gave her anonymously." I handed him the card that Kasi brought home to show me.

He was quiet and serious as he looked the card over. When he looked up at me, I could see that he had tears in his eyes. I knew that he was very protective of all of his Lao tenants, but he was especially protective of Kasi. It reminded me a bit of how my brother Seng was protective of me.

"This is very serious. The parents of this child should be alerted to the fact that their son brings these attitudes into school. It may be that he thinks this makes him macho. But it may be that his parents have similar attitudes and that they may be instigators or supporters of the vandals that have been heckling you and throwing garbage on my property," he said.

I was very happy to hear that. It didn't matter, at that point, whether he would be able to do anything or not. All that mattered to me, right then, was that we had an American citizen on our side. We were not crazy feeling this treatment that our family and my daughter had received was wrong. He didn't stop there, though.

"I would like to go with you to see the principal of the school and show him this. I would like to take pictures of the garbage that those vandals have been spreading on the property, and I hope you will both come with me. This is not the way things should be in our school and community." That was his proposal. Khamphet and I welcomed it and accepted it. That was exactly what we did.

That meeting did not settle the question or stop the bad behavior, but it was what turned the tide in our favor. Mr. Smouse was also a member of the Chamber of Commerce of the town, and he took the matter up with them, too. After a few carefully worded letters to certain strategically placed people of high standing and rank, the word seemed to come down from on high that such behavior was not to be tolerated. The bullies stopped teasing Kasi at school, and the drive-by heckling subsided as well. I learned the importance of staying connected and engaged! For a time, the bullying subsided.

Kasi finished 4th and 5th grades without any further issues, and consequently moved on to middle school, while Huck still had two more years to go in the elementary school.

Naturally, middle school was very challenging because Kasi was going through puberty. As Lao parents, we had to start thinking about how our children's lives would be preserved and protected. As I mentioned, I wanted to pass on Lao culture to my children. Part of that was in speaking Lao to them at home. Another part of that was providing them with the food that is part of the Lao way. I took the time and care to prepare home-cooked meals that Kasi and Huck could take with them to school. I never imagined in my wildest dreams that such good home-cooked meals could become another source of conflict in the schools.

Kasi started school as a 6th grader on Monday, the 21st of August 1978. Although by this time, she was more proficient with English, bullies still existed at a different level. They were older and meaner, and mostly they were girls.

In spite of English being her second language, I had never seen a single grade lower than an A in her progress reports.

In 6th and 7th grades, I would pack lunches for Kasi almost every day. Naturally, I would include sticky rice, or whatever Lao food we had. So, she didn't think anything about it and just took it to school.

For a while, I didn't know that kids made fun of her. The bullies would even touch her food, make fun of her, and make comments like, "What kind of crap are you eating here?"

For months, this bullying continued. Kasi told us and Mr. Smouse about it, and he helped write another letter to the principal of the school. The office administrators tried to talk to her and to the bullies, but obviously the bullies didn't seem to take it seriously. They continued to pick on her on the bus and even followed her home.

Kasi's Diary 7-Nov-1978

Yesterday, before I went to school, I asked Pa, "Can I push back those bullies if they touch me?" and he said, "Go ahead." That freed me.

When I was coming home from the bus that day, the bullies, Yvonne and Cassandra, were following me as usual. I just kept walking straight ahead even after they started calling my name (but they never said it correctly.) Then, with Pa within my sight, the two girls ran up behind me and started pulling my hair as they had before. Now, I was ready for them. I just turned around as fast as I could and gave one of them, Cassandra, the biggest kick that I could. I hit her just below the knee on her left leg and she let out a yelp and fell to the ground. Yvonne just stood there for a second, not knowing what to do. I was so ready to give anyone that came near me another kick. Yvonne helped Cassandra up and they turned around and went the other way. I didn't even know I could do that! I totally surprised myself.

And boy, did that scare them away!

The next day, they were all nice to me at the lunch table. Cassandra apologized to me. I noticed the girls all went to tell their friends what happened, and that I knew karate or something, and they all seemed to be much nicer and wanted to be friends with me.

Haven to Heaven

I didn't understand that, but it was much more peaceful to accept their friendship and move on.

Ironically, later in 8th grade, because she excelled in school, she was asked to tutor those students who needed help in math. Kasi wanted to help other students and agreed to volunteer before and after school. She told me later that it surprised her that so many students were very weak in calculations and that many students did not even have the simplest understanding of mathematics.

Kasi was taking Algebra in 8th grade, but some other kids did not even understand the basic idea of an assumption like: "if a + 1=3..." To teach them effectively, she had to learn the material very well herself. Doing so helped her to improve her English and communication skills as well, so she didn't mind. In fact, it gave her a sense of satisfaction to be able to give and help those "in need". Some of those kids included the ones who had bullied her. They listened well and appreciated her help. So, it all worked out well in the end.

Summer Years

"Good evening, folks! This is your Friendly Fred Fry newsman extraordinaire of WTWR 99.3 FM Seattle, Washington. Here is our big international news for this day in summer of 1980.

The Carter Administration joined Sakharov's appeal and set a deadline by which the Soviet Union must pull out of Afghanistan or face the consequences, including an international boycott of the 1980 Summer Olympics in Moscow.

The Nong Khai Refugee Camp, built in May 1975 after the influx of Laotian refugees, was recently closed to new refugees by the Thai government. It was deemed overcrowded and unsafe for human health. The Thai government, claiming that it has too many refugees, is sending them to Loei and Ubon, and has even returned some refugees to the Laotian authorities.

And that's what happened so far in the year 1980!"

"A mentor is someone who allows you to see the higher part of yourself when sometimes it becomes hidden to your own view."
~Oprah Winfrey

As a general rule, the Fair Labor Standards Act (FLSA) sets the minimum age of 14 for employment and limits the number of hours worked by minors under the age of 16. Also, the FLSA prohibits children from working in certain hazardous occupations or for extensive durations or at unusual hours. In spite of these restrictions, Kasi was eager to find a paying job to help out with the family expenses, and to earn some personal spending money.

It was the summer of 1980, just after her 14th birthday, Kasi had just been notified that she was accepted for her first job at McDonald's. We were still living in the rental house with no central heating or air conditioning, so Kasi would look forward to the opportunity to have some place to go during the day. It would be a nice refuge for her to be in an air-conditioned place. Summers were always packed with opportunities for us, though. These opportunities did not involve spending money, but rather, making money and earning a living.

Most kids look forward to summer to be free and to have fun. Instead, Kasi looked forward to summer to learn English with the intention of enrolling in one of the ESOL classes. Kasi knew that she would still be able to hang out with some of her immigrant friends. They sometimes learned English by listening to the lyrics of their favorite music. I still remember her singing the lyrics to Kenny Rogers' "The Gambler" and Carly Simon's "You're So Vain". What better way to spend the summer than to learn English and to earn money?

In addition to her first job at McDonald's, Kasi also had other jobs crushing soda cans (for ten cents per can) with her father and Huck; and peeling off shrimp heads with all of us as a family. That was opportune family time we took advantage of – earning a living together. The crushing of soda cans, by foot, became "embarrassing" when some of the kids saw them doing it and would tease them. The next day at school, they were laughed at. But by this time, they were numbed to such teasing. We all learned to ignore that and continued to do what we had to do to simply survive. I often reminded my family of the American dream of "success comes to those who work hard, and hard work builds character." So, for at least fifteen years for the Champa family, there was no such thing as a vacation or dining out. Holidays, overtime and weekend hours were the best opportunity for earning extra pay.

From the age of fourteen on, her jobs included McDonald's, Wendy's, then a clothing store in the mall. Kasi also worked in a factory that reminded her of the "I Love Lucy" scene in which Lucy and her side kick, Ethel, are frantically trying to keep up with an assembly line belt with chocolates on it.

No account of her summer jobs would be complete without mentioning the Jamaican-born factory supervisor who unforgettably became her mentor. Kasi was not well suited to factory work. She was not fast enough and would often make mistakes. It was very challenging to keep up with the moving belts which transported the little pieces of electronic components to the workers for assembly. One of the tasks for the workers was to sort out which parts were good, and which were defective. One day, after Kasi had made several mistakes, she was called into the supervisor's office. Kasi was sure that she would be fired. Instead, the supervisor sat her down and talked to her. She wanted to understand why Kasi was making mistakes. Instead of reprimanding her and making her feel ashamed, the supervisor talked to her like a human being and encouraged her to try harder to not make the kind of mistakes that they had just discussed. The supervisor also encouraged Kasi to go to college instead, so that she would never have to do this kind of job again. Some people, she told her, are stuck doing this kind of job for their whole lives. That talk was a real inspiration, and it motivated Kasi to do better at that job; but more importantly, it inspired her to seek a better station in life through higher education.

Every year, Kasi continued to secure better summer jobs. She was mentored by a high school accounting teacher, who later helped her get an intern position at a local bank. Kasi excelled at the bank, which resulted with them providing her with a glowing letter of recommendation for college. It helped her obtain a full scholarship, and with a little help from a Pell Grant, Kasi became the first girl among the Lao refugee community to attend college.

Never underestimate the power of a mentor!

Haven to Heaven

Rebellious Years

*"We are all rebellious teenagers. Sometimes we grow out of it,
and sometimes we don't." ~Kelly Asbury*

After coming to the United States, I realized that there was much to value in my Lao culture. In addition to the humility, there was an appreciation of the symbolism of culture and meanings and the beauty of nature. There was an emphasis on kindness, good deeds, and the authenticity of everything from one's dedication to Buddhism to the ingredients of the food and the simplicity of life. These were not the values that I saw in the urban and suburban culture of the United States. Those who showed off and were loud and abrasive seemed to get the greatest respect. Those who were disrespectful and unkind were idolized, especially by the youth. Even the churches seemed to be infected with this spirit of brash showmanship. We watched some of the televangelists and felt very disappointed. Of course, McDonald's was not our idea of a good meal or a good eating place. Naturally, I wanted to be sure that Kasi and Huck would know the difference between the humble Lao culture and the brash American one.

Unfortunately, those aspects of the Lao culture were not the ones that were front and center as Kasi became a teenager and went through puberty. I had rebelled against the patriarchy that had held me back in Laos, but I had accepted the special role that women were assigned in the context of the family. It is a simple fact of biology, really. When men have sexual relations, they have nothing to show for it afterward. There is no biological evidence. Not so with women. When women have sexual relations, they may get pregnant. Pregnancy is a necessity for the creation of families, but it is also evidence that a woman has had sexual relations. Unless those relations are sanctioned by the community, the single parent or the illegitimate couple will not have the social support that they will need to sustain their family. These expectations are universal. They are not specific to Lao culture. Every culture speaks to these social values in a different way. The Lao culture focuses on the purity of the woman. Women who do not get pregnant prior to marriage are pure. Those who do are not. It's as simple as that. As the mother, I was expected by my culture to enforce those values. I knew this instinctively, and I went about it with dedication and even fanaticism. I had not made all of the sacrifices of the refugee life just to be deprived of social status by the behavior of my daughter.

It was a consequence of my overzealous monitoring of Kasi, that she and I encountered the most acrimonious of all of our mother-daughter conflicts.

Both Khamphet and I had objections to the unsupervised interactions between girls and boys that we all refer to as "dating." We prohibited Kasi from going on dates. I think it is quite obvious why her father and I did that. As a result, she and I fought a lot about that.

I think that the first time she asked about meeting a boy was in the summer of 1982. It must have been just after her sixteenth birthday in June of that year. Still, she seemed so young to us. It was very close to the end of the school year and all of the kids were making arrangements to see each other over the summer. She came in after school and set her books down on the kitchen table.

"Mai, could I go to the mall with my friend David this Saturday?" she asked. I was cooking dinner, so I had my back to her. She wasn't able to see my face, but I winced.

"Who else is going?" I asked.

"It's just me and David. He invited me to go to a great movie. It is *The Outsiders*. We even read the book in class last year," she said as she began snacking on some food that I had left for her on the kitchen table. I really felt uncomfortable having this conversation. So, I didn't even turn around. I just kept looking at the food that was cooking on the stove even though I didn't need to.

"Who is going to chaperone you?" I asked. She was very quiet. She stopped eating.

"Chaperone?" she asked. "What do you mean?"

"You know," I said matter-of-factly, "an adult that goes with you to the movies to supervise you." You would think I had asked her to wear her bra on the outside of her dress.

"Mai!" she exclaimed. "Are you kidding me?"

"Why would I kid about something like this? What would your father think if you went to the movies alone with a boy?" I admonished.

"Everybody goes to the movies with their friends!" she said with exasperation. "Why should I be any different?"

That was a good question. I am afraid that the answer I gave only made things worse.

"Well, you are Lao. Good Lao girls don't go to the movies alone with boys. You can only go if you have a chaperone." I didn't say this with anger or any emotion, really. I was just stating the way things were. She didn't even answer me. She just broke out crying and went to her room. I was sure that dinner that night would be difficult, and it was.

However, that was only the opening bell in our conflict.

For the same reasons, we could not allow her to go to unsupervised parties. The same was true of attending concerts, or proms, or homecomings. She could have gone to her friends' weddings if they were Lao weddings where we would be there and could supervise her, but she wanted to go to weddings of her friends outside the Lao community. She did not want us to attend with her. That was not going to work for us.

Meanwhile, this culture clash was occurring in the context of events in the Lao community as well as in the larger American community. In the larger American community, the high school dropout rate was quite high. In the Lao community, the dropout rate, while not as high, was rising and so was the rate of arranged marriages.

In order for you to understand the conflict that arose between me and Kasi, it is first necessary to understand the arranged marriage – something not practiced in the U.S. and generally not part of the Western European culture, either.

We like to believe that what is true now has been true forever. The truth is more complicated, and complications are uncomfortable. When we are more thoughtful, we realize that the world we live in now is different—sometimes dramatically different—from the world that existed before us. That does not always mean that it is better. Progress is not guaranteed.

The most important prejudice about arranged marriages is that they are primitive. This assumption, like all others, is based on ignorance. There are many kinds of arranged marriages and some transition quite smoothly into the kind of pairing that we call romantic love.

Of course, it is different when we are dealing with arranged marriages between an adult man and a child bride. That is very objectionable. We were not considering that at all. We only wanted two things: that Kasi would consider prospective grooms that we chose and that we could have veto power over her choices. That is rather civilized, don't you think?

It was the first weekend in June of 1983 that Khamphet and I decided it was time to see about getting Kasi married. She was already seventeen. Of course, we had been discussing this privately for at least a year. That June, though, we decided to take some action.

There weren't really that many prospective Lao families to choose from. First of all, they had to have a son closer to Kasi's age. We didn't want to marry her to a man who was much older than her. She might end up taking care of him when he grew old and sick while she was still young. Then, of the families that met that condition, they had to be of the proper station. Some of the Lao families that we knew of in the area were clearly above our station. The Savanh and Dara families were in that category. Some of the Lao families that we knew were clearly below our station. The Vixay, Vongsa, and Rhatsavong families fell into that group. So, that left only the Savanh and Dara families. Naturally, I preferred the Dara family, while Khamphet liked the Savanh family.

Alauyath and Kanoi Dara lived about ten miles from us in a house that they had just recently bought. Kanoi was tall with sharp features and spoke English well, much better than we did. They were well-educated and were both former teachers in Laos. That was one of the reasons I liked them better than the Savanh family. Alauyath, whose name means "the light of dawn," was a bit shorter than me and a little plump. She was the kind of person that you feel comfortable to talk with immediately.

Haimi and Liko Savanh lived a few miles closer to us, and they were still renting like we were. Haimi was one of those women who knew she was attractive to men, so she had to be careful around other women. Khamphet seemed indifferent to her, so that didn't really worry me. Liko got along very well with Khamphet. While I would often speak English with Haimi, he and Liko always spoke Lao when they were together.

Haven to Heaven

Both the Dara family and the Savanh family had sons that were Kasi's age. The boys used their English names. Bruce Savanh and Paul Dara were strikingly dissimilar. Bruce preferred sports to school work. He was outgoing and handsome. He was also brash and impulsive, or so I thought. Khamphet said he was manly. Paul wore glasses and was taller and gracile. He played piano and excelled at school. I liked him, but Khamphet thought that he seemed lacking self-confidence as a man. That was from another man's perspective. Of course, these were just first impressions, but it was all we had to go on in the beginning.

We knew that we would have to arrange a meeting, and the obvious question was who she would meet first. Being first gives you certain advantages. Khamphet thought that we should arrange a gathering in which all three families would be present. I didn't think that was a good idea at all. First of all, it would put the Dara and Savanh families in direct competition. It also would present the boys with the possibility of developing animosities. That would not help at all. We talked a bit, and I finally convinced him that it would be best to arrange meetings one at a time.

Khamphet and I didn't know at the time that Kasi already was seeing another boy! That complicated things in ways that we were not able to understand at the time. Kasi had her 17th birthday party on June 20, 1983 at which only our family members were present. She seemed happy enough during the party, but she wrote something different:

Kasi's Diary 20-June-1983

I am furious! Mai and Pa are so stupid! Why can't I have a birthday party with my friends like every other damn person in this school? I am 17 now, not 12! I had to tell Randy that we couldn't see each other on my birthday. That made him very sad, but it made me really mad. I don't want to live in this house with my parents anymore. I have been doing everything that they ever wanted since I was a little girl, and they won't adjust even a little bit to the way things are here in the United States. Why did they even want to come here if they only want to do things the Lao way?

I must make a decision. Either I am open and honest, and I let them run my life completely; or I keep little secrets from them and get to have a little bit of my own life. I have been thinking and writing about this problem for almost a year now. It is time for me to stop writing and start acting! I have to think of a fool-proof plan for fooling them.

At the time, Kasi had found a way to hide her diary from me. And I didn't even know it. She is very smart, that girl! She must at some point have discovered that I was snooping in her private diary. Instead of confronting me about it, she started another secret diary. But she didn't stop writing in the one that I had access to! She would just write things that were not very interesting or detailed. Of course, I noticed the difference at the time, but I explained it as her taking more interest in school than previously. It was really that she was learning the necessity of duplicity when she was being spied on. I can't really blame her.

Anyway, it wasn't until she went off to college that I discovered her secret diaries. I took pictures of all of her secret diaries and then made sure to put them back undisturbed. It is strange how seeking the truth can motivate you to do underhanded things. Nevertheless, it was all for a good purpose. If it weren't for my sneakiness and nosiness, we wouldn't have this clear picture of what was actually going on between us at the time.

So, while Khamphet and I were making arrangements to introduce Kasi to Bruce and Paul, Kasi was seeing Randy secretly, behind our back! She would sneak out the window of her room in the middle of the night and sneak back in before or even after midnight. She was very angry at us and very determined to make her own choices.

Now, back to the unfaltering arrangement.

We were equally determined to arrange a marriage for her. We didn't want to do that without her consent, exactly, but we were not going to let her make a decision without our input. Khamphet and I decided to visit the Dara family first. I think it was on the Friday after Kasi's birthday.

Alauyath came to the door when we rang the bell and welcomed us in. School was out, so Paul was home. Kasi was at my sister's house. Or so I thought.

"Please come in," she greeted us in Lao. Then, in English she said, "Excuse the mess. I have been working all week." Of course, the house was immaculate. She was being humble. She had probably been cleaning and organizing things until late last night. She had taken the time to do this for our visit. I really liked her. It showed that she valued what other people thought of them and she was honoring our family by providing a comfortable and appealing place for us.

Paul was sitting at the piano playing a classical piece that I didn't recognize.

"Can I get you something to drink?" asked Kanoi in near-perfect English. I knew that made Khamphet self-conscious and put him off.

I looked at Khamphet and asked him, in Lao, if he would like anything. I tried my best to make him feel how much I appreciated the sacrifice that he was making by coming here and enduring this encounter with a family that sort of made him feel less than what he would have liked. He looked at me and I think he understood my sentiment.

"Just water, thank you," he replied in his best English. I was proud of him.

We didn't really stay long. We talked a bit about the weather and other small talk. We really couldn't be explicit because Paul was right in the next room still playing piano. We didn't know that he was just practicing, because his piano teacher was picking him up. After he left, it was easier to talk frankly.

"Let's be honest," I began. "The children are not going to like us arranging their lives for them this way. What should we do about that? What can we do about it?"

"I want to be honest as well," said Kanoi. "We have heard that Kasi already has a boyfriend. Is that true?" Alauyath took his hand and gave him a look that indicated it was too soon to talk so frankly. Khamphet and I were shocked! I squeezed his hand under the table to get him to let me speak.

"We are very strict with Kasi. She is never allowed to be alone with any boy. I will not deny it categorically, but I hope you will share with us how you know about this," I said with restraint and great embarrassment.

If they were right about Kasi, Paul would not be her husband. We would leave the home of the Dara family in disgrace, and it would be hard for us to recover the trust of either the Dara or Savanh family. I wanted to break down and cry, but that would not have made things better, so I just held on.

They looked at each other and Alauyath spoke first.

"Well, we were at the mall late in the evening earlier this week – it must have been nearly midnight – and there was Kasi with another boy that we don't know. He was not a Lao boy. Do you mean that you did not know about that?" she asked.

"We absolutely did not know about that!" shouted Khamphet. "Are you positively sure that it was Kasi?"

"Well," Alauyath said, "She was wearing the school colors and she had on that necklace that I always see on her. I mean, I know her. I was her substitute teacher for math last year. She hasn't changed that much. I am so sorry that you are learning about this from us."

"I really don't know how to thank you for telling us about this," I said. All I wanted to do was to get out of that house. I barely remember the rest of the conversation as it passed in meaningless, polite chit-chat. The explosions went off in the car when we were driving back and then when Kasi got home from my sister's house.

"Kasi Champa," I shouted, "You have shamed our family!" She was not exactly apologetic. She was just silent. She looked directly at us, though. She did not look away or look down as I would have expected for someone who was ashamed of what she had done.

"What do you have to say for yourself?" demanded Khamphet in ominous Lao tones.

"What do YOU have to say for yourself? If you had trusted me a little and let me have the freedom that we supposedly came here to experience, this would never have happened." She was not embarrassed or cowed. She was furious. I knew that we would have to reassert our authority, or this would go in the wrong direction.

"I am in school, not dropped out like so many other Lao kids. I get straight As in all of my classes. What do I get for being good like that? I am permanently grounded. That is what Americans call it when their kids are punished for doing something bad. But I am always being punished for doing what is right and good. If that is the way you are going to treat me, then I am not going to keep being good. I will do whatever I want just like all of the other Lao kids. Is that what you want?"

This incredible attitude on Kasi's part was not making Khamphet happy. I saw that he was removing his belt. That worried me. I didn't want to challenge his authority. Here in the United States, Kasi was no longer a child, and we were no longer in Laos. Parents could get in very serious trouble if they beat their children and leave marks. I wanted to remind Khamphet of that, and I had to avoid it at all costs.

Kasi was in no mood for a beating. She turned around and was out the door and down the street before we knew what was happening. Khamphet tried to catch her, but she was young and determined. She outran him easily. When I caught up with him, he was trying to catch his breath with his hands on his knees and tears in his eyes. I felt so bad for him. All of this had been one event of losing face after another for him. I hugged him, and we walked back to the house together embracing each other the way we used to do when we were both much younger.

All that had happened on Friday. We expected that she would return that night, but she didn't. On Saturday, we put out the word that Kasi was missing. Huck was also worried about his sister, and he even got all his friends out on a search. That turned out unfruitful. We expected that we would find her, or she would come home of her own accord. We didn't find her, and she didn't come home.

It was not possible, any longer, for us to sleep. We both knew that we would have to get up on Monday morning to go to work, but we still could not sleep. Sleep deprivation is a terrible thing.

Khamphet and I were traveling opposite emotional paths. He started out angry, but by Sunday morning he was grief-stricken. He had no desire to eat, but as expected, he didn't cry. I was very worried about him. I was initially saddened, but I realized that Kasi was probably right that we were being too strict with her. She was certainly right that we did not trust her. I could see how her attitude had come to be as a consequence of our intransigence. She had found a way around us using deception and deceit. What a terrible lesson for a child to learn!

Now, however, with Khamphet completely distraught over this whole affair, I came to see what Kasi did – and was doing – as essentially selfish. I remembered looking into those willful eyes when she was born, and I recognized now the coming to fruition of her personality. It was my responsibility to ensure that she was not selfish and did not shame the family. I had failed in that, and I was furious about it.

That Sunday night, we got the call. It was Kasi.

"Kasi! Where are you?" I demanded with a completely confused mixture of anger and sadness.

"That doesn't matter, Mai. I will not come back to live with you. Pa will beat me, and you will let him. That is wrong, and I am no longer going to let that happen. I want to go live somewhere else," she said with a determination that made me realize that she was right, and that her words were prescient.

I had made calls to all her friends – including her Cuban immigrant best friend, Rita – but none of them revealed to me where she was. I even threatened to report them to the authorities if they didn't tell me the truth, but these kids were not anywhere near being intimated!

When she was away, Kasi would sometimes call us, but would never give us a number where we could call her. We arranged for a sort of truce in the calls that we had. In early July, we got the first call. I answered.

"Hello, who's calling?" I asked.

"It's me, Kasi."

"Oh Kasi, please come home. Where are you? We are worried sick."

"No, Mai. I am not coming home yet. I have been thinking a lot about what will happen when I come back home – if I come back home – this August, before school starts. Some things will have to be different," she said.

"What do you mean?" I asked softly.

"Well, first of all, I have to be able to go out with my friends without an escort or chaperone. No one else in my grade has to endure that. If that condition isn't met, then I won't come home. Secondly, I just want to raise the topic of driving. I already passed the exam for learner's permit, and I have been practicing driving a little. Will you be okay with me continuing toward getting a driver's license, or is that only for boys?"

I looked at Khamphet. I could see that he wanted to talk to her, but I just didn't think that was a good idea.

"Give me your number there and I will call you back. Your father and I need to discuss this," I told her.

"No, Mai. *I* will call *you* back in a few days after you have a chance to discuss it. I really hope you are both doing well, otherwise. Let's take things one step at a time. Goodbye, Mai," she said. She didn't hang up on me. She waited for me to say good bye. After I did, she hung up. I had to explain everything to Khamphet.

We really wanted Kasi to come home for one more year before we would lose her forever when she would leave to college. For

207

our mentality, at the time, this was a very difficult decision. However, we got past that, and decided that we would not enforce our dating rules any longer.

When she called back a few days later, our conversation was a bit more open and friendly, but still guarded.

"Hello, who's calling?" I asked, as usual.

"It's me, Kasi," she said.

"Kasi, thank you for calling back so soon. Pa and I have discussed the point that you raised, and we agree with you."

She didn't reply immediately. She seemed to be waiting for me to say "...but..." Only I didn't. So, she continued, "Thank you, Mai. I am feeling better about the prospect of coming home in August. How is Huck? Can you believe that I actually miss him sometimes?"

That was an ice breaker. We continued to discuss issues like her getting a driver's license and there being no more beatings. These were things that I could not oppose under these new conditions. She finally said that she would be home on the 13th of August, just in time for school to start that following Monday. I was very happy, and I told Khamphet everything. He was relieved, too.

We were not sure where Kasi would take this topic of a driver's license. Did she think that we would take out a loan to buy her a car? That was out of the question. We didn't think that debt was a good thing. We didn't want to be indebted to anyone if we could help it. That was another difference between us and some of the people around us. We worked hard to save up, and then we paid for our home in cash with no mortgage.

Of course, I understood her point about boys having advantages that girls don't. I had always hated that. There were a few aspects of this topic that Khamphet and I had to discuss at length. The real issue was not her getting a driver's license. Driving when she was with us was one thing; driving when she was with others was something else entirely. Of course, if she were out with her friends and one of her friends was driving, how could we be sure that she would be safe? It was impossible to avoid worrying about that when you began to talk about teenagers and driving licenses.

These conversations with Kasi are just a taste of how we were getting pulled into the currents of the American way of life.

Adapting to a new culture is a bit like learning a new language. Unfortunately, many Americans never learn a second language. So, this analogy may not be very enlightening. Maybe that is the point. What is the shared experience that will help most Americans understand and empathize with the lived experience of refugees and immigrants? Multiple languages, cultures, and geographies are a fundamental part of the lived experience of refugees and immigrants. When we try to share our stories with an audience that speaks only one language, knows only one culture, and never travels internationally, how are we to find common ground?

Those of us who are trying to adapt to new circumstances – we speak multiple languages and know more than one culture or one geography – have a responsibility to ask the difficult questions that others don't ask. Why don't most native-born Americans speak more than one language?

As my husband and I were getting ready to accept our daughter back into our home for her last year in high school, I was asking myself these questions. Kasi spoke Lao and English. Most of her classmates were monolingual. Why? Kasi had lived in three different countries before the age of 18. Most of her classmates had never traveled outside the U.S. Why? It is hard not to propose a simple hypothesis to explain these facts: the educational system in the United States does not prepare its citizens to be humanitarian citizens of the world.

All of the foreign language courses—if they are offered—are optional. When high school students study geography, it is just book learning. Why isn't foreign travel part of the core high school education of United States citizens?

Once I get hold of an idea like this, an unanswered question, I can be as determined as my daughter is to get to the bottom of it. At the end of the previous school year, in August of 1982, I had gone to the school to talk to the guidance counselors to ask them why the foreign language courses were not mandatory and why there was no built-in international travel in the high school curriculum. They prudently said that they didn't know. However, they had a hypothesis of their own. They suggested that the reason that foreign languages were not part of the core curriculum was because the United States is so big that most students would never need a foreign language at work and the core curriculum was to provide a foundation for students to become productive workers. The reason that there was no foreign travel as part of the core curriculum, they suggested, was because it was too expensive. I thought that those were sensible conjectures. Of course, they also told me that the decisions about the curriculum and the budget for the schools were made by the school board and others. So, I decided that I ought to contact some school board members with my questions.

You may think it is a bit strange that I had taken up this investigation at this late point in our life in the United States. However, everyone knows that it takes time to understand the foundations of one's living conditions. When they were throwing trash onto the front yard of Mr. Smouse's house, I was not yet ready to ask about how the perpetrators had been educated. Now, I was ready to ask that question. When those girls were bullying Kasi in elementary school, I was only concerned about her safety. I was not ready to ask what responsibility the school had in the education of those bullies. Now, I was.

So, near the end of July of 1983, I had made some progress along these lines. I understood that perhaps the purpose of the American educational system was to serve future workers in the United States, not humanitarian citizens of the world. This knowledge only raised additional questions for me, though.

As a refugee from Laos, I must never forget what happened there before we began our exodus. I remembered some facts about the relationship between the United States and Laos. Between 1964 and 1973, as part of the secret war in Laos, the United States conducted 580,000 bombing missions. Each of those planes in those bombing missions was piloted by United States high school graduates. While I don't know for sure, I suspect that most of those pilots spoke only English. I suspect that their bombing missions were probably the only time that they had been out of the country, too. Certainly, those bomber pilots were not educated to be humanitarian citizens of the world, and they knew very little of the working people that they were bombing.

The bombing of Laos was not a small thing, either. Laos was bombed relentlessly. It was as if a planeload of bombs had been dropped on the country every eight minutes, 24-hours per day, for nine years. Laos is the most heavily bombed country per capita in history. This historical knowledge about the relationship between my country of origin, Laos, and my country of refuge, the United States, forced me to ask the question that gets at the material basis of that relationship. Who paid for all those bombs? How much was spent on that bombing? How many innocents were killed by the bombing? Who voted for the representatives in Congress that in turn voted to spend the money on those bombing missions? Who voted for the President and Commander-in-Chief that ordered those bombing missions? What if the Americans—at that time and just before it—had spent that money on an international component of the educational system instead?

These, too, are questions that can be answered. We don't seem to like the answers, though. That is why the questions are never discussed in polite company. The people who pay for the bombs are the same people who pay for the educational system. United States taxpayers are also high school attendees or graduates. That is the connection to the high school dropouts that Kasi threw in our faces in her anger. When I decided to hire Phoemkhun at the stand in the refugee camp in Thailand, I hired her because her work would render more than what I paid her. Without her work, I would not have been able to make those profits. It is the same in the larger economy. When we say that taxpayers are the ones who pay for the bombs and the schools, we mean the people who actually do the work. Making war is a very profitable business, and it was beginning to become clear to me that those war profiteers—the ones who profited from the bombings of Laos and the ones that are profiting from the current wars—are the ones that do not want a more humanitarian population in the United States.

Parents, unlike most politicians, have a time horizon that extends to the lives of their grandchildren. Kasi was not even out of high school yet, but Khamphet and I knew that she would get married at some point, and that she would have children. We wanted the best for her, and it was for that reason that we tried to arrange a good marriage for her. We certainly also wanted the best for her children, and that was what motivated my current focus. As I look back on Kasi's 11th grade school year, I remember how much I was thinking about what kind of world we would be leaving for Kasi's children, my grandchildren.

As I write this, I am looking ahead to a time after Kasi is married and has children. I am envisioning a time when those children will have grown up and will be ready to have children of their own. If Kasi is fortunate enough to get into college and finish her studies before getting married—which we now realize is a real possibility for her—she will probably be 22 before she will even think about having children. She would be 22 in June of 1988. Getting pregnant isn't always as easy as we make teenagers think it is. If she was not able to get pregnant until 2 years later, her first child might be born in 1990. It would not be before 2008 that my first grandchild would graduate from high school. I wanted the things that I was doing now, advocating for mandatory foreign language classes in high school and the funding of a year abroad for every high school student, to affect the kind of school system that my grandchildren would encounter.

I imagined that, if I were successful, Kasi's children would grow up in a world where even those with no more than a high school education would have an international humanitarian outlook. That was my goal.

When I put down the phone after the conversation with Kasi that settled her coming home, I realized that *I have truly become an American.* Kasi did this to me. It was for her that I had to be a super mom. I am still working almost full time, although I need to have two jobs to get that many hours. I am taking care of the house, taking care of the domestic needs of Khamphet, Kasi, and Huck. In addition to all this, I have been attending the meetings of the Parent-Teacher Association and the Board of Education. I am even considering running for a position on the Board of Education.

Finally, I am writing this book. I haven't made a big deal of all this within the family. Just as I had given birth to Kasi alone, I was giving birth to a new educational system and a book about our family, secretly.

Haven to Heaven

Part II: KASI

Haven to Heaven

Bicycle Ride

21-June-1990

I am Kasi, the daughter of Khamphet and Kim Champa. I just celebrated my 24th birthday yesterday. As a present, my mother gave me this unfinished book that she had been working on for twenty some-odd years. It was not the best present I ever got. I have a long history with this book. Today, I have decided to accept the responsibility for finishing it. I find myself revisiting the story of my relationship to this book.

About six years ago, my mother had an accident on her bicycle. Mom was riding a bicycle to work when she fell and hurt herself badly. I didn't hear about that bicycle accident for a whole day because, even though I was just seventeen and going into 11th grade, I was living at my best friend Rita's house. I called that day just to let them know that I was alive and well and to confirm my return that weekend. My father answered, which was unusual, and he told me about her fall. But, he didn't tell me the whole story. Mom seemed to want to keep it a secret, I guess.

Everything changed the day I found that that she had read my journal. In the summer of 1982, I went in to the desk of my mother's study to see if I could find a piece of paper for my homework. There, at the top of a stack of papers, right next to the used IBM Selectric that I always heard her typing on, was a piece of paper with the word "Foreword" at the top. I read that whole page. Then, I read the next. As I read more, I read faster. By the time I had finished it, I was not thinking about getting paper for my homework anymore. I was thinking about getting revenge. I left the house immediately to go for a walk.

On that walk, I made some decisions. Until then, I had always tried to be a good girl in every way. I studied hard and got good grades. I was obedient to my parents, even if I often felt they were unfair or too strict. I never got in trouble at school or anywhere. Still, I had been longing for a taste of the freedom that we supposedly came to the USA to enjoy. I knew that none of my friends' parents were as strict as mine were. Despite that, I respected my parents. I did not rebel by lying or cheating to get away with breaking their rules. Until that day, I thought that at least my mother respected me. Realizing that she had been spying on my writing all these years, reading what she wrote in that *Foreword* to this book, I no longer believed that she respected me. I felt betrayed. I decided to create two journals, just so that I could have one that was private without the need to confront my mother. I never told her that I found out about her reading my journal, and I never told her that I created a "public" journal just for her. Those were my secrets.

I realize now that my mother was just trying to collect information that would have been lost otherwise. She was not reading my diary to violate my privacy or to hurt me in any way. However, that was not the way I took it when I read those few pages that day.

That willingness to remain hidden and avoid confrontation changed after my 17th birthday. That was the day that I wrote the entry in my public journal about how stupid my parents were. I wrote it there so that Mom (as I now sometimes call her) would read it, and she did. That day, something happened to me. I decided that I was no longer willing to live a double life. The idea of a chaperone was the straw that broke the camel's back. I don't really think that either of my parents is stupid. Far from it. But then, I was seventeen and rebellious.

When Mom gave me this unfinished draft yesterday morning as a birthday gift, she said that she knew all along that it was really my story. I realized that she was doing it for us, for me and Huck, and I began to understand how deeply she had been committed to us and to bettering our lives by bringing us to the United States. She also apologized for having violated my privacy for all those years. I accepted her apology, and I think we both felt a sense of reconciliation.

She told me that she stopped writing after I ran away, and never began again because of the bicycle accident. My mother believed that her ends justified her means. You could see that in the way she pursued our escape from Laos and our arrival in California. I am more moderate than that. I believe that my means are just as important as my ends. Like my mom, though, I realize how important time and space are.

Mom was quite idealistic. You could see that in her idea for developing more humanitarian citizens. My practical reasoning tells me that perhaps affordability may have been an important factor. She was also a bit of a disillusioned and radical thinker. For example, here is one of the drafts that she was not able to incorporate yet, into the body of the book.

When you are in hell-on-earth and you imagine heaven-on-earth, you are unlikely to acknowledge that less-than-savory elements may inhabit that heaven. We had escaped from Laos, and then from the Nong Khai Refugee Camp in Thailand, and finally arrived in what we had imagined would be the heaven-on-earth United States. We were transformed from refugees into immigrants. We—or at least I—had not really considered what it would mean to be an immigrant in the United States.

First, it is important to realize that the United States of America is not America. America includes all of the countries of North and South America. To refer to the United States as America is an implicit way to say that the rest of the countries on the two continents don't really matter. Even more importantly, it is an acknowledgement that many other distinctions don't matter, either. I am Lao of Chinese ancestry. Those that refer to the United States as America refer to me as Asian. But I know that, linguistically and culturally, I am different from other Asians. Some of those differences don't matter—we are all human—but some of them do.

I had neglected to imagine that being an immigrant—especially an Asian immigrant to California—would subject me to the ignorant attitudes of my neighbors and employers. As I became aware of those attitudes, the bright and shining image of the United States that had drawn me here was tarnished. It was tarnished by certain individuals, but I could still see the good in most Americans.

Just as I had encountered prejudices in Laos against foreigners that forced families to change their last names so that they sounded more like a Lao-native name, here in the U.S. I encountered prejudices (or rather, a positive stereotype) against Asian immigrants that encouraged me to act in certain ways to gain what I wanted. Asians were considered to be hard working. To get the benefits of that stereotype, I had to work harder than anyone around me. All I ever wanted was freedom for my family.

Unlike my mom, I am quite an optimist. I feel assimilated into the U.S. society. I have no resentments against the success that others enjoy. In some ways, though, I am more critical of people than she is. Part of her radicalism is an inclination to blame systems rather than people for the problems that we face. Here is another snippet of what she wrote and didn't incorporate into the story:

What I learned when I got here was that immigrants are not free here in the U.S. Freedom would mean the possibility of being selected for a job that you are good at, and for which you are compensated appropriately. Immigrants in the U.S. are not able to take any kind of job, and the ones that they could get were not compensated appropriately. Now, I realize that *life is only as good as the freedom that you can trust.* None of us Lao immigrants could trust our neighbors or employers to permit us the freedom to get those good homes and good jobs, no matter how qualified we were. We were Asians. Those are the facts that I confronted when we began to try to make a living in the U.S.

First of all, it was very difficult for Khamphet to get a job. His English was rudimentary, and his progress in learning was slow. So, I was the first to get a job. As a waitress in a Chinese restaurant near City Hall off Main Street in Oakley, I quickly realized that we could not live on what I made. So, I had to find another job. Having two full-time jobs—which was what we needed before Khamphet was able to get a job— means that you do not have enough time to sleep. As an educated person, I knew that sleep deprivation could have long-term negative effects on my health and well-being. But until Khamphet got his first job, I knew that I had to endure. Life in America was not easy. We incurred more expenses just on the basic living, but we wanted to save up to get a car and a house. Riding to work on bicycles was dangerous and exhausting, but we did it anyway for seven years.

I think that capitalism is the best possible system. Sometimes, Mom didn't seem to agree with that. I think we are all free, both immigrants and citizens. What we make of our freedom is what distinguishes the successful ones from the unsuccessful ones. I believe that you create your own destiny.

I have the motivation that I need to take on the writing of this book. I do it, in part, because I know that Mom can't do it anymore.

Let's begin where my mother left off.

Just before she had the bicycle accident, her life was pretty harsh. I have to admit that. I don't blame her for it, either. It is just the way things were for her—and both of them—at that time. Their educational background from Laos did not qualify them to be in the field of Education, and it was looked upon as equivalent to a high school education in the U.S. Basically, they were just thankful to be able to pick up any jobs available, often multiple jobs—one full-time and one or two part-times, including on weekends.

Mom was working two jobs. Her first job started at 6 AM working in a factory assembling electronic components. It lasted for 9 hours because they insisted that everybody took an hour for lunch (even if they only took 15 minutes to eat), because the company wanted to conform to the regulations. Of course, our family had no car and couldn't afford a taxi or even a bus, so she had to get to work by bicycle. It took about 40 minutes for her to ride from our rented home to work. Then, it was the same amount of time to get home. The route to the second job was a little shorter—it took only about 15 minutes—but that one was slightly more strenuous because there was a sunken underpass beneath a train track with an incline on each side along the route.

So, her day began at 4 AM when she got up to shower, dress, and eat. By 4:30 or so, she was on the bicycle. She usually got to work by 5 or 5:15. She always tried to get there early because, if she was late, they would fire her. That was her greatest fear. Then, she would get off at 3 PM and peddle back home through the traffic—and sometimes the rain—to arrive close to 3:30.

Bicycle Ride

Her second job as a waitress in a Chinese restaurant started at 6:30 and required a uniform, so she had to shower, eat, and dress before she could leave for that one. Of course, Huck and I would arrive from school at just about when she got home from work. That was fine before Dad (as we now call him) got his first job because he would be there even if she was late. After he got his first job in a factory assembling airplane parts, she had to rush home because she understood that if Huck and I were found to be home alone, the authorities could take us away from our parents. Mom often told me that she lived with the constant terror that she might be late to work and get fired, or that she might be late to home and have us taken away from her. Those terrors were stressful enough, but were made worse when layered on top of the sleep deprivation.

Unlike Mom, I am very aware of the fact that this stressful existence was not a unique circumstance that was forced on us by a system. It was the same stressful existence that many low-wage workers faced then and now. If you are resilient and resourceful, you are able to endure that kind of life until you are able to get out of it. That is just the way it is.

A stressful, hurried work schedule was the situation that she faced on the third week of December, seven years after we arrived in the United States. Dad was working, and she arrived home just before Huck and me.

I learned the story from her at the hospital bed when I visited her on Thursday, the day after the accident.

We spoke in Lao for privacy, and I called her Mai just as I always used to.

"Mai, how are you feeling?"

She was bandaged and swollen in many places. Her face was black and blue, too. But she was conscious. It was hard for her to see and hear, though.

"Kasi, is that you?"

"Yes, Mai, it's me. How are you feeling?" I repeated.

She began to sob.

"It's okay now, Mai. You are safe in the hospital."

"Where is my bicycle? I need that bicycle to get to work." She was quite disoriented.

"Mai, don't worry about work or the bicycle. You had an accident. You are in the hospital."

"I am in the hospital?" she asked with a genuine uncertainty in her voice.

"Yes. You are in the hospital because you had an accident on the bicycle. Do you remember that now?"

Something seemed to click, and her usual lucidity returned.

"Yes. Now I remember. What day is today?" she asked.

"Today is Thursday, Mai. You had the accident yesterday, on Wednesday." I tried to remain calm.

"Oh. Oh no. Did I lose my job? Is Huck safe? Where is your dad?"

It was difficult to get her out of the mindset of being a low-wage worker that had to perform to very high standards all the time or face devastating consequences. I finally got her calmed down and focused enough to answer my questions about what happened, although I had been briefed by the doctor before I got to see her.

Bicycle Ride

"Why didn't you tell anyone that you were pregnant?" I really needed to know the answer to that question. She was quiet and took a long time to answer.

"Well, I didn't think anyone needed to know. It was very early. Nobody could tell. What happened? Did I lose the baby?"

"Yes, Mai. You lost the baby. You are lucky to be alive."

"I don't feel lucky, really. What am I going to do now?" she wondered aloud.

"I just want to know what happened. Could you tell me what Wednesday, yesterday, was like for you? I don't really understand. Where were you when you fell?" That question seemed to bring back the details of the day for her.

"Well, I hadn't been sleeping well all week. I think that was because of the pregnancy. When I got back from the first job, Huck was already home, so I told him to go wash up quickly because dinner would be ready very soon. Then, I started making his dinner. As soon as that was done, I went to take my shower. I finished my shower and started getting dressed before I realized that I was putting on my regular clothes instead of the uniform that I needed to wear to that second job! I looked at the clock and realized that I was going to leave the house a few minutes late because I had to change. Your father arrived just as I was getting on my bicycle to ride toward East 18th Street. I had to take that road to Main Street, and then turn left onto Bridgehead Road. My job was down by the marina, you know. Do you know where that is?"

"Yes Mai, I was there with you once when you first got that job. Remember?" She just wanted to continue with the story now, and she didn't answer me.

"I was pedaling very fast to make up for the time that I had lost changing into my uniform. Bridgehead Road is mostly flat, so I could make good time. Suddenly, I felt a cramp. I looked at my watch. There was no time for me to stop for a rest. I just kept pedaling. As I came up on the underpass, where the train passes over the road, I relaxed a little. I knew that I would be able coast down one side, and it would give me momentum to go up the other side. I was tired and let myself relax as the bicycle accelerated down the underpass. I closed my eyes, just for a second, and let the bike coast. When I opened them again, it was already too late to avoid the pot hole, right under the train tracks where Bridgehead Road leveled off before rising again on the other side of the tracks. I should have remembered that stupid pothole, because I had seen it the day before. But I was in a rush and I forgot." She seemed to recollect.

"Do you remember anything after that?" I asked.

"No," she replied, "the next thing I remember is waking up with you here asking me questions. Do I have to go to work?"

I took her hand and talked softly to her. "Mai, it's okay. You don't need to go to work."

Mom was never the same after that accident. She not only lost her child, but her spirit to write further. She has finally transitioned that responsibility to me, and I hope I have fulfilled that duty in honoring my mom. She struggled through life, so we wouldn't have to. She escaped the political tyranny, so we would be free. She sacrificed her education and career, so we could succeed. She endured poverty, so we would have in abundance. All for us, so that our lives would be better than hers.

I finally understand that now.

Bicycle Ride

Haven to Heaven

Relationship and Family

"You don't choose your family. They are God's gift to you, as you are to them." ~Desmond Tutu

When Mom gave me her unfinished manuscript as a gift at age of twenty-four, I did my best to fill in the missing pieces and bring it to a close. It was my gift back to her, and I truly thought that was the end of the story. I could not have been more wrong. Here, twenty-four years later, I am reflecting on recent events and realizing that my mother's gift – and my mother's story – live on. They live in me and will continue with the generations that follow. Life and love are precious. I realize that now more than ever, and I am inspired to continue the story – writing for my own children just as my mother did for me. I hope these words will pay tribute to my mother and provide words of insight to my children as they face success and failure, love and heartache, and continue their own stories of struggle and hope.

****

I finished high school without much trouble or much fanfare. In September of 1985, I finally got to experience my full freedom. After all of the battles I had to fight against the restrictions of my parents and the Lao culture, when I got to the University of California in Berkeley and met my first roommate, I began to feel as though I was equal to any other American. My perception of myself as a liberated person blinded me, however, to just how much Lao culture had seeped into my psyche. In the very beginning, I was blind to how Lao I was, but I soon discovered that blindness.

My roommate could have been a model Miss America. It's not that she was the most beautiful or talented or determined person in the world; it was just that she was a typical American. I know, I know. I probably shouldn't say that about her. Still, if you had met her, you would have agreed with me. The way she behaved, and the way she reacted to me was so significant that I simply couldn't just skip over this part.

Her name was Alice. Alice came from the New York suburbs. Now, I had never been to New York. When I heard that she was from there, I didn't really know what to expect. I knew that New York City was in the State of New York and that it was – and still is – the largest metropolitan area in the United States. That knowledge gave me no idea about what to expect from this girl who lived in the suburbs of that city.

"Hi, Alice, I'm Kasi," I said when we first met. I walked right up to her with my hand extended for a handshake, and she sort of backed away and didn't give me her hand.

"Hi, Kashi," she said, mispronouncing my name and without looking at me directly. "I'm sorry, I am a germophobe. It always makes it difficult when I meet a person for the first time. I hope you won't take it the wrong way."

"No, no." I reassured her, "It's okay. I have some idiosyncrasies of my own. I won't hold yours against you if you don't hold mine against me!" I said with an embarrassed enthusiasm that I was surprised by. At least that got her attention. She looked at me directly so that we were then able to have what I considered to be a normal conversation.

"What are your ... ideo...?"

"Idiosyncrasies?" I completed her question for her. "Well, for one thing, I eat many different interesting foods, and I do speak another language, too, especially with my family."

"You do?" she asked with her eyes open wide. "What language do you speak? Spanish?"

I wasn't sure if that was typical. Why would she suppose that I spoke Spanish as a second language? I think it is because that is the only other language that she is familiar with. I was quite sure I already knew how the rest of the conversation was going to go. I won't bore you with the details.

Fast forward to the first time my family came to visit me in college during my freshman year. Of course, they brought the foods that they knew I loved so that we could enjoy and share some family time together. What else would you expect? It seemed to me like the most natural thing in the world at that time.

The Lao culture has some foods that are uniquely ours. We grow up with them in such an intimate way that we forget how foreign they are to other cultures. My mother always prepared the Lao specialties in a way that made us all feel at home when we sat down together every day to share a meal. It was nothing fancy, but it was good, fresh food prepared in the Lao style. Some of these common dishes that I grew up with were: *tum mak hoong* (papaya salad), *laab* (beef salad), *gel bong* (spicy sauce to dip with sticky rice), bamboo shoot soup, and blood sausage.

Some of the Lao staples and delicacies that my mother prepared for that day and brought were sticky rice, papaya salad, and *balut* (a boiled fertilized egg). *Balut* is the Filipino word for that food. In Laos, we call it *khai look* (ໄຂ່ລູກ). They have other names for it in Thailand, Vietnam, and Cambodia where it is also eaten.

While we were enjoying our meal in the dorm kitchen, Alice came into the room. My family said "hello" and invited her to taste some of the delicacies we were sharing. Since she had told me that she was a germaphobe, I was sure that she would decline the offer.

"Oh, thank you," she said. "What are you eating?"

I began pointing to things on the table and giving their Lao names and English descriptions. When I got to the *balut*, I showed her the one that I was about to eat. It was already open, and you could see the duck embryo clearly. As I was explaining to her more about eating such a delicacy, she immediately put her hand over her mouth and ran into the bathroom. After she came out of the bathroom, she ran down the dorm hall yelling, "That's so nasty!" Naturally, everybody who could hear the commotion was looking toward us with curiosity.

Up to that point, I hadn't given much thought to the kinds of things we ate. Since then, I have educated myself on the reasons for our wide variety of edibles. It turns out not to be very complicated, really. One characteristic of all Asian cultures is the density of our populations. The most densely populated cities in the world are primarily in Southeast Asia. This is not only true today but has been true historically. Doesn't it seem reasonable that, if many people must survive in close proximity to one another, waste must be minimized? Asian cultures generally abhor waste; and therefore, find ways to use resources very efficiently. We learn to eat and cook anything edible. It is sinful to waste food. For example, take the banana tree. We eat the fruit from it, but we also use the leaves for cooking or wrapping food. In addition, we use the banana flower for many dishes. As for meat, if you're going to kill an animal for food, it makes sense to eat every part of it: the head, the tongue, the ears, the intestines, the feet, etc. We especially don't like it when waste is created as a consequence of being "picky." My mom instills that value in me.

Eggs are a good source of protein, and protein is a necessary part of any diet. Eggs may be fertilized or unfertilized. There are too many fertilized eggs to hatch them all. Too many birds on a poultry farm will eat too much and may not all be sold. There is an economic reason for the consumption of excess fertilized eggs. To not eat those excess fertilized eggs would be wasteful, and so a cultural norm was established. But my simple rationale remains: If you eat eggs and chicken, what's wrong with eating a chicken in the egg?

However, even without a cogent economic argument, one should respect the culture of another and refrain from judging the foods and practices of other cultures, based on your own culture. I can see that now, even though as a nineteen-year-old college freshman, I did not.

After my family left, Alice and I reunited in our room. I was so embarrassed that I couldn't even look her in the face. Her run to the bathroom was not so much an abstract moral judgement as it was a visceral moral judgement. I couldn't blame her for it. She couldn't help herself. However, I now see it as a learned response, not a natural one.

"I am sorry..." I began to apologize when she interrupted me.

"Oh my God! How could you eat that? That is disgusting! Please don't bring your parents here anymore. Stay on your side of the room. You stink and now I know why," she said angrily.

I ran out of the room crying. I walked around campus for a long time trying to make sense of it all. I gradually came to see her point of view, and I wanted to distance myself not only from that particular food, but from Lao culture generally. I did not want to be associated with it.

It was sometime after that horribly embarrassing encounter with Alice as a representative of American culture that I met Lawrence. He introduced himself to me.

"Hi I'm Lawrence. I'm an ABC. And you?" That was the first time I had heard of an ABC—American Born Chinese.

We first met in the school cafeteria. He smiled to me and said, "Isn't cafeteria food the best?" I thought he was sincerely funny.

Unlike other non-Laotian friends, Lawrence enjoyed Lao food and was very interested in my Lao culture. His friendship was very refreshing. We studied together and got along well. I enjoyed his company, but I didn't feel that spark that draws you into an intimate relationship. As we began spending more and more time together—I really did enjoy his company—I realized that I was going to have to be honest with him. I was a little bit afraid that he would not want to be my friend anymore if I told him that I was not interested in a romantic relationship. Still, I knew it was the time to say something.

"Hi Lawrence," I said when we met after class. "Do you want to go over to the Student Center and get a bite to eat?"

"That would be great. Let me go back to my room for a few minutes, and we can meet there in...15 minutes?" he suggested.

I agreed, and we met at the Student Center. I had found a nice booth that would give us some quiet space to talk.

"Sorry it took a little longer than I expected," he said as he sat across from me. "Have you ordered already?"

"No. I just got here myself," I replied. We ordered and after the waiter left, I began, "Lawrence, I just wanted to talk a little about our relationship, okay?" I really didn't know what I should say or what I would say.

"I have been trying to do that for at least a week. I just never found the right time," he said with some relief. I was afraid that meant that he wanted to take our relationship to the next stage and I winced inside at what I was going to have to say next.

"Well, what I wanted to tell you is that," I paused a little. "Well, I just want to be friends. Is that okay with you?"

"Are you kidding? That is exactly what I was going to say to you!" he replied.

I was not convinced initially. I played along though. I wanted our friendship to work out. We had a very nice dinner together, and it certainly didn't seem like he was holding anything against me. That was unexpected. I mean, I hadn't rejected him, really. Still, I was expecting that male ego to kick in and reject me. Instead, he just stayed with me and gave me his presence and friendship. I will always remember Lawrence for that.

In my junior and senior years in college, I was working on campus in the Political Science and Public Policy Departments as an interpreter. They were doing a project in the Lao community, and I worked closely with several of the professors in those departments. Consequently, I started to get involved with the Lao community again. I ended up regularly attending different Lao community social events in the Bay Area. As interpreter, I was often invited to attend social events by people who became friends. It was at one such Lao New Year Festival that I met a Laotian man named Dade.

At the party, women were all over Dade, but he had his eyes on me, and I knew it. I returned his glances, furtively, and eventually he came over to talk to me. One by one, the other women came over to where we were talking and would touch his shoulder and glare at me as they passed. Dade stayed focused on me, though. We were involved in an interesting conversation that moved seamlessly from topic to topic.

Dade was highly educated. He was charming and very charismatic. He said that he was new in town. He had just moved from the Northeast and was working as an architect in a big architecture and engineering firm in Berkeley. He was also fourteen years older than me. I was almost twenty-one. But his age didn't matter to me or my parents. For some peculiar reason, in the Lao culture, people tend to equate wisdom with age and prefer older men, maybe as an indication of stability. Besides, he didn't even look his age.

"Where are you from?" he asked.

"My parents and I live in California now – Bay Area," I replied. "Where are you from?"

"My parents were living in Massachusetts. They passed away last year," he told me. I gave him my condolences, and we talked a bit about losing those that you love. I told him the story of the death of Keo. He was very empathetic and took my hand when I was overcome by emotion at the memory of her.

I was quite taken by him, and we began to see each other frequently. We would go out and have meals together at nice restaurants, and he would call me from work, sometimes, and we would talk and laugh about a lot of things. He was naturally charming, and he made me feel special.

Even my parents fell for him. During the summer between my junior and senior years, while I was visiting my parents in Oakland, California, he was in the suburb of San Francisco in the last two weeks of June for business meetings. Since he was only fifteen minutes of driving distance away from my parents' home, I was ecstatic because that made it possible for me to present him to my parents during my birthday celebration. Naturally, he was his usual polite, well-educated, multi-lingual self. He talked to my father about education, and he even engaged my mother in a conversation about French literature. He listened carefully and never interrupted them. He did not flaunt his profession or his accomplishments but described them with humility when asked. I couldn't have been prouder or happier. That birthday celebration seemed to mark my coming to terms with my relationship to my parents and to the Lao community. He made it possible for me to have it all. That was such a relief.

The only problem, really, was my friendship with Lawrence. He accepted my relationship to Dade only because he cared so much for me and wanted me to be happy. However, it became obvious to both of us, despite what he'd claimed earlier, that Lawrence wanted more than just the friendship that I was offering. Besides, I didn't have much time to spend with Lawrence now that I was seeing Dade. But when Dade discovered that Lawrence and I would still get together as friends, he was irate.

"Why do you want to see him? Isn't our relationship enough for you?" Dade would ask.

"He is just a friend. You are very busy, Dade. Even on the weekends, you are always working. It's not fair to ask me to stop seeing my friends. Best friends are difficult to find." I tried to explain to him.

I was unsure about making this complaint because I didn't want to lose Dade. I didn't want to lose Lawrence, either. But I had to tell Lawrence that, for a while at least, I would not be able to see him only because I didn't have enough time. Lawrence did not trust Dade and warned that I should be careful of him. I knew that he had strong feelings for me, but he said that it was not right to hold me back.

"I will still be here for you, if things don't work out," he said. He had been my best friend since my college freshman year. We could have a heart-to-heart talk about anything. I was so grateful for him.

On the Friday before Christmas, I decided that I would drop by unannounced to surprise Dade with an early Christmas present that I bought for him. I had visited his home twice before, and it was still fairly empty as he had just moved in and had little furniture.

237

He had even asked me to go furniture shopping with him. When I got to his house, I noticed that there were teenagers playing in the front yard. That surprised me because I didn't think there were any neighbors nearby with teenaged sons or daughters. I walked up and knocked on the door and had to wait quite a while before Dade came to answer it.

"Uh—Hi Kasi," he said in a strange way, probably wondering what in the world I was doing at his front door.

"Hi, can I come in? I have something for you."

"Actually, it would be better if you came back at another time." By now, the teenagers had stopped playing and were looking at us. I looked back at them.

"Do you know those kids?" I asked.

"Yes," he said matter-of-factly. "They are my children. My wife is coming in a few days. That is why it would be better if you came back another time."

"You're married? With kids? Come back another time?"

This caught me completely off guard, naturally. I looked at him trying to understand why it was so hard for me to believe what he was saying in such a matter-of-fact way. It was as if he thought that I knew, or should have known, or should have asked if I didn't know. Of course, these were his kids. Of course.

A little voice inside me was saying "No! No! Somebody should call it what it is: duplicity, deceit, dishonesty. This breaks all the rules! You could not have known this. He was supposed to tell you this! He is a liar. He is a user and a cheater. He created an illusion for all of us. He created it for me, for my parents, for the whole Lao community. He did all of that, and now he expects me to believe that I was a fool to have believed in the deception that he created

238

for all of us? No. This is wrong. He has cheated me!" That's what my inner voice was telling me.

Outwardly, I don't remember much what I said or did. Except for one thing. I slapped him as hard as I could across the face. I slapped him so hard that his kids heard it and so did his next-door neighbors. He was so shocked that he stumbled backward into the house and had not regained his equilibrium until I was opening the door to the car. Then, I just remember driving back to my apartment with tears blurring my vision. I was hurt, but I was already angry, too. How could I have been so blind? Needless to say, that was the end of that relationship.

It was only the beginning of my disillusionment and of my healing from that period of time. It took the longest time to get over my shame in front of the Lao community for having believed in the lies that Dade was selling. I avoided the Lao community for many months, if not years, because of my shame. Shame is something that you feel. It is not something that you can stop feeling just by talking to yourself. It took a long time before that feeling went away.

It was a period of healing because I had to understand why *I* felt shame when it was *he* who had done the shameful thing. I had to understand why *I* felt shame before the community when the *community* had been witness to the shameful act and had not warned me or shunned him for what he had done. It seemed that everyone had known except for me and my family.

Finally, there was a complex reckoning that I had to undertake with my parents. They were supposed to be my protectors, but they had been taken in as much by Dade's performance as I had. His presence in our family had solved so many problems, we thought, and now, his absence presented those problems to us all over again.

"Mai!" I cried when I told her of the discovery. "Dade was a fake! He was married all along. He has a son and a daughter! How can I ever trust a man again?" She didn't say anything, but I could feel the fury of the lioness in her thumping heart. If he had been within reach, she would have torn him to shreds. We just hugged each other, and we both cried for the injustice of the indecency of con artists like Dade.

My father was not nearly as emotional. He was stern and sad, but he really didn't have much to say – it didn't surprise me, because he had always been a man of few words and was not accustomed to dealing with emotions. He turned to the practical, instead, and asked how my studies were going otherwise and what my plans were for the future. I thought that disguise was the great tragedy of manhood.

Dade showed me how someone could use deceit and dishonesty to abuse my trust. That demonstration raised the issue of the grounds for trust going forward. I realized that not everyone is a con man like Dade. To assume so would be prejudicial on my part. Mistrust can breed mistrust. How would I be able to avoid that downward spiral?

Lawrence was my answer. It was clear to me now that his distrust of Dade was appropriate and not at all due to jealousy or any other emotional instability. He had an intuition that was tuned just right. I wanted to learn from him. Of course, he might have moved on and not wish to reestablish our friendship. I hadn't seen him for a long time. I couldn't even remember how long ago it had been. Perhaps it was when we had that talk about suspending our relationship because of Dade. I certainly owed him an apology. I decided that I would call him. It was Christmas Eve, just a few days after my discovery of Dade's deceit, so my emotions were very near the surface.

"Hello, Lawrence, this is Kasi," I said. There was a silent pause, and I was worried that he would hang up on me.

"Hello, Kasi. I have missed you. How are you?" he asked. Now, I was the one who paused. I swallowed and wiped away a tear. I didn't want him to know that I was crying.

"Oh! I'm fine. I..." before I could continue, he interrupted me.

"I heard what happened. I am very sorry you were hurt by him. I did try to warn you, you know?"

"Yes, Lawrence. I know you did. That was the reason I wanted to call you. I wanted to apologize for not believing you or for not taking your concerns more seriously. I want to ask your forgiveness. I hope I didn't hurt you."

"Kasi, you remember what I told you when we spoke last? I said that for a reason. I expected that this day might come. You have nothing to apologize for. Not everyone, not every man, is like Dade. You may find that hard to believe right now, but you will have to come to believe it if you are going to move on."

That was too much for me. I was not able to pretend that I was not crying anymore. I broke down and told him everything. He listened for over an hour to my recounting of the story of my relationship to Dade. I told it from my new perspective that cast everything that had gone before in a new, painful light. He said very little, because he knew that I just had to tell the story. I had to tell the story to make sense of my life anew. I had to tell the story so that I could begin to learn from it. That was the main thing and was necessary. Lawrence knew that and listened in the most caring way possible.

Lawrence was such a comfort. He helped me get over the betrayal of my trust by focusing on our friendship and our common activities – such as the Asian Student Association, debate team, and community organized events which we were actively involved in. Simultaneously, our friendship deepened to a new, more intimate level. We tenaciously finished our senior year and subsequently graduated together in the Spring of 1989.

The graduation ceremony was very emotional for my family because I was the first in our family to graduate from an American university. In some ways, it was a culmination of Mom and Dad's great struggle. For me, it was a sort of vindication as well. After all of the bullying and all of my struggles to overcome our poverty as new immigrants, I had succeeded in getting my degree in Education, and I had done so with distinction.

My relationship with Lawrence continued to become more serious. A year later, he asked for my hand in marriage before he left for medical school in the Dominican Republic. It was not a formal proposal, and we did not make a public announcement. With both of us still working towards our graduate degrees, we were going to wait a few years to see where our relationship would take us.

In the spring of 1990, Lawrence's long-time friend, Wayne, from medical school came to visit with his colleague, Richard from Singapore. Lawrence wanted me to bring two of my girlfriends to dinner with them. I suggested I could bring along Sarah and Lisa, so it was informally a triple-date night.

"Oh, that would be great!" exclaimed Lawrence.

We both were excited to get together with both his friends and mine. Besides, both Sarah and Lisa were always fun to be with. Sarah was a little on the quiet side. Although I think I'm a bit of an introvert, she was even more quiet. Lisa, however, had no problem conversing with anyone in the room. Guys had a tendency to gravitate towards her, and I thought she was one of the prettiest and outgoing girls I knew. But she had made it very clear to all the guys she met that she was not looking for commitment. That was perfectly fine. We were all just friends going out to enjoy an evening together.

We all had a wonderful time at dinner, and we sang karaoke all night. Richard did not know who was dating whom at that time, so he was friendly and conversed with everyone there. I enjoyed his lively conversation. At the end of the evening, when we were saying goodbye, I shook hands with Richard and felt him pass me a piece of paper. I secretly hid it away to read when I get home. The small piece of folded paper, from one of the fortune cookies, contained a simple message: "It was nice meeting you tonight." I have to admit, this made me smile.

Hanging out together, having dinner and singing karaoke were among our favorite activities at that time. So, every weekend for the next few weeks, the six of us would do exactly that. Richard continued to leave a nice little message when we shook hands to say goodbye at the end of each gathering. Unbeknownst to Lawrence, the messages I received went from "Thanks for a lovely evening," to "I had fun with you tonight," to "You look great tonight." Secretly, I was flattered. And without realizing it, I was falling in love.

As the weeks and months went by, Richard and I became very close friends, spending more time together. He and I had a lot in common — as we talked about life in general, tennis, traveling, family size we wanted, work-family responsibility, and our Asian culture — and we shared some laughs. The conversation was natural and effortless, and always interesting and fruitful. He was kind, patient, smart, and a real gentleman. Richard was very encouraging and empowering, too. For instance, when I told him I wanted to continue with my studies, he responded that I should and was very supportive. When he heard the story of my family's escape from Laos to Thailand, he was intrigued. He even encouraged me to write a book one day. This book is that book.

To my surprise, Richard took it upon himself to learn the Lao language, so that when he met my family, he could speak to them in their tongue. My parents were quite impressed with this

243

handsome, charming and intelligent man. He was genuinely good with my parents. He took interest in their projects and helped my dad with home repairs and my mom with her garden projects. As for me, I wanted to spend all my time with Richard, and hoped to travel to Singapore to meet his family one day.

Richard and I continued to date for six months, during which time my fondness for him turned to love. Naturally, my relationship with Richard deepened. My gut told me that he was the one, and I followed my heart. Consequently, I broke off the relationship with Lawrence. He said to me, "I knew that there was something different between you and Richard. That was when I realized I had lost you. It's the way you looked at him. You would never look at me with that same level of passion."

Richard and I spent a great time deal of time together during our courtship days. He was living two hours away from my apartment in Berkeley, so we always looked forward to spending the weekends together, after his work and my studies concluded for the week. One of our favorite things to do was watching the sunset together at the Bay Area beaches.

Six months after we met, on one Friday afternoon, he asked if he could pick me up for a picnic date and watch the sunset together. Naturally, I was very excited and got ready for him that evening. Richard showed up looking all nice and tidy, as usual, in his white ironed shirt and gray trousers, probably too nice for a picnic at the sunset. Just about an hour before the sunset, we drove down through the beautiful mountains and beaches along Point Reyes in Northern California. I realized how beautiful this place was, and I would never want to leave.

We drove farther down the mountains when we came upon a car that had stalled in the opposite lane. A man was struggling to push it uphill and away from traffic while a woman steered it in neutral position.

Without hesitation, Richard pulled our car safely to the side, and helped push their car out of danger. When the embarrassed and grateful couple explained they had run out of gas, Richard smiled reassuringly and drove thirty minutes back up the mountain to return with a container of gas.

It was nearly dark when we were finally able to resume our journey. Richard got back in our car with a stained white shirt and slightly concerned look.

"I'm sorry, Kasi," he said, looking in my eyes. "I made us miss the sunset."

I just smiled and threw my arms around him. He had won my heart with his act of kindness, and I knew there would be thousands more sunsets for us.

My intuition proved to be right later that same evening. At the picnic – beneath a bright moon rather than a setting sun – Richard proposed. This time, it was me who acted without hesitation.

Another six months later, Richard and I were married on April 30, 1991. I was overjoyed to be Mrs. Yang. One of the meanings of the name is the Sun. Coincidentally, Yang is just like the yellow Champa, which in our family represents the Sun – the true provider of all resources.

We knew we would wait several years before starting a family – mainly because I was still pursuing a graduate degree in Linguistics and Public Policy with the goal of attaining a position as a university professor. When I subsequently achieved that goal, it was a culmination of another milestone celebration for the Champa family.

When I finally did find my dream job in the Bay Area, Richard and I began to think about starting a family. We were much more deliberate about this step than my parents were. We waited until we were financially and emotionally ready to have children before

I got pregnant. Being financially ready was very different for us than it was for my parents. We did not pay for our house in cash. Like many Americans, we took a mortgage, but we both worked, and we had health insurance to help us pay the anticipated expenses of childbirth and other unforeseen events.

During that second month in 1993, Mom called me one morning. It was worrisome whenever I received a phone call from her, especially when she started her sentence with, "What are you doing? Are you sitting down?"

"Kasi, I have some bad news," she started. I had gotten used to this. It sometimes seemed as if she was so engrossed in her own world that the world of others didn't register.

"Tell me, Mai. I am listening," I said.

"Your father took me to the doctor a while ago, and they did some tests. Yesterday we went in to get the results," she reported. "I have degenerative kidney disease. The doctor said that I will need a new kidney very soon. He gave me some medicines to take until I can get a new kidney. I will probably need dialysis at some point. That depends on the progress of the disease."

I could sense she was close to tears. So was I. She had always prided herself on being independent. Now, she would be completely dependent on doctors and medicines and the kindness of her family. After all of her struggles to get us to the United States and after the trauma of losing her unborn child, it was heart-wrenching to realize that her last years would be saddled with burden.

"Oh no! I am so sorry, Mai. But we are going to get through this. There are many challenges ahead, but we have the will and the means to make it through this," I said.

I knew that she needed to hear that someone competent would be able to help her with this struggle. She knew that Richard was a doctor, and I had friends, like Lawrence, who were also doctors. Our resources were considerable when compared to those of many others, especially other refugee immigrants. It did give me pause when I imagined what we would do if we did not have all of those advantages.

In August of 1993, when I was nine months pregnant with Vanita, our first child, my mom called again.

"Kasi, I want us to have a family dinner together tonight," she said on the phone.

"Mai, I am about to give birth anytime now, so..."

"Then, we'll go somewhere near the hospital. That way, if you're in labor, we can quickly just drop you off the hospital."

"I'm not sure if I want to check in to the hospital that way, Mai."

"Why not? This is the wonderful thing about America. Everything can be done in express way. Express delivery."

So Richard and I, my dad, mom and my brother Huck all went out for a nice Thai dinner together, just five miles from the hospital. No kidding. That decision actually turned out to be quite fortuitous.

Halfway through dinner, we heard a buzz, and it sounded like Richard's on-call alert. But he checked, and it wasn't. And we all searched to find where that sound was coming from. Finally, I tracked down the sound to Mom's purse. Richard looked at the unit and explained that it was an alarm that she had a perfect match for her kidney, and she would need to get to the hospital within the next 24 hours. And it just so happened that we were only five miles away!

So, we all ended up taking her to the hospital where she received a new kidney, after six months of being on dialysis. It happened to be a kidney from a nine-year-old girl who was lost to a car crash. I had requested for us to meet the family of the little girl, to thank them, but they preferred to be anonymous. It was understandable, and we respected that. We were just so grateful and moved to know that there were people who would choose to do good things – to save someone's life – and would not want any recognition or acknowledgement.

Fortunately, the kidney transplant went without incident, and Mom got her wish to dedicate the rest of her life to her grandchildren. From her hospital bed, she told me and Richard, "I don't want to go until I see my grandchild. From today on, I only live for my grandchildren." And that, she did.

Just a week after Mom's kidney transplant, our first child – our daughter, Vanita – was born in 1993.

Two years later, our second child and our only son, Kevin, was born in 1995.

Three years later, our last child arrived – our daughter, Lee. Our family was complete.

Mom was the most dedicated, doting, hands-on grandmother that I had ever seen. She would have given anything just to see our children and be with them. There were times when she would just show up at the door, more often than I would have liked – sometimes daily. It didn't matter that I was in the middle of work or if I had company; she would drop by just to see the kids when they were in the preschool days. Clearly, Mom's greatest joy was her grandchildren. In retrospect, if only we knew how much time we each were given here on earth, we would likely react to everyone and every situation differently.

Third Freedom ~ Transition

"The world breaks everyone, and afterward, some are strong at the broken places." ~Ernest Hemingway

With the establishment of our family, Richard and I began a generational transition. My mother became more ill just as my children were coming into the world. Once our family was complete, and everything was looking up, we were suddenly confronted with a real nightmare.

Haven to Heaven

Ups and Downs

"In the end, we'll all become stories." ~*Margaret Atwood*

The fortunes of the Yang family were on the rise from the time that Richard and I married in 1991 until the events after July 2011. Richard, ten years older than me and already established in his medical career, had been able to buy a home before we were married. We lived there for about a year before building the house that would be the birth home of all of our three children. Richard and I liked to plan our life, and we began looking for the right neighborhood with good schools as soon as we decided to start a family.

Travels

What beautiful years those were! Every summer we would travel to different states. We visited the national parks and saw the wildlife and rugged landscapes of every place we visited. We taught the children the names of all of the animals and even the names of the special monuments and landmarks. I made a travel diary for each of our kids, and made sure they wrote down what they liked and learned from each of the new places we visited.

We chose Hawaii as the first state for our little family of three to visit. Of course, its natural beauty was a primary reason. However, it is also the only state in the United States with an Asian plurality. We wanted to see what the United States would look like if Asians were the majority. We also wanted to see the threatened native species of animals such as the Nene, the Monk Seal, and the Hawaiian Hoary Bat, for ourselves just in case they were unable to survive the onslaught of humanity. Vanita was too little to be able

251

to appreciate this adventure, but we bought books and took pictures that we shared with her for years to come.

Then, a year later, we went to South Carolina. There, we learned that the Great Migration in which blacks left the south for better prospects in northern, mid-western, and western states led to a white majority in South Carolina for the first time since 1708. We also learned that the relatively non-violent struggle for civil rights in South Carolina was a consequence of the willingness to accept some change on the part of the established political power structure in negotiations with the civil rights movement. However, we were surprised by the fact that the same power structure rejected the 19th amendment in 1920 that gave women the right to vote. It was not until 1969, just three years after I was born, that South Carolina finally ratified the amendment. It was important for us, as immigrants, as a racial minority, and for me as a woman to understand that South Carolina was an integral part of the mosaic of American culture.

We had our first and only son, Kevin, in 1995. That year, we went to Washington.

The variety of wildlife and climate in Washington State is what drew us there that year. We were able to see some species that neither Richard nor I had ever seen in the flesh: elk, moose, wolves, coyotes, black bears, and cougars. We got to see Killer Whales, as well as one Humpback whale breaching off the coast, and were enthralled by the western red cedar and ponderosa pine forests that we were able to experience. The changes in the climate from the arid eastern part to the extremely wet western parts taught us about the effects of mountains on local climate.

We noticed that Hispanics were most numerous in the areas east of the mountains because they were the agricultural workers in that part of the state. We recognized the value they added to the rich variety of foods in the American diet. We also noticed how the majority of the population of the state was centered in Seattle, which is the home of Starbucks, Amazon, and Microsoft with all of the associated technical firms that are residents of that part of the American mosaic.

We had our third and last child – our second daughter, Lee, in 1998. The following year, we went to Kansas.

Several features of Kansas interested us. The fact that immigrants from other states – abolitionists from Massachusetts and pro-slavery advocates from Missouri and Arkansas – determined the nature of the state that was accepted as the 34th state of the union and a free state revealed the role that internal immigration had played in the formation of the United States.

Eventually, by the time all three children reached high school age, we had covered 46 states and some foreign countries.

I recognize that good fortune is not exclusively a matter of hard work and will power. It is also a matter of luck. The difference between the fate of our family and the fate of the less fortunate was a consequence of chance at every turn. It was chance that Mom's brother had a boat that we could use to escape Laos. It was chance that it was Keo, and not me that was drowned in the Mekong River. It was chance that the guards on the shore chose not to hurt us. It was chance that my father was not like Phoemkhun's father. It was chance that we were given opportunities to go to France, Australia, and the U.S. as refugees. Our success came from being ready to take advantage of opportunities and from recognizing opportunities when they presented themselves. But the opportunities themselves were not made by us either by our will or our hard work. We were lucky. We always remember that, because it is what connects us to all of those who are less fortunate than we were or are. Humility is a hard lesson to learn when you struggle for so long and so hard to get what you have.

Pay It Forward

I don't know exactly what prompted me to walk to the post office that Wednesday. Of course, I went there to mail our taxes. It was 2009 tax filing time, after all. Still, there was no need for me to walk off campus. I could have mailed it on campus. I guess I just wanted to take a walk. It wasn't far from my small office near Sproul Hall and – although it was cooler than usual for this time of year and there was a little wind, too – the day was clear and pleasant in my down jacket. The post office on Durant Avenue was a sordid little hole-in-the-wall. There was a long walkway between Cafe Durant on the right and Johnston's Market on the left. It was a walkway that looked like it led to nowhere. There, at the end, was the door to the post office.

Then, on my way back to my office on the UC Berkeley campus, I met Margaret. She was sitting on the right side of that long walkway as I came out of the post office. Normally, I didn't pay much attention to the homeless. They were everywhere in Berkeley. It had always been that way. To me, that day, Margaret was different, though. She was Japanese. She was about the age of my mother. She had extended her hand which I understood to be a plea for some money. When I looked at her face – just for a fraction of a second – she smiled. It was that smile that conquered me. You see, she had a mostly toothless smile. I fumbled in my purse for some money. While I was standing right in front of her, she spoke to me.

"Hi. How are you, today?" she asked softly.

"I am fine," I replied. "How are you?" I had found a few dollar bills, and I was about to hand them to her. She withdrew her hand. I looked at her, confused.

"Don't you want the money?" I asked.

254

"No. I really don't need money. I was hoping you would give me your down jacket. I'm cold."

The jacket that I was wearing was an Eddie Bauer Sun Valley down jacket. It cost more than $100. Of course, there was no question that it would fit her. She was my size, for sure. In that moment, I wondered what I would have felt like if our positions were reversed. I could see that she was cold. She was shivering, actually. It reminded me of when I had gotten out of the Mekong River and onto the river bank in Thailand. I had noticed her mostly toothless smile before. Now, I could see that she was wearing a thin white shirt – a man's shirt – and a pair of black sweat pants. She was sitting cross-legged on her bare feet. I felt warm and safe in my hiking boots and down jacket.

The sun was shining, and I didn't have to get back to the office right away. I told her that I would be right back, and I went to the end of that desolate walkway and around the corner to Thompson's Market. I went in and found a nice quilted jacket, my size, in a discreet color. I paid the $39 for it and brought it back to Margaret.

I could have left it at that. Instead, I actually surprised myself when I simply decided to sit down next to Margaret and talk to her. She didn't think it was a big deal, either. In fact, she just started to smile more broadly and began to talk to me as if we were old friends.

I asked her how she had come to the point of begging in the streets of Berkeley, California. This was what I learned from Margaret: Her parents were Nisei, Japanese immigrants' children who were born with American citizenship. So, her parents were American citizens for the same reason that my children are American citizens. They were all born here. Margaret was born on February 20th in 1938. She was 71 years old on the day that we met. She was almost of the age of reason when Roosevelt signed Executive Order 9066 on February 19th, 1942 which authorized the forcible relocation of Japanese Americans to internment camps and the confiscation of their property. Margaret's family was forcibly relocated in the spring of 1942. Even though they lost their house and their business, her father joined the army and fought with the 522nd Field Artillery Battalion that had the distinction of liberating survivors of the Dachau concentration camp from the Nazis in 1945. Her father paid the ultimate price for his patriotism and never returned to their family. Margaret's mother had to raise the children alone.

I imagined what it would have been like if my father had chosen to go to France instead of staying with us. I understood how difficult it must have been for her mother to raise the family without the help of a father for her children. The consequence of having been raised by a poor single mother was that Margaret wasn't able to go to college. Instead, after high school, Margaret married another high-school graduate when he got a job in Kern County, California in the oil industry. The deepest well in the world was drilled in North Coles Levee just three years before they graduated, so good high-paying – though dangerous – jobs were still available.

The Interstate Highway Act of 1956 inaugurated the largest public works program in history. So, she got a job in the auto industry at the Chrysler Los Angeles plant. She joined the Union and was part of the 1958 strike at that plant. Margaret and her husband both were able to stay employed in those industries and to stay together. Their employment was affected by the 1969 Santa Barbara oil spill, and the 1971 closing of the Chrysler Los Angeles plant. They bought several houses as they were forced to move from one place to another to follow their jobs. In 2006, they finally bought their dream home. Then, in 2008, they both lost their jobs as a consequence of the downturn. Their house lost almost 20% of its value between 2006 and 2008 so they were unable to sell it. The bank took the home that represented their life's savings due to their unemployment, and that was how Margaret became homeless.

This was a troubling story. However, I did not want to come to any hasty conclusions. When I left Margaret and retraced my steps back to my office on campus, I was just looking forward to the weekend that Richard and I had planned for more than a month. We were going to fly to Santa Barbara to housesit for one of Richard's patients. He had a very nice condo overlooking the beach and had offered it to us because he was off on a vacation. I couldn't wait to have a weekend alone with Richard. We had arranged for the kids to stay with my sister-in-law, and it was the first time in a long time that we would be able to relax and be together.

By the time we reached the beautiful condo overlooking Hendry's Beach in Santa Barbara, I had already told Richard about the conversation that I had with Margaret and how unsettled I felt about it. He was kind and empathetic, as always, but we didn't have time to get into the details as we were busy getting the kids off to my sister-in-law's house and ourselves to the airport that Saturday morning.

We found the key to the condo just where his patient had left it for us, and we carried in our bags in a single trip. Then, we decided to have our brunch. There were fresh oranges, eggs, and coffee, which was all we needed. I made orange juice for us while Richard did the coffee and boiled the eggs.

"Let's go down to the beach right after we eat, shall we?" he asked. I agreed. I was looking forward to a walk on the beach. However, in that moment, I was just enjoying the sweet sourness of the orange juice and appreciating how attractive Richard was. I could feel myself settling in and relaxing. I walked over to the big picture windows that looked out at the Pacific Ocean as Richard turned on a local radio station that was playing jazz.

Later, we walked down to the beach. We had been to Hendry's Beach before, so we knew exactly what we would do. We walked along the boardwalk that was closest to the beachfront restaurant. When we got to the steps that descended to the beach, we held hands and walked toward the leash-free area to the left to watch the dogs play. We could hear the screeches of the crows and hawks. The sky was a bit cloudy, so the light was not dim but subdued. We watched as a group of pelicans floated in a V formation from the cliffs toward the ocean where we could hear the sound of the Pacific Ocean punctuated by the occasional barking of the dogs. Richard and I looked at each other and smiled silently, knowing that we had the whole weekend to be together again.

"There is so much I would like to talk about," I said.

"We have time, Kasi. Let's talk it all through one topic at a time. When we finish with one, we will move on to another."

It was that patient thoroughness that I really appreciated about Richard. He was not only a great doctor, but a great partner in our marriage, too. I was quiet for a while just thinking about how lucky I was to have him as a husband.

"So, first of all," I began, "I just wanted to explain why I didn't give her my coat when she asked."

"Well, Kasi, I would have been concerned if you had. I gave that to you as an anniversary gift last year. I hope it means something to you beyond what it costs."

"Yes!" I exclaimed. Richard almost always got it when we spoke. It was the symbolic significance of the coat that made me want to keep it. You can't buy symbolic sentiments.

"I also want to say how grateful I am for the good fortune I have had compared to Margaret. I had two parents and an extensive network of aunts, uncles, cousins as well as nephews and nieces to help me. I would not have been able to get my education if I had to go to work to support the family full-time when I just got out of high school like Margaret. I am grateful for that opportunity."

"I know how you feel. I feel the same way about all of the support that I got from my family to go to medical school. I did the studying, got the good grades, and spent the time doing my post-graduate internships. That was hard. I certainly couldn't have done it if it weren't for my family. Besides, you and I would never have met!"

"That is the other part of it. What if I had to marry a laborer? There is nothing wrong with that kind of physical work. But, we would not have been able to buy our home and the cars that we have if you had been a manual laborer. I am grateful that I met you through Lawrence and that you were able to become a doctor." After having told Richard those things, I felt unburdened and was able to go deeper.

"How would you have felt if you and your family had been stripped of your property including your business, home, and even your car as happened to those innocent Japanese Americans, the Nisei?"

Richard didn't answer immediately. I could see that the question troubled him, too.

"Well," he said, "that is sort of what happened to the Champa family, isn't it?"

"Yes, sort of. But my parents chose to leave everything. The Pathet Lao took it only after we abandoned it. I think it matters when your own government – the one you believe in, and even love – takes your property from you and puts you in a camp against your will, even though you have done nothing wrong. How can you continue to believe in a government that does that to you and your family? How can you leave your wife and children and give your life to that government the way her father did? I just can't understand it. I feel terrible questioning his patriotism that way. Still, I wouldn't feel that I was being honest with myself or with you if I didn't." I really wanted to know what Richard would say about that, but I also felt much better after I had gotten it all out.

"You are absolutely right. It is very uncomfortable to think that your country could put you in that moral predicament. He had to choose his family or his country, and he chose his country. That is an extreme form of patriotism. I am not sure I would have chosen that way, frankly. However, when I think about that possibility, it makes me realize that dictatorships and representative democracies are similar in one way: the power of the state is exercised by human beings. Human beings – including doctors – are fallible. Sometimes, when representatives or doctors make mistakes, people are injured or killed. Perhaps that just means that we should not revere the laws of legislatures or the decisions of doctors as though they are above humanity. Sometimes, when you understand that a law is unjust, you have to stand against it. That is what conscientious objectors do. They have an important role in our democratic society. Sometimes, their self-sacrifice results in changes to unjust laws. In part as a consequence of those extreme patriots and several conscientious objectors, Ronald Reagan did issue an apology to all Japanese Americans for that internment program." He finished and suddenly became silent.

That was very unusual for Richard. A man of few words, he usually did not speak so extensively about anything. At first, there was a sort of awkward silence between us. But, I was looking at him carefully. Then, I said, "Are you OK?" When he finally looked at me, I could see that his humility had returned, and he was a bit embarrassed for his outburst. His guilty look made me laugh, and when he realized how funny the situation was, he began to laugh raucously, too. Nevertheless, I agreed with him. I told him so and kissed him. We continued our walk down the beach.

Our walk was surrounded by the sounds of the crows, the dogs, the children and the ocean. I snuggled up to Richard as the cool winds began to blow the sea spray toward us. We turned around and started walking back to the condo.

When we were about to start dinner, we looked out those incredible picture windows and watched the sun set into the Pacific. We had started a fire in the fireplace, and it crackled in the background amid the pinkish-red silence of the dining room where we had even lit the candles. We looked at each other and were so grateful that we were able to sit in that room at that time and just listen to the sounds of silence and the crackling fire.

"Sweetheart," I said, "do you ever feel overwhelmed? That is what I felt after my conversation with Margaret. How do you handle that?"

"I do feel overwhelmed, sometimes. I have a very reliable way to deal with it, though. I do one of two things. Either I set it all aside and come home to you and the kids, as if none of the troubling aspects of the world existed. Sometimes, I have to do that to get back to my center. Or, at other times, when I have more energy or time, I participate in some of the activities at the Asian Health Services facility in Oakland." He looked like he wanted to tell me more.

Even as he was telling me this I began to form a plan. First of all, I realized that I was not alone. Richard was my partner in this. Just as he had connected with a network that helped him to contribute in an organized and efficient way, so could I. Besides, I realized that I was not alone in another way. I had a responsibility to teach my children. Our family was not saved from the situations in Laos and Thailand only to ignore the troubles that we left behind. Our whole family could act together to help. We don't need to take a vow of poverty or sacrifice our lives the way Margaret's father did to make a difference. We could find a way to make volunteering

261

for the right projects a part of our lives without sacrificing more than is reasonable.

I realized that encounter with Margaret and this talk with Richard was just a beginning.

When we arrived home, Richard and I returned to our routine. Since the kids were back home and school was not out for the summer yet, I had meals to make, stories to read, and homework to help with in addition to preparing for my lectures at the university and grading exams and such.

Since I wanted to involve all of the kids, and since they all have summer birthdays, I came up with the idea of a reverse birthday. On a reverse birthday, instead of receiving gifts, you give them. I would encourage the gifts to be intangible. That seemed like a nice idea to me, as an adult that wanted to find a way to give back. However, I thought that it might be too much to expect the kids to give up their birthdays to give back to the community. I certainly didn't want them to feel as though this was a punishment. I decided it would be a good idea to elicit their birthday wishes first, and then make gaining that wish contingent on some kind of giving back. That way, they would be rewarded in terms they could understand, for doing the right thing. Of course, we should all do the right thing, simply because it is the right thing to do, but I was going to have to start with baby step.

Of course, I had to take into consideration their ages. Whatever volunteering we would be doing, their understanding and their activities must be age appropriate. Lee, our youngest daughter, was 10 and in 4th grade, the same age and grade as me when I came to the United States. Kevin was 13 and in the 7th grade. Vanita was 15 and in the 9th grade.

I really wanted the whole family to be involved in this volunteering effort, but I didn't want to make it seem like I was some kind of dictator that was demanding obedience from my children. Richard and I had talked about that, and we both agreed that this ought to be a lesson in democracy as well as a way to give back. As it turns out, that is a perpetual problem for democracies. How do you encourage participation?

It was hard for me to let go of control and allow the process – a family democratic process – to determine the outcome. However, that was what Richard and I had decided we needed to do. All I could do was to make the preparations. In doing some research into democratic process in the family context, I discovered that there was very little to give parents guidance about that. We seem to tell ourselves that ours is a democratic, open, participatory society, and we may even believe it. However, in our most intimate associations – our families – we are mostly authoritarian. The parents are the undisputed rulers until the children become teenagers. Then, rebellion erupts. I wondered if that might be just a consequence of the lack of education about democratic process in our homes. After about a week of carefully considering the problem of the process for that meeting, I decided that the best way would be to present it as a game.

Since May Day was just about two weeks away, I thought that would be a good day to have a Friday family dinner and discuss the upcoming summer. I prepared a delicious Lao dinner with everyone's favorites in mind – Richard's papaya salad, Vanita's salmon *laab* dish, Kevin's lemongrass grilled chicken, and Lee's mango sticky rice dessert.

It was our habit to give thanks at meal time, and I decided to use that tradition to set expectations.

"We would like to thank God, our country, and our family for the wonderful meal that we are about to share and to give thanks for all of the opportunities and advantages that we have. Hopefully, this summer, we will all find some way to give back to our community and to those less fortunate than us. Amen."

Richard asked me to tell the story of Margaret. I did, and it was well received. Lee was rather more curious why Margaret was toothless.

"I would like to play a game. Who would like to play?" I asked. All of the kids wanted to play.

"Okay. This game is called the Reverse Birthday Game with Rewards," I announced.

"What kind of rewards?" Lee asked.

"That is the best part," I replied. "You get to choose whatever reward you want!"

There was a noisy discussion of what each of them wanted the most.

"Okay. That's good. Now, the Reverse Birthday part is that you have to do something nice to get the reward that you have chosen. Just like the reward, you get to choose the nice thing to do. The only catch is that it has to be something that we all want to do with you!" I explained.

Suddenly, there was silence in our dining room. For a moment, I was afraid that I wouldn't be able to explain it.

"Oh, I get it!" exclaimed Kevin. "You will give me that computer I want if I can get a majority of the family to agree to join me for some charity event that I pick. Is that it?"

"Yes," I replied with relief. "We each need to choose a charity – or maybe more than one just in case – and then we need to sell the rest of the family on that charity, enough so that when we take a vote about participating in the activity that supports the charity, at least half of us are willing."

Richard decided that he would donate his time to give free medical examinations to those who would not have been able to afford it.

"I saw that there were a lot of people that couldn't afford to pay for a visit to a doctor. I asked the question: How can I help the uninsured and the poor to be able to see a doctor. I actually found something that we could all do. There is an organization called Direct Relief and we can go to a designated facility and help those who need medications or other services. You don't have to be a doctor or nurse to help," he explained to us.

"Of course, you know your Mom. I have a list of charities if you want to take a look!" I entreated.

"I already know what I would like to do," said our oldest.

"What is that, Vanita?" asked Richard.

"How food insecurity affects children at school and over the summer," she replied.

"Wow," I said. "I'll vote for that!"

"Me too," Lee chimed in.

That was how our May Day dinner went. Kevin chose Habitat for Humanity to address homelessness. On the 25th of May, we celebrated his birthday by helping to paint a house. I chose to do some work on voter registration on my birthday. The whole Yang family joined in, too. Lee chose an environmental group that helps sea life. On the Independence Day weekend, we celebrated her birthday by helping to save turtles. The beautiful result of our efforts that summer was that the Reverse Birthday idea is now a Yang family tradition. Kevin got that new computer that he wanted that summer. During the next summer, though, none of us were even thinking about our rewards. And that is as it should be.

Mom

Although our fortunes were rising throughout the period that began in 1991 when Richard and I married, there were signs of the cruel winds of misfortune gathering. When I looked back, it was clear that Mom's decline began when she lost the child as a consequence of that fatal fall on the bicycle in 1983. It was a definite break with her past. She became disabled and was forced to stop working. She had time to reflect on her life, but she also broke a bone in her hand that prevented her from writing any more. Reflection without prospect of expression is a terrible thing. It seemed to affect her emotional stability.

Eventually, she was not able to attend parent-teacher meetings or board of education meetings. Her dream of creating a national program of international travel and multi-cultural, multi-lingual education faded into her reveries and, she even began to doubt that it would have changed anything. I was captivated by the idea, but I really didn't have any time to pursue it. You see, the Champa family began to face crisis after crisis, and I was right at the center of them all.

Then, the kidney failure. Although Mom received the kidney transplant successfully, and it extended her life another twenty years, the medications that she had to take for the rest of her life were many. They did something to her, I'm sure. It was harder for her to talk or think as sharply as she used to.

Mom was incapacitated, physically, for years after the kidney transplant. During that time, Dad and I were her primary caretakers. Huck moved out years ago to pursue his dreams in traveling and living abroad. When Dad called me at work on the 15th of December 2010, the day after she took a fall that damaged her hip and leg, I knew that I would have to go home to help. My teaching semester was almost over, anyway, and everyone was preparing to go home for the Christmas holidays.

Ups and Downs

At first, she was bed-ridden, then she graduated to a wheelchair. Finally, she was able to use a sort of scooter that freed me from some of my more onerous duties.

During the time I cared for her, we got to spend a lot of time talking and reflecting on life and everything we wanted to talk about. Well, it was mainly Mom doing the talking, and I was just lending her my ears. It was quite interesting to hear all the "stories" or "dreams" she shared with me.

Mom was very focused on the loss of her child. She often referred to the child as her third child or as her American baby. I knew that every human life was sacred to her. I remembered the care she took to account for everyone when we lost Keo. And she would tell me that the child would often "visit" her. Sometimes she referred to these stories as her "dream." But sometimes I didn't know where or when the truth actually ended.

"One day, I heard the cry of an infant, a newborn, and I turned to see a crib in the distance, under a tree. I began to make my way to the crib and had the feeling that I knew that newborn. As I got closer, I could see that the tree was full of Champa flowers of all colors. I thought that it might be you or your brother or even both of you when you were infants. It made me feel good thinking that you both might be able to live in a land of plenty. As I approached, I knew this child was different. Instead of a blanket, the child was covered by leaves that had fallen from the tree. So, the harvest was upon us. All of the fruit on the trees was ripe and ready to pick. I wanted to uncover the newborn so that I could know if it was a boy or a girl. Then, I knew – as if I had always known – that this newborn was the child that I had lost when I fell from the bicycle. It was in that moment that the name of the child came to me in Chinese: Yong Yuan (Forever). But I was overcome by the desire to know if the child was male or female. So, I began to brush away the leaves that had fallen from the tree. The shock of it woke me," Mom said with her eyes wide open.

"How can you dream such things!" I exclaimed. She looked at me as if I had caught her with her hand in the cookie jar. Then, she made light of it.

"Oh, it is just a silly dream. It probably doesn't mean anything. The Champa flowers were beautiful though!" she said. I was too tired, to contest her expression or to pursue the dialog any further. I just accepted it as a matter of fact.

Another week went by, another visit, another story.

"Kasi, I have had a dream that troubles me greatly," she said in a whisper in my ear. I looked at her and saw the seriousness on her face. I took her by the arm without saying anything, led her into a nearby bedroom, and closed the door.

"I am so sorry that I dreamt it," she said apologetically.

"Mai, a dream is a dream. You can't control what you dream about. If it reveals something that is true, you just need to deal with it. We are all here to help." I hoped that would reassure her as it did me.

"I dreamed of your two older sisters, and another one – but that one was your half-sister."

I was shocked, but was trying to appear calm and reasonable, as this was not a story that had ever been shared with me before. Could this even be real?

She, however, went on telling me that she lost two children prior to me and my brother – one from stillbirth and another girl from malaria. She often "dreamed" of the lost children during her demented years and talked a lot about them. She sometimes vividly described how she was visited by these children dressed in white singing sweetly to her, welcoming her with open arms as she entered the gates of heavens. The place, she told me, was filled with beautiful, fragrant flower gardens – *dok champa* among them, and she was so content.

"Wait, who was my half-sister? I don't think I'm following this well," I said, trying to bring her back to that part.

"That was the child your father had with another woman. That child is your age."

I had to reflect on this. There was so much more to the revelation than just having a half-sister. It meant that my father was duplicitous with my mother in the same way that Dade had been with me. Not in exactly the same way, but what each of them did required duplicity, deceit, lies – all of the behaviors that I despised. Now, I had to face the fact that my father, too, was guilty of these sins. But, still, that was between him and my mom in their marriage. As far as I was concerned, my father had been a good man to me.

Again, visits after visits, talks after talks, stories after stories, dreams after dreams. Sometimes they were repeats, sometimes new.

"I will never forgive your father, that is for sure," she said again during another visit.

"What did Dad do, Mai? You shouldn't be so mean to him. He is a good man," I said.

"Oh yes! He is a good man now, Kasi. But not then. Not when he left me for that other woman and had a daughter with her!" she exclaimed angrily. I was used to her angry outbursts. The doctors had told me to expect them. This one seemed particularly animated, though.

"Mai! Come on. Dad doesn't have any other daughter. I am his only daughter," I said with denial and some annoyance. Secretly, I had hoped maybe her previous revelation was just another one of her dreams.

"Oh yes he does. You ask him some day when I am gone. Then, he will tell you. Her name was Luna. Her mother was that woman in France. That was why he wanted to go to France instead of America. But I would not consent to that. I wanted to keep our family together," she ranted.

"Mai, our family IS together. You are talking nonsense. Just stop it!" I scolded. And she did stop.

Suddenly, she was silent, and she said nothing else for the rest of that day.

That was as much conversation as I could muster that time. However, her vision haunted me. I couldn't stop thinking about her revelation about my half-sister. I didn't know how to register all that in my head.

I had to admit that I was too tired that day to engage with her. I had been staying up late to grade papers for the class at the university. Along with taking care of the kids, one of them sick with a fever all night, I was not sleeping well. Besides, a dream like that might make you think that there was something going on with the mental state of the dreamer. I made a note to myself that this might be a symptom of dementia, and I decided to mention it to her doctor the next time I took her.

Forgive me for my silent diagnosis: I decided that my mom was demented. I sometimes couldn't tell where the truth actually lay and where her imagination set in.

"I've forgiven your father. And I have encouraged him to try to reconnect with this daughter Luna, because it's not the child's fault, and she should not have to miss out on a chance to know her father. The poor child, she's not as lucky as you, Kasi."

Our conversation continued as I made my weekly visits.

"Do you believe in the after-life? You know, a better place?" she asked out of the blue. Still, this didn't seem to be the right time to have a discussion about heaven with my incoherent mother.

"Yes, of course, Mai. Do you?" I replied. She didn't answer me for a long time. Then, she looked directly at me.

"I do now. Lately, I have been thinking a lot about it," she said.

This was the beginning of her conversion to Christianity.

"Everything makes sense now," she said. I really didn't understand what made sense to her. But this time, I'm glad she carried on that conversation further.

"It was Christ all along, even as I had wondered 'where was God' in the midst of our escape, and in the harsh conditions we had to endure in the refugee camp. It was Christ disguised as the USCC people giving us food and water when we needed it most. It was Christ who gave us blankets when it was cold, clothes when we were naked, and shelter when we were homeless. You see, all the sufferings of this present time are nothing compared to the glory that awaits us."

That was deeply profound. I had to take a moment of silence to absorb this new view of events.

Even in the state of dementia, my mother recognized the kindness in humanity - the altruistic agents of our escape; the aid received from USCC and other charity groups like Meals On Wheels, Direct Relief, Feeding Children; and people who demonstrated kindness to us through their acts. Similarly, it was all these life experiences that made me think about the Christian faith more seriously. The love of my life, Richard, had also been a big part of my faith. I took my mom's advice to marry someone whom you can see yourself with tomorrow, not just today – someone who

271

is not only kind to you but respects every person as a valued human being. Mom always said that God was in everyone, and it wasn't hard to find Him in Richard. It was why I fell in love with this man.

During another visit, another event took place. My mother finally gave me that gold necklace that she had hidden while we were in Thailand and that she had told me about to allay my fears when we were all so vulnerable. When she gave it to me, she reminded me not to tell my father about it. Then, too, I had reprimanded her for being so hard on my father. She was unrelenting. She made me promise that it would only be passed on to my children. I promised, but without real commitment. Now, finally, that promise was made clear to me, and I cried with sadness for its reason.

Mom had unburdened herself to me, because she had begun to come to terms with her own mortality. She wanted to be sure that she shared with me issues that weighed heavily in her heart, and what she had learned in her "dream world" just in case she suddenly passed away. That is the way she thought about those things.

My mother had been experiencing the progressive effects of Alzheimer's disease for a decade, and the effects of the disease on her cognition were very pronounced. According to the doctors, it was very likely that she had been living with the disease for ten years before she was diagnosed. That means that the disease was already affecting her around the time Lee was born.

Still, we thought that her troubles were all that we would have to deal with and we adapted – as a family – to the burdens that dementia imposed.

Cancer

But our troubles were about to increase enormously. While we were on a family trip on July 24, 2011, Lee began complaining of stomach pain. We didn't know the source of her pain. There were no visible signs of any injury. Still, her pain was persistent, and we all decided to take her to the emergency room to let them check her. It was good that we did.

That day, Lee was diagnosed with Burkitt's lymphoma, a very fast-growing form of non-Hodgkin's lymphoma. Fortunately, it is treatable. However, the treatment must continue for five months, is debilitating, and is very expensive. Lee had her first treatment that very day because waiting even another day might have been fatal.

From that day until the 13th of November, our whole life revolved around Lee's treatments and recovery. Actually, it would have been a luxury if our life could only have revolved around saving the life of Lee. In reality, it also revolved around Mom's increasing dementia. Richard continued to work and the lives of our other two children had to continue. There was no reprieve from any of the other life commitments. *We had to do it all, all at once, and all together.*

The treatments required Lee to be in the hospital for a week. Then, she would come home to recover for 21 days. Then, she would return to the hospital for another week of treatment. That meant that she was in the hospital for five weeks starting on July 24th, August 21th, September 18th, October 16th, and November 13th that year.

Warriors speak of the fog of war. Certainly, there is also a fog of life. Too much is happening too quickly. There is no time to plan or the planning gets lost in the doing. There is no time for accounting or the accounting is swamped by the sheer emotional weight and number of the events that need to be accounted for. Even if I could recount the day-to-day activities of each member of my family or even just of mine alone, the details would overwhelm the significance. It is only by stepping back, by stepping out of the details, that it is possible to make sense of the events of that time. Your imagination can help.

Imagine that you are torn between your desire to honor your mother who saved your life and your soul more than once and your desire to save the life of the daughter that meant so much to you and your mother, too. We have our culture, expressed in language that tells us to honor our parents. I was caught between these primordial imperatives, and every decision I made illuminated that dilemma. Of course, that dilemma is not just my dilemma. Our whole society faces the same dilemma in the way we provide for our elderly and our children when disease descends on them.

There is a great disparity between the way we treat the young and the old. I saw that disparity the way my daughter received care and the way my mother received care.

When we took Lee into the hospital for her treatments, we were greeted by a young enthusiastic nurse practitioner. She explained everything that we needed to know and answered all of our questions. We were escorted through a facility that was clearly well maintained. It was obvious that the physical building was cared for in the sense that money was spent to pay people to take care of it.

It was also obvious that there was a coordinated team of caregivers to help Lee and our family with the stresses of cancer treatment. We met most of the team members. We understood how each one contributed to the overall care of our daughter. We were told about the extensive research and development that was done by those that we would never meet to ensure that the chemicals that would be used to cure her condition were as effective as possible and had minimal side effects. Everything administered to her was double checked and tripled checked by several health practitioners present.

These five treatments were not cheap. I do not know how much our insurance company paid for the treatments, but we incurred expenses of close to a million dollar to save our daughter. The insurance company covered most of that, but we still spent about one percent. We would have done anything to save our daughter, and we had the money or access to the money. It is difficult to ignore the question of what a family without our means would do. Certainly, they would do anything to save their child. We have that in common. But our access to the means to save her is uncommon. I couldn't help but wonder about something fundamental of our health care system – are some people's children worth less than other people's children?

Dementia

As my mother's dementia advanced, it became clear to me that my father and I were no longer able to care for her. Just as she had decided for the whole family that we should come to the United States, I decided that she should begin to stay in a facility that offered 24-hour care for dementia patients. Mom did not really want to go. Dad did not have much choice in that matter. However, it was the best for the family in both instances. In any case, since I could not visit her as frequently as I wanted, especially after Lee was diagnosed with cancer, one of my closest friends, Evie, would often go to visit her.

Evie is a devout Christian and would often talk to Mom about God and religion. Evie is a kind person with compassion and loves to offer her time and help to those in need. Sometimes our presence and availability are the best gifts to people, especially the elderly. Most of the time, they just need someone to listen to them and talk to. I think those talks also influenced Mom in her transition to Christianity.

Haven to Heaven

The critical scene in the story of her progression into dementia happened when I was not present. One day, when Evie was there instead of me, the nurses came into Mom's area for some routine purpose. Evie told me that a confrontation ensued between my mother and those healthcare workers. She was not able to tell me exactly what happened except that the workers were not very empathetic or attentive to Mom's difficulties in understanding and speaking English. In any case, the conflict erupted into a physical confrontation that resulted in them invoking the involuntary commitment statute and taking away all of my mother's rights. When I finally arrived, Mom was taken to a locked facility, and the staff told me that I no longer had any right to determine or recommend any course of treatment for my mother.

In California, there is a law referred to as 5150 that permits certain people with credentials to confine patients to a mental health hospital against their will, if they are a danger to themselves, to others, or unable to care for themselves. They don't even need the consent of the family. This law, with all its specific qualifications, applies only in California. However, there are similar laws in every other state (such as the Baker Act in Florida.) The point is that these laws are state laws.

When we say that something tragic occurs, we usually mean something that is unfortunate, but that could have been avoided if only some independent variable had been different. Here, it seems to me, the tragedy is in mutual misunderstanding. My mother probably did not understand what was being asked of her or the reason why it was being asked of her. The health care workers probably did not understand the need for empathy with my mother, her modest competency in English, and the Lao expectation of how younger people respectfully address and treat older people. All of these factors may have been at play. For that reason, it was tragic that she was committed.

Imagine the injustice from my perspective: My mother's loss of her baby, her struggle with kidney disease and her transplant. We had gone through so much after our struggle to move her to an assisted-care facility and I was overwhelmed by the competing twin demands of a cancer-afflicted daughter and a demented parent. After all of that, for her to be taken away from me and the rest of the family by the state – to which I had been paying taxes for years – and over a cultural misunderstanding was just too much. It may have been legal, but it was absolutely unfair. The state, in this case, acted inhumanely.

The state would have acted just as inhumanely, regardless of the immigration status of me or my mother. However, the fact that we had struggled so hard to become successful in the United States and yet still were not immune to such treatment just added insult to injury. It is not that we should have any special privileges; it is that such indignities should not be visited upon any person or family.

Haven to Heaven

Passing

"I had endured so much in life, if it were up to me, I would never have left this place" ~Malala Yousafzai

According to the doctors, by November of 2011, Mom was completely engulfed by Alzheimer's. However, I have since begun to wonder about that judgement of her mental competence. This realization has caused me to question whether or not it was wise or correct to dismiss the things that my mother said just because the professionals said that she was demented.

With the advice of her doctors, I decided to place Mom in a nearby well-maintained facility that offered 24-hour care for dementia patients. When I first took Mom to the residence to stay, she was not happy about it. I was conflicted as well because, in the Lao culture, the care of elderly parents is the responsibility of the children. However, several factors led to my decision to place her in the residence.

First of all, Lee was still going through her cancer treatments. I had to be available to her for the twenty-one days between treatments when she was extremely fragile and staying at home. Second, taking care of a person in the advanced stages of Alzheimer's disease is a full-time occupation and often requires training or knowledge that I did not have and could not get. Finally, I was still fulfilling my responsibility to take care of my parent because I was bearing the financial burden of her care. I was not abandoning my mother in any way.

None of this really mattered to Mom. First of all, she had great difficulty understanding anything that required the retention of context over the course of several minutes. If it took you two minutes to explain something to her, she would have already forgotten the premise in the first sentence by the time you got to the last. She would ask the same questions over and over again, because she could not remember the answer that you gave her just five minutes before. Needless to say, that was extremely frustrating.

As a consequence, she and I had a terribly emotional exchange the day I brought her to stay at the residence.

"When are we going home, Kasi?" she asked for the third time.

"You are going to stay here tonight," I told her again.

"I am not going to stay here tonight. I am going home. You are a terrible daughter. You always leave me alone to fend for myself. That is not what I taught you to do," she said, raising her voice this time.

"Mai, I only leave you alone so that I can take care of Lee. I am always with you. I feed you and drive you wherever you want to go," I replied.

I did not want to have this conversation, actually. I wished that someone else had been available to help me to get Mom settled in, but even Evie had said she couldn't come until later. Of course, my father would have been more trouble than help. He didn't want Mai to go away to the residence, either. He couldn't take care of her by himself, and they would constantly argue because she couldn't remember anything. Still, he said that he didn't want her to go and refused to help me move her on that day. Huck was out of the country and was not available to help with the move. Richard would have done it, but he was on-call at the hospital emergency room and had been up for eighteen hours straight two nights earlier. I didn't even want to ask him. The only reason I felt capable of moving her this day was because there was a home health-care worker that was able to stay with Lee for a few hours. So, I took advantage of the opportunity to do something that was painful for both of us, but that had to be done. Mom had made those kinds of decisions many times over the years. Now, it was my turn.

"You are a liar!" she said, suddenly. "You don't love me. You only care about your husband and your children. All the years I spent raising you, and this is how you treat me. I've raised you for 45 years! Shame on you! Shame on you!" I was not going to argue with her about the 45 years.

Even though I knew that was not really what she believed, it hurt me to hear her say it. I was standing right in front of her, thinking about how my daughter's life was hanging in the balance, and I just broke down. I started crying and I just couldn't stop. I made my way to the bathroom with my cell phone, and I closed and locked the door.

"You come out of there! What kind of daughter are you? Come out of there, right now," she yelled as she began banging on the door. Then, it got even worse. She forgot who I was.

"Who are you? Why are you in my bathroom? I am going to call the police!" she shouted at the top of her lungs.

Through my tears, I called Evie. She had told me earlier that she might be able to help later that day. I called and called and left message after distressed message. Evie finally called back, and I asked if she could please help me with my mother. I couldn't leave her in this state without anyone she knew, but I couldn't endure the insults any more. She said she would be right over. Still, I had to listen to Mom's semi-cogent tirade for another half hour before she arrived. When Evie got there, all I wanted to do was to get away. I didn't say goodbye to Mom. I just left, crying, hearing her begging me to stay. That was one of the hardest departures I've ever made.

The one benefit of dementia – from the point of view of the caregivers – is that events of one day do not carry over to the next. The dementia patient doesn't remember what transpired the day before. I visited many times after that, and she never had that reaction to me again. Some days were very happy, some days were not. I didn't know what to expect each time.

Another year and a half passed, Mom's mental condition seemed to deteriorate even more.

One day, as happened from time to time, she seemed unusually lucid. Three days before another visit, I had recently heard from Uncle Seng. After all these years, he and Mom had never seen each other since he visited us in the refugee camp in Thailand. Now, he was in the United States and wanted to make the trip to visit her. He planned to come on March 25th. I told Mom about his impending visit, and she was very excited about it. She did something that was quite unusual for her. She went to get a piece of paper and wrote his name on it with the word "visit." Every morning after that, when she went to the table where she had left the note, she would read it and ask me when he was coming. Each day, I would tell her that he would be there on the 25th. She was elated and looking forward to his visit.

On March 24th of 2013, my mother passed away peacefully in her sleep.

It was in the same time during the sad news of my mom that I received the good news of my daughter being completely cancer-free, and she was regaining her health. This was a great celebration. But it was also a day of great sadness.

In the same day, one life regained and one life lost.

When Uncle Seng arrived the next day, I had to tell him the bad news. He was devastated and so was I. They had both been looking forward to the possibility of seeing each other again after the tumultuous events that had brought them together and then separated them. The currents of the Mekong were a metaphor for the currents of history that sealed their fate. The lesson from this is simple and unforgettable. Time is of the essence.

It wasn't part of the plan, but Uncle Seng stayed for the funeral. My father and my brother were there. Huck showed care during the last years of our mom's deteriorated condition. He tried to be there when ever he was able to come back from his travels. Despite our distance and differences in life choices we made, it was good to see Huck there, because it reminded us of what Mom always taught us – family is family, no matter what.

Evie, the friend who had spent so many hours keeping my mom company, was present. All my aunts – her three sisters, who traveled from afar – were all there together. Richard, my husband and great love, who had provided for all of us during these twenty-two years of progress and regress, was right next to me. Our children, our great loves – Vanita, Kevin, and Lee – were sitting next to Richard in the pew of the church. My Uncle Seng sat on the other side of me, with Dad and Huck next to him. There were so many others, who were friends of mine or Richard's or friends of my parents, filling up the chapel. Even Lawrence came to pay his respects. However, Dad was emotionally distraught – in his own stoic and quiet way – and was oblivious of everyone's presence. He didn't even pay the slightest attention or recognize half of the people in the room.

The most surprising and unexpected attendant of all – Luna showed up at the funeral and introduced herself to me. She approached me as if we had met before. She told me that Mom had contacted her in recent years and was trying to reconnect her with Dad. She was very touched and excited for a chance to meet Dad and all of us, in the hope of becoming part of our family, as she had only recently lost her own mother. I expressed my sympathy for her loss. However, I didn't want to add another set of emotions to the room or distract from my mom's funeral, so I decided to postpone the family introductions until after the funeral. Luna looked so much like me. I felt that strange instant connection. We embraced and enjoyed the celebration of life together.

In the same day, we lost one family member and gained another.

It was a day of many emotions, but for that moment, I wanted to stay focused on Mom. We were all there, gathered in sorrow and in the presence of the sacred, to pay our last respects to my mother and her indomitable spirit. She was a woman of strong character and determination, who would sacrifice anything for what was right and for her family. Through her valiant struggle in a very tough life, my mother suffered and sacrificed so we wouldn't have to. Her perseverance gave her children, my children, and the subsequent generations the chance to lead better lives.

Final Freedom ~ Afterword

Although my mother has passed, her story lives on through those whose chapters are still being written. I believe my mother's spirit lives on as well. I close this story, for now, with thoughts she shared after one of her final visions. She believed the vision to be true, and for her sake – and for all of ours – I choose to believe it, too.

~Kasi Yang

My name is Kim Champa. I am in a better place now – no more pain, no more struggles, all is serene here, forever. And I am in good company. I have a splendid view from heaven. It is as I envisioned it in my dream: full of beautiful gardens and flowers, especially the *dok champa* in abundance.

I've discovered some truths. I feel called to express my feelings and reflections on life; what it means for us all and what my wishes are for all of you.

I was born a Buddhist, but later became a Christian. The acts of love and kindness I had witnessed in my lifetime, through the people who were there for us during our struggles, and through the life of my daughter Kasi, led me to the Christian faith. The Dalai Lama once said that the best religion is the one that gets you closest to God and makes you a better person. A better person can still fall short in God's glorious standard, but through that relationship with God, I know that I am loved.

"Not only that, but we rejoice in our sufferings, knowing that suffering produces endurance, and endurance produces character, and character produces hope, and hope does not put us to shame, because God's love has been poured into our hearts through the Holy Spirit, who has been given to us." –Romans 5:3-5. Now that I am free in my final freedom, this passage led me to reflect on my struggles on earth, and it revealed to me that my struggles were for a reason.

In the beginning of our story, I said that I was the one who had decided to make our family become refugees. That is true. However, as I taste this final freedom, I now know that in some sense, *we are all refugees on earth*, because our earthly existence is temporary – but the love and kindness we share with others transcend death and endure forever for generations.

Your earthly life is short, and so is my message to you. Love and forgive one another.

May you always feel God's loving embrace. Peace be with you all.

Made in the USA
Columbia, SC
12 June 2018